HIS
LORDSHIP'S
ARSENAL

HIS LORDSHIP'S ARSENAL

A NOVEL BY

CHRISTOPHER MOORE

FREUNDLICH BOOKS *New York*

This novel is a work of fiction. Names, characters, places and incidents are either the product of the author's imagination or are used fictitiously. Any resemblance to actual events or locales or persons, living or dead, is entirely coincidental.

Copyright © Christopher Moore

Library of Congress Cataloging-in-Publication Data

Moore, Christopher, 1946–
    His Lordship's arsenal.

    I. Title.
PR9199.3.M618H5   1985   813'.54   85-13175
    ISBN 0-88191-033-3

Published by Freundlich Books
(A division of Lawrence Freundlich Publications, Inc.)
80 Madison Avenue
New York, N.Y. 10016

Distributed to the trade by The Scribner Book Companies, Inc.
115 Fifth Avenue
New York, N.Y. 10003

Manufactured in the United States of America

10 9 8 7 6 5 4 3 2 1

FOR
JULIE AND ALISON

There are some men live in darkness
While the rest have light for free
You can spot those in the limelight
Those in the darkness you don't see.

ACT THREE, SCENE FIVE
The Threepenny Opera
BERTOLT BRECHT

HIS
LORDSHIP'S
ARSENAL

PART ONE

CHAPTER 1

THE pictures from the scene of death were gruesome. Two dead men inside a burned out room in the Delrose Hotel. One, an elderly man, had been tied to a cross. The flames from the fire had eaten away his clothes; his flesh dried and cracked, peeling in strips, falling away in clusters from his hands and face. His lips were blistered and puffed; and a large scar on the right side of his face looked like an open mine, the flesh tufted along the edges in little ridges. The naked man on the bed was less horribly burned. He was curled up like a child, his hands wrapped around his knees. His legs and arms and sides were scorched by the flames. Next to the bed were two tribunal masks. They bore the image of a lion—no, lioness.

The police report was unable to identify the two men. They were recorded as transients, homosexuals who'd been involved in a strange ritual of drugs and fire. The police theory was an ugly one of torture and masochism. The gay community in Vancouver complained when one local newspaper published a photograph of the death scene and described the two men as homosexuals driven to sexual frenzy. There were no arrests. The police closed the file. All that was left was to try the civil action between the hotel owner and the insurance company. There had been a question as to whether the policy was in force at the time of the fire. Slum hotel owners often neglect paying their bills on time, and in this case, their default stood to cost them a lot of money. The Chief Justice assigned me to hear the case. He thought I should have more experience in commercial cases. Before, my cases had tended to be criminal, family law, and contracts.

Each time I started to work on the case, I thought of the two lioness masks. Throughout the trial they sat on the table with the other exhibits with the empty eyeholes staring up at me. With the short golden mane, they vaguely reminded me of an Egyptian goddess mask. They looked too small for the heads of the dead men. The police said that they fit their heads; but that didn't take into account the shrinkage of the skulls from the fire.

Twenty-four hours after reserving judgment I'd written one sentence, stopped, torn up the paper, and tossed it towards the wastebasket. Thirty-three crumpled paper balls lay in and near the basket. The room took on the appearance of a basketball camp for handicapped boys. On each piece I'd written exactly the same sentence.

> Flames were seen rising from the rooftop of the Delrose Hotel at four o'clock Sunday morning, the nineteenth of November.

The evidence revealed that much. Beyond this one fact, I did not share the views of the witnesses as to why or how this rest home on the doorstep of Stanley Park burned to the ground.

I was stuck. Midafternoon in my oak-panelled study, trial exhibits scattered across my desk, I rose and walked to the window. Arms stretched out, I closed my eyes. What was behind the one sentence? The three shareholders of Warnell Enterprises, the owner of the Delrose, sought to collect three million dollars in insurance proceeds against the Federal United Insurance Company. One million dollars each. Federal United said the shareholders burned down the Delrose. Someone burned down the Delrose, but the shareholders said it wasn't them. Buildings don't just burn themselves down. No one disputed that flames were seen rising from the rooftop of the Delrose

Hotel at four o'clock Sunday morning, the nineteenth of November. That makes thirty-four times I've repeated the sentence; like a Buddha marooned on a koan and no vocabulary to pass around it.

Under the pleadings, exhibits, and briefs was my lunch. The case seemed to consume my food. Somewhere there were cream cheese bagels. The insurance policy balanced on a half-empty glass of wine. Soon everything would be stuck together with food. If the case went on appeal, I'd be reversed on the basis of bad diet. So what could I infer from the evidence? I was the judge. Judges infer things; but I could not. As I stared out the window I caught a glimpse of Dr. Hershey Rosen who lives to my west on Marine Drive. Dr. Rosen, wearing a Sony headset, pedalled an exercise bike on his swimming pool deck. He had a pulse meter strapped to his wrist. A psychiatrist who became a property developer, he had gotten very rich in five years. We had two things in common: we were both forty-three and divorced. Although I didn't know Hershey well, our age and marital persecutions formed a bond between us: like war veterans who had survived their wounds to fight another day.

I had great faith in the healing powers of doctors. Edgar had been a doctor. A gynecologist who worked twelve-hour days. Most of the time with his hands fishing around in dark, wet places; checking the ecology of the marsh. His father and uncle had been doctors. Seeking medical advice was as easy as giving a urine sample in my family. I include these facts as support for my decision to cross the lawn and stand at the end of Hershey's pool deck after writing the same opening sentence thirty-three times. I needed a doctor's point of view.

Hershey was sweating and singing along on his exercise bike. I watched him for nearly five minutes before he saw me. He removed the headset and slowed his pedalling to a crawl.

"Hey, Matt," he said. "How goes it?"

That was the moment of truth. Judges lead secluded lives on a pedestal so they can't be compromised. Secular monks with the power of the Pope. Not really monks, more like surgeons—Edgar would like that better—who remained permanently scrubbed and sterile. Anyone who wasn't a judge was a potential germ-carrying fatal infection. But coming from a family of doctors I immediately trusted Hershey.

"You all right?" Hershey asked.

"I've written the same sentence thirty-three times," I replied after a moment.

"You should get a word processor."

"Without a mistake," I interjected.

Hershey puffed out his upper lip and stared at me for several seconds. I knew the look well. From my years on the bench, it wasn't uncommon to see some prisoner in the dock slobbering out stories of his genealogical horrors transmitted down the family tree; branches missing, and standing before me was the bitter pulp. I was about to mention this to Hershey when he pulled a cordless phone from his belt and rang for two glasses of dry white wine. Within several minutes, Nancy, his daughter, clad in a tiny white and blue bikini, came onto the deck carrying a tray, two glasses and a bottle of champagne. She had her own idea of dry white wine. She placed the tray on the deck table and adjusted the umbrella canopy, delicate, tanned hands working the lever. I watched her disappear back through the sliding glass door, where she lingered for a moment. Flames were seen rising . . . I watched Nancy's young, slender figure from the distance as she lingered framed in the door. Then she was gone.

"Bet you've not seen one of these," said Hershey, showing me his mini-push button, auto redial, computerized cordless telephone. A little antenna rose from the top. He had that Secret Service man's *The-President's-safe* look, as he put it to his mouth. He'd phoned a computerized weather service. He turned up the volume so I could listen.

"Handy for the pool," I said, as he gestured for me to take a glass of champagne.

"Twenty-six Celsius. No rain in the forecast," said the announcer.

"Only two hundred dollars. Picked it up in Seattle last week," he said. "You can't get them here yet. Want me to pick one up for you on my next trip?"

Dr. Rosen didn't think smuggling was a real crime. Like low-grade tax fraud, this type of misconduct was as morally neutral as the weather report. I hadn't come to provide legal lectures on smuggling to Hershey; so I let the question hang in the air.

"I really need some professional advice, Hershey."

He leaned back in the chair, his feet crossed near the edge of the pool. He swirled the champagne around the inside of his glass. A smile started and aborted. He saw that I was serious. A critical expression passed across his face; a little crinkling of skin gathered between his eyes. I thought how exceptionally young Hershey looked. Lean, relaxed, a nonaggressive manner. He looked at women and they returned his attention. Nancy could be mistaken for his second or third wife.

"Matthew, it'll pass on its own."

"What will?"

"This writer's block. Most writers suffer from it at some stage in their career."

"But I'm a judge, Hershey. I don't sit around writing television scripts."

I guess I protested too much. Hershey smiled as he filled our glasses again.

"That's all judges do—write stories about people who have problems. You wear a robe. Hemingway wore a hunting shirt. He got a Nobel Prize. David Mamet wrote 'Fuck you. Fuck your mother. Fuck your boss.' And he got a Pulitzer Prize. You, Matt. Well—you'll get a nice pension."

"Have you ever read a judgment?"

"I've been sued now and again. The judge decides who's the good guy and who's the bad guy. Then he writes a story about them."

Between a slum hotel owner and insurance company that was a hard distinction to make. It felt hotter than 26 Celsius. I touched the ice-chilled glass to my cheek, and unbuttoned my shirt. A drop of sweat ran down my dolphin-white stomach. Hershey had a valid argument. So I wrote little melodramas: sex, violence, drugs, death, greed, stupidity, and stings were the central plots and subplots. What I call the Wongness of human existence. Judges became drunks, senile, or lazy but they always wrote their stories. But I was blocked and sweating on Hershey's pool deck. The sort of weather that makes you prefer Mamet to Hemingway.

"You're a special kind of artist, Matthew."

That was the second time he'd called me Matthew. I'd ceased to be Matt. The automatic professional touches kicked in like overdrive in his sports car. I'd become Hershey's patient.

"It's not a stigma," he continued, choosing his words with more care. "Nothing to be ashamed about. Just an unavoidable occupational hazard."

"I can't go fishing for six months. I've got to decide this case. At the moment I can't decide any case." I'd overreacted. Even to myself, I began to sound slightly crazy. I filled my own glass, and leaned forward with my elbows on the table, head resting on my hands.

Hershey played with the antenna of his cordless phone. "It's simple then—write. Write something like *The plaintiff wins*. Or substitute defendant or Crown or accused for plaintiff. Just leave out the story." He was sounding like Stew, the Chief Justice, a father figure to me, who decided hard cases with the flip of a quarter that he kept hidden away inside his office desk.

That wasn't the way I decided cases. Each decision needed a plausible story line to justify the result. The Court of Appeal wants to read these stories. Like editors, their very job depended on telling a good story from a bad one. Not that anyone expected a lyrical, richly-textured, moving tale; not even publishable—merely a narrative so that everyone knew from all the lies what lies the judge has decided were facts. And there was the great power and authority: to impose your story as fact and dismiss all the others as fiction. Only this time the story wouldn't come from the conflicting testimony and evidence. Like the lioness masks in the photographs, the case had a mystery at the core. Only fragments stood out. The Delrose Hotel had suffered damages on the second floor. Two people, one old and one young, both male, had died—one from fire and one from drug overdose. This wasn't a complex case, no uncertain legal principles were involved, and nothing was at stake but the insurance money. A perfectly unoriginal, straightforward little incident that even the gay community had forgotten.

When Nancy returned to the pool deck she was wearing sunglasses; the kind in which you can see your own reflection, like a two-way mirror. She put down the tray with a jar of salmon mousse and a baguette. On the side were cutlery and a chilled champagne glass for herself. Smiling shyly, she poured champagne. The suntan lotion glistened on her shoulders and arms. I felt her brush against my leg with her arm. She paused. I saw myself in her glasses; the sweat-streaked face looked tired.

"Take a swim, Nance," said Hershey.

"Can't. Just have time for a short commune. Then two appointments."

As she sauntered into her father's fourteen-room house, I wondered with whom she was about to commune. A few moments later Nancy reappeared framed in the sliding glass door. Ten or more high-strung, exotic birds clung to her arms, shoulders and hair. I glanced at Hershey, who faced me as he spooned salmon mousse onto a baguette. Curiosity drew my attention back to the door. Nancy had peeled off her bikini top, stretched out her hands, palms up, and tilted back her head exposing her throat.

The flames of red, yellow, green and blue feathers spread down to her fingers. Her body shook slightly then was very still. At that moment, she looked like a child who stepped from a jungle, an innocent who occupied a space outside of the place and time shared around the pool by Hershey and me. An air-conditioned jungle with carpets and stereo equipment. A calm, reflective expression crossed her face as if the feathers were brightly colored flames that had cleansed her body and soul.

"Of course this will be kept strictly confidential," Hershey said, biting into the baguette.

"Yes, of course." I used my stern Judge's voice to mask my preoccupation with Nancy's ritual. The libretto of confusion and irony, polished and sharpened by the sexual fantasy, dissolved. She crashed through layers of perception and thought, smashed through emotional levels cluttered with computers, tennis rackets, television sets, heated swimming pools, and cordless phones, and walked out on a plateau heavy with animal sounds, amongst cloisters of rock, earth and caves splashed in light and fire. She traversed a subconscious slope, climbed to the top, unfrightened, alone, and experienced emotions long lost to the shopping mall world of liquor stores, tax returns, divorce, traffic accidents, and lawsuits.

"Strictly confidential," Hershey repeated, slowly drinking his champagne. "Nothing goes beyond here." Had he seen Nancy in her commune mode? Was this some weird father and daughter stroke patient routine? Maybe this was part of Hershey's cure for blocked writers.

"I merely want some insight," I said, as if I were talking to a lawyer standing below me in front of the bench. A flicker of a smile wove across his face. "As to your fee," I began, but Hershey waved his hand midway through. Even the way he lifted his hand reminded me of the Chief Justice. As I looked back at the door, Nancy had disappeared . . . vanished.

Hershey had a difficult task. One could reform the law but one couldn't reform a judge who no longer knew the cause of flames. Working that lattice of truth and fiction, good and evil, fact and opinion caused warps and bends and the entire fragile edifice threatened to collapse. Perhaps Nancy had never been in the door; perhaps it was the heat splitting my psyche into atoms, showering the pieces like shards of crystal through a wind tunnel of forgotten traumas and passions. The voice inside my head sounded like a tiny far-off echo bouncing from the debris. I sat and listened, trying to tune in a clear, strong signal, as if the door was a television screen that had lost its picture. An empty, remote screen on the other side of the deck. This had happened before. The reception faded and nothing but static came through.

I plowed through the remembered images of Nancy, making my best guess about the kind of birds; exaggerating the intensity of her shudder, playing a stop-action rerun over and over again inside my mind. All my faith, trust and integrity hung delicately in the balance as I examined the sliding glass door. Like in the Delrose Hotel case there could only be one right answer.

"I've got an idea," said Hershey. "You must write." I watched him spread the salmon mousse on a piece of baguette.

"But I am writing. The same sentence. Over and over again."

He took a bite, then sipped his champagne. "But that's the point. To clear the block you have to write about something else. Another kind of story. Maybe a little sex." He winked.

The ploy was clear. Challenge my ability to write anything at all. Put my pride on the line. Of course, I could write. My judgments are widely reported in the law reports, the subject of scholarly articles, cited in other courts, quoted in textbooks, taught in law schools. As judges went, I knew the techniques well, and had refined my own voice. I even had what one colleague called "a real *flare*" for writing. I enjoyed writing; no, I loved writing, putting the facts together, describing the events in detail with elegance and style. "Flames were seen rising . . ." was a dramatic touch. A one-sentence drama in the making. A story waiting to rise from the ashes. But this time there wasn't even a possibility of reaching the second sentence.

"I don't know where to begin," I said.

"That's definitely not healthy." Hershey was sounding more and more like a doctor. It was possible that property developers said this sort of thing about deals over salmon mousse and champagne.

"Right now I feel like I'll never finish another decision."

"You will, Matthew. But one stage at a time."

Obiter. That's the Latin term that flashed through my mind. It means to lawyers and judges a personal or incidental remark that is unimportant to the main decision. Since law school I've had an obsession with *obiter*. Judges aren't supposed to use it. It's like flying off the handle about all things that are wrong in life—all the Wongness in the world—when you're only concerned about one concrete dispute. When Hershey trotted out the old chestnut about one stage at a time, I found myself muttering, "Obiter."

"Matthew, you'll have to bear with me," he replied, no doubt thinking I'd lapsed into foreign tongues, when I only dream about people speaking in foreign languages. "Writer's block is a mental attitude. One you can detach from. Trust me. Pretend we're taking that little fishing trip you mentioned. Not for six months. Just for a couple of days. A little pleasure trip away from all the pressures and anxieties of the job."

Hershey climbed back on his exercise bike. I watched his legs pumping up and down on the pedals. Working off the champagne and salmon mousse before he'd digested it. The secret to a fit and lean body. My bleached white stomach, swelled from the drink and food, rose and fell, spilling sweat down my side. I remembered now why I had avoided Hershey. Any young woman in my presence would never be confused for a wife. He made me feel like I'd gone to seed; like other writers who spend their days and nights at a typewriter, smoking and drinking, I was the worse for wear. I was coming apart.

"What do you suggest?" I asked Hershey as he ticked off thirty kilometers an hour on the bike.

"An autobiographical sketch," he said. "Everyone can write about themselves. Tell your own story. Throw in a little sex and violence."

"With only one sentence?" I felt the toxins build up. I tried sucking in my stomach; it looked like a badly terraced Peruvian mountainside. What sex was there to write about? And why did shrinks always want to know about sex?

"Start at the beginning. With your parents. School. University. Women. You can write about that stuff." He placed the headset back over his ears. He gave me the thumbs up. Back at thirty-five kilometers, his eyes closed. Our session had ended.

I didn't speak or write French well, though I should. I was married to a French Canadian for nearly twenty years. Some things float back on occasion. Walking back from Dr. Hershey Rosen's pool, I recalled one phrase Danielle sometimes used: auto-da-fé. It came from the medieval times when heretics were put to the torch. As my one-sentence judgment indicates, I have developed an enormous sensitivity to fire.

CHAPTER 2

THE psychological walls of my life were erected by very few people. Novice craftsmen and women who had little connection with one another. No, I want this to read more like a judgment. Like a first-rate judgment. So I will deal with facts and individuals and circumstances seriatim. And like most of the judgments I've written that will be a small lie because there is no natural order in the way you can put the bricks into a wall.

Three days after my seventeenth birthday I entered law school. The next youngest member of my first-year class was Joan Bildson. She was a mess physically—fat, with unkempt hair and clothes, yellow nicotine fingers and a sullen, pissed-off air about her. Joan was twenty. Most of the guys in my class, returning war veterans were nearly ten years my senior. I'd just begun to shave every day. But I wasn't old enough to drink a tankard of beer with the boys. That created an immediate barrier. Joan and I spent a lot of time eating ice cream and smoking; sometimes at the same time. My age established a myth in the law school that I was a genius, a boy wonder with the highest IQ in Canada. Most reputations for brilliance can be accounted for by either accident or fraud. In my case, the vaulted reputation was the result of both.

It doesn't lie well in the mouth of anyone to yak about their parents screwing up their lives. Most times lives go wrong for the best-raised children. The no-hopers play this routine in the courts through their probation officers and social workers. Yak, yak about their broken homes, child-abuse, lack of understanding and love, no Sunday school, no allowance. The neglect of the accused by his parents was the simple reason for his decision to squeeze off five rounds into his wife's upper body. When I talk about Edgar and mother it's not a yak-yak session about why I can only write a one-sentence judgment, but to explain how I came to be admitted to the Faculty of Law at the University of British Columbia. Edgar Walter Burlock, MD, the gynecologist who was married to my mother, arranged my admission. Edgar, who adopted me when I was five, was always there when I needed a male role model. He assumed—indeed the whole family shared the assumption—that I would continue the Burlock family tradition and become a respected doctor.

But boy-wonder flunked first-year biology. That was the accident. I mean the untimely failure that put an end to the assumption about another Burlock, MD. In the second week of lab we were given tasks by a teaching assistant called Nelson. We weren't given a choice. Nelson wasn't big on democracy. He assigned students to cleaning test tubes, wiping down the counters, storing Bunsen burners, and feeding and caring for the lab animals we experimented with. During the first week, Nelson had a dossier from the registrar's office on each of us. He inspected the records and then interviewed us in his airless little office which he shared with another teaching assistant. Nelson, a prairie boy from Regina, had been rejected by the medical school the year before. He bore a considerable grudge as a result. When he discovered that I was a doctor's "kid" (as he put it), Nelson's forehead knotted and he had the look I have subsequently noticed in many prisoners in the dock charged with manslaughter. His theory was that only doctor's kids got into medical school. The conspiracy theory. The Jews ran the banks; doctors' kids in med schools; Communists reading Marx and Hegel in the Ministry of Foreign Affairs.

On Monday, the second week of lab, Nelson called my name last. My duty consisted of baby-sitting an eight-foot boa called Louise. Nelson regularly starved Louise for two-week periods. Then, as Louise's keeper, he had the job of feeding her white mice. Most of the time Louise slept coiled in a container beneath the lab sink in the far corner. No one used the sink during the second week of Louise's fast. My instructions were to check Louise's container first thing in the morning and last thing at night. Unlike the run-of-the-mill lab animal, Louise was an expensive asset. Nelson remarked once that she was worth about four thousand dollars and had a million dollars worth of hate inside. Nelson took me aside and said that Louise had been named after a mass killer in Regina, and if Louise disappeared that I'd better turn up inside her belly. Bitterness made Nelson exaggerate risks, punishment, and his own abilities.

Under no circumstances was I allowed to feed the snake without Nelson's personal written permission. Having been cautioned about Louise's foul temper, the bell rang and I left Nelson's office and filled my lungs with fresh air. On Thursday I was scheduled to feed Louise a half-dozen white mice. Open the cage, drop them in one by one and slam the top closed. But I never had the chance to execute my duties. Louise escaped Wednesday night. On my way back to the dorm (Edgar insisted I live on campus), I stopped by the lab, flipped on the lights, and walked over to the sink. The top of Louise's cage was open, and she was coiled around the three-inch drainpipe below the sink. Her head, the size of large apple, moved back and forth in a strange, angry manner. The same eccentric quality I'd noticed in Nelson after he found out that Edgar was a doctor.

Louise's jaws sprang open like a trapdoor. At night, when

you're alone in a large lab, things look larger than life. I saw those jaws swallowing all the king's horses and all the king's men. But I also remember feeling surprised how calm and controlled (at a distance) I felt. This was, after all, one very hungry creature. It wasn't in my job description to untangle Louise from the sink pipes and put her back in the cage. The simplest solution was to throw a few mice into the cage and she'd happily drop back inside. But I was under orders not to feed her until the next day.

So I phoned Nelson from the lab. The phone rang a long time. He sounded like he'd been drinking. The television was blaring in the background.

"I want to feed Louise the mice now," I said.

"Negative," he replied.

"She's bolted," I said.

"Whaaa?"

"Fastened herself like a nine-inch-thick rope on the pipes," I explained.

"Permission denied," he said, and slammed down the receiver in my ear. Believers of the conspiracy theory of life tend to have a military manner.

"Louise's escaped," I whispered into the dial tone.

I was an inexperienced beginner. I'd been largely ignorant about people like Nelson in society. Lack of exposure and opportunity fostered the distorted view that people in authority were like Edgar or Potter, my boarding school housemaster. Responsibility was packaged with upper-class manners, social grace, and a rational, coherent grip on reality. At no time did it occur to me that Edgar's well-laid plans would be in the hands of a police constable's son from Regina.

As ordered, I didn't feed Louise. Neither was I found in her belly. She disappeared into the maze of ducts, electrical wiring, and pipes in the ceiling, no doubt mistaking them for a jungle habitat stocked with monkeys, birds, rabbits, and mice. Two days passed and Louise silently roamed unseen above our heads. Nelson cancelled her Thursday feeding—something of a formality given the circumstances, and reported my dereliction of duty to the department head. I dreaded the inevitable confrontation with Edgar. My second week at university and I was at the lowest point of my life. Edgar would detonate when he got the bill from the department: one snake, $4,000. The money he'd set aside for my medical education would find its way into the pocket of some jungle poacher.

Potter had taught me to examine a problem, find a solution, and act forcefully and quickly. Back at the dorm I loaded my Colt .45. I wished I'd taken a lighter weapon. But I didn't want weapons hanging out of every desk drawer. University wasn't like school where I had boxes of guns under lock and key. Potter, my boarding school mentor, had the rest of my arsenal in the basement of Alpha House. There was no point involving Potter. I would make do with the Colt. So I packed the gun in my briefcase that Edgar had bought me. The case was black leather and would be carried through my long career as a doctor.

As I walked across the campus, a few extra rounds rattled in the bottom of the case. The cowboy image of guns was repellent to Potter. Guns were crafted tools: instruments of foreign policy. Diplomats controlled their development, deployment, and use. They were the underlying element of basic political management and day-to-day business cycles. Gunslingers were aberrations, spin-off mutations. I didn't flash the Colt around. During the next two days, Nelson's personality blossomed. Most of the students, secretaries, and professors had their heads pivoting like gun turrets at all times in the building. Nelson had never been happier or more carefree. He started to smile, combed his hair, pressed his clothes. He was grooming himself for power. Charts and maps of the building were pinned to the wall. The lab took on the appearance of an operational headquarters. He started calling us men.

I was mystified. Soon enough, I was convinced Nelson's true colors would begin to float slowly to the surface. On Thursday afternoon he called the ten members of my lab class together. Hands behind his back, he walked back and forth in front of us.

"Men, we have a problem." The problem was that all our lab work had come to a halt. Instead we were all reading maps and charts Nelson had worked up the night before.

"The problem concerns your safety," he said, with a heavy emphasis on safety. My lab partner, Wong, squirmed. Nelson gave him a knowing smile: war-is-hell. For nearly fifty minutes Nelson told stories about dangerous snakes. He had acquired a reasonably wide knowledge on the subject; in fact, it was clear he'd read every book on snakes in the library. Something that must have greatly impressed those who interviewed him for medical school. He knew snakes' habits, where they burrowed, fang dimensions, the toxicity of venom.

"Men, boas like Louise are fast and strong. Before you can react she'll sink her fangs into you." He liked to exaggerate. He told us Louise had one hundred hot needles in her mouth. Most everyone in the lab discounted Nelson, and didn't like the idea that military school and a paranoid commander had become their door to science.

The problem was Wong. He was fractured with fear. In Canada hardly anyone ever dies of a snakebite. You have to go out of your way to even find a snake in Vancouver. Not true in South China where Wong had been born. Thousands of Chinese peasants were eaten by snakes every year; and millions of snakes were eaten by the Chinese. A roughly balanced ecology. Wong had left China so he'd never have to worry about being ambushed by another snake or finding another one cut up on his plate. His eyes constantly surveyed the ceiling as Nelson told, and retold, his snake-devours-man stories. Even at seventeen I had a reasonably good idea that Nelson's hopeless indifference to the truth would have caused his patients considerable confusion if he practiced medicine. But Wong hung on every word.

On the evening of the second day, Wong and I were alone in the lab, working up an experiment that involved dissecting a mouse's reproductive organs. Wong wasn't even his old monosyllabic self that night. Having been cloistered in a posh private boarding school, I'd never known a Chinese before Nelson paired us up as lab partners. I was sorry about the whole mess. I told Wong so. He worked hard and carefully, pulling back the skin on the mouse. He just let me talk. He dropped the knife a couple of times. Then he knocked over two beakers, spilling a yellowish-gray liquid on the floor. Looking up at the ceiling, he'd heard some noise. It came from outside. He knocked a Bunsen burner over. The mouse caught fire. I poured a beaker of water over the sizzling carcass. The lab was starting to smell something like a Chinese restaurant where Edgar and I had once eaten lunch. Wong was on his hands and knees cleaning up the mess on the floor while I dealt with the flambéed mouse.

I glanced at the lab clock. It was ten past eleven. I wanted to reassure Wong so I took him aside, and opened my briefcase. I reached in and took out the Colt. Sometimes good intentions run against the reefs of cultural differences. As many of Wong's people had been dispatched by pistols as by snakes. Wong again knelt on the floor. His hands clasped over his head; tears spilled down his cheeks. In retrospect, I suspect it was the smell of the mouse cooking. When I looked up, I saw Louise.

"Don't move," I said. "Freeze."

Wong wet his pants and farted. I had the palm of my hand pressed over the top of Wong's bent head. He must've thought—in some genetic flash—that he would die in Vancouver of multiple gunshot wounds and "one hundred red hot needles" from a snake.

"Please," Wong pleaded. Maybe breaking beakers and burning mice was a capital offense in China.

"Shh. It'll be over in a second," I whispered. I squeezed off the first round. It caught Louise right above her right eye as she dangled several feet above Wong's head. She'd come out of nowhere. Maybe snakes do prefer Chinese. It was a close call to determine whether Louise had been aiming for the fried mouse or Wong. She hung from the ceiling for a moment. Then Louise dropped like an anchor from an oil tanker on Wong's back.

Louise was, of course, quite dead. But Wong had thrown up in my briefcase. This guy was a complete mess. The lab reeked of gunpowder, barf, piss, broiled mouse and the yellow-gray liquid stuff around Wong's knees. You had the idea this was what it was like to be sharing a cell in one of Mao's prisons. Louise was sprawled out on Wong's back. He lifted his head from my case. He was still alive. For what seemed like a long moment Wong remained frozen in a half-stooped position. Then he let out a scream. The sort of scream you never forget the rest of your life. Nobody is safe. That's what Wong's scream was about. Change your climate, your politics, locale, but don't ever think you can forget about the lethal little horrors left behind.

He pushed back slightly and Louise fell to the floor. I handed him a towel from the table. He wiped his face. I had no idea where to put my Colt. My briefcase with all my lab and course notes and two textbooks was ruined. I tucked the gun in my belt and reached down to help Wong to his feet. He nodded, no it was more a bow, and walked over to his own briefcase and took out a red brick. Then he walked back to Louise, knelt down and hammered her until she was flattened to a surface no more than half an inch thick. She became eight feet long and four feet wide. She no longer resembled a boa. It was hard to tell exactly what kind of animal she was. He quietly placed the brick back in his case and left the lab.

I looked around at the lab, and then phoned Nelson.

"I found Louise," I said.

"Oh," he said. He sounded disappointed. He was going to be a civilian again.

"But she's dead." I could've lied and told Nelson that something had inexplicably fallen on Louise as she slithered in the air ducts.

"You're personally responsible, Burlock," he shouted over the phone.

"I killed her," I said, and put down the receiver.

The next day I phoned Edgar at the office. I told him that after two weeks of first-year biology I wasn't cut out to be a doctor. Nelson gladly gave me a note saying I'd failed the course. When Edgar ordered me down to his office, I showed him the note. He was heartbroken. How could I fail biology without taking a single examination and after two weeks? I told him there was a new department policy. The idea was to weed out the students early so no one would waste time on false expectations.

MOST afternoons mother sipped apricot brandy from a Royal Worcester cup in our sitting room with the curtains drawn. She sat erect and pointed her little finger outward as you'd imagine the Queen Mother in her private Buckingham Palace would. In the late 1950s most of mother's friends sat in their big Shaughnessy mansions and played bridge and sipped gin late into the afternoon until no one could remember the score. Mother had more reason than most. She'd lost her first husband in the Spanish Civil War; not a killed-in-action, nothing so neat, just a missing-in-action casualty. He left us behind for Edgar. Like the others, mother had many shared values about life. Wives had faith in their husbands; they trusted the conservative government; they supervised servants who ran the household and planted and tended the garden; and believed in God and that things would always turn out for the best.

She seldom left the house. A panic disorder would take hold outside the Burlock estate, she'd feel faint, start screaming, legs became rubbery. The same symptoms appeared if I asked questions about my father. I put it down to the fact that he left the house and "disappeared" and mother interpreted that as some kind of cosmic message that outside the front door was a great abyss where there was danger of being listed as missing-in-action. Mother rarely saw Edgar. She'd seen even less of me since I'd been sent to boarding school at an early age. When I did come home I gave mother plenty of advance notice. She had a highly structured life inside the house and loathed unexpected interruptions in her daily routines.

All this nonsense (as she put it) about failing biology gave her a migraine. She had an ice pack pressed against her head. I saw her standing in the window as my taxi arrived. The curtains were partly drawn, and she looked like she'd been standing in the window for sometime. Waiting for father to return from the war? As I walked up the drive I could tell that she'd been crying. She looked more fragile, tender, and sad than I'd remembered her from my last visit home. Like a film actress who played the part of a mother who watched an olive-green army car stop in front and some strong, rugged Major climb out with a telegram saying father was lost somewhere in Spain.

Mother exaggerated the importance of things. Or maybe in the course of time different things seem more important than a person previously thought.

Nothing much had really happened, I explained. A snake named Louise had gone missing-in-action. I'd killed her just about as she was about to dine on Wong. My morals were still intact; I hadn't committed any crime against humanity; I hadn't contracted some unusual disease. I'd survived quite nicely outside the Burlock house. And by my own standards I found nothing particularly regretful in my actions. This was the reason I didn't understand all the violent emotions and censure. I'd spent so little of my life with Edgar and mother, and so much of my life with Potter, that the conditions and responses I'd acquired didn't comply with their expectations.

I wanted a job that wouldn't take too much time away from my avocation as a gun collector and sharpshooter. Professionals like Edgar would never know the exquisite feel of an 1892 Winchester. Nelson had done me a favor. I was glad but I tried not to let on in front of mother.

"We are so sorry, Matthew," mother said, as I sat the sitting room and stood with my shoes on the planted floral pattern of the Persian carpet.

"I did my best, mother," I said, looking at the brandy glass and bottle on the table behind her. On formal occasions such as this she dispensed with the Royal Worcester cups; it was her way of throwing the full freight for her drinking on you. Several times after too much brandy she'd tell me about the time she met Brecht in New York. In those days, she wasn't afraid to go outside. Brecht was some lifeline to the past when she had control, happiness, and hope.

"It couldn't have come at a worse time."

I knew she'd say that. Everything in her life had arrived at the worst possible time. There was some irony in this. She was bloated with excess time. No schedules or appointments to keep. But all the things that happened outside the house made her heart race. In the 1950s Shaughnessy housewives had a generally distorted view of reality. Mother's was merely more blurred than most.

"Why are you twitching your nose like that, Matthew?" she continued. "Are you all right?"

"I think I have an allergy." I wasn't about to tell her the Wongness from the place of Louise's slaughter had been released in my nose.

It was a signal of fear somewhere in the house. Mother fingered her glass and watched me disappear into Edgar's study. He sat behind a large polished cherry wood desk with a stethoscope around his neck. He still had his white frock on. His neatly trimmed beard made him distinguished looking; the black horn-rimmed glasses added a scholarly touch; and the tufts of gray hair around the temples the image of worldly wisdom. He emitted respect. The Wongness was overpowering. It was Edgar's fear. For a moment he didn't look up from Koestler's *Darkness at Noon*; no doubt getting pointers from Rubashov's interrogation. Smoking a cigarette, Edgar quietly turned the page, placed his bookmark, and motioned for me to sit down.

"I shall pay," he said, quoting Rubashov. "And of course, in the end, he will."

[23]

I couldn't think of an appropriate reply and remained silent, my hands folded behind my back. He looked at me for several moments in silence. He thought of me as some sort of medical problem. Like a malfunctioning ovary in one of his patients, I was something to be treated and cured. He was very different from mother. No recriminations; no strained show of emotions. On the surface he was scientific; a rationale, empirical type of man. I was an experiment which had not quite worked. Edgar put out his cigarette. The smoke curled from the corner of his mouth.

"You've made up your mind?" he asked me, leaning back in his chair.

"Yes," I replied. "I don't want to be a doctor."

He formed a bridge with his fingers, hooking his thumbs under his nose. Beside his desk was a full skeleton he called Ray. After a moment, as was his custom when deep in thought, he ran his right index finger down the right side of Ray's rib cage. Like father, the rest of Ray had gone missing-in-action.

"I've investigated several alternatives, Matthew." He lit another cigarette and blew smoke through Ray's chest cavity. Not even Koestler's Gletkin could have established such a perfect atmosphere for cross-examination. The vague menace in his tone, the rattling of Ray's bones, counselled me to cooperate. Only seventeen years old and my life was in the hands of a gynecologist whom I didn't know very well. He had less sentiment than logarithms. For the better good, a decision about my future was about to be made for me.

"I might be suited to a military career," I said, thinking of the excellent training from Nelson.

Edgar held up his right hand, shaking his head. He gave Ray a little shove, setting the bone clanking like a wind chime.

"No," he said. "I have something else in mind for you. Law School. No cutting, grafting—or dissecting."

I was utterly confused. I'd assumed that Edgar would ship me off to McGill or Queen's—or maybe Mexico where I'd get a fresh start and eventually go to medical school. Later I discovered that Nelson had written him a long, rambling letter about my unsuitability for science. Edgar accepted the verdict from the son of a Regina policeman about my abilities.

"I don't know anything about law," I said, staring into Ray's empty sockets.

"You'll learn soon enough."

"But aren't I too young?"

"In your case, I don't think we should waste any time."

So that was that: law school was the decision. Later in my room, I sat in bed cleaning my Colt. I thought about Edgar and mother. They read different things. He read Koestler and Shaw. Mother read and reread all of Bertolt Brecht's plays and drank brandy. She played bridge; he played chess. He liked golf but she never left the house. Yet they shared one common bond: at all possible costs, I shouldn't be allowed to slip into a lower social class. Mother's father, a Boer War veteran, had been a fireman in Vancouver. He'd died fighting a fire in the West End in 1917. It was a story I'd heard many times. At seven, I dreamed Grandfather "Wild" Bill Anglin had walked into my bedroom, his arms spread out like he'd stepped down from a cross, on fire from head to foot. I was in boarding school at the time. Potter took me down to the kitchen and made me some hot milk and wrapped a blanket around my shoulders. I was very upset—my first real Wongness in life— and drank hot milk from a chipped mug.

I thought that I might swallow a piece of glass. I was shattered. I started to cry again. That's when Potter (as he told me many years later) decided to take me downstairs and show me his gun collection. It always cheered him immensely to handle guns when he was afraid or depressed or angry. But young boarding school boys fall prey to such emotions all the time. I found out the real reason I had been selected over the other boys for this special privilege with the housemaster.

"Wild" Bill Anglin, my maternal grandfather, had been a British Columbia gun collector. His photograph (taken in his fireman's uniform), his name, the dates of his life (1894–1917), were carefully recorded inside a glass case housing the gun collection he'd left by his will to a North Vancouver museum. Potter took me to see the collection the weekend following my nightmare. I studied the grainy old photograph of "Wild" Bill. I thought I had his eyes. Potter explained the guns inside the glass case, while my chest swelled with pride.

Neither Edgar nor mother had ever mentioned "Wild" Bill's important and famous gun collection. For them, grandfather Anglin was an example of what would happen to someone who didn't study hard and prepare himself for a proper profession. What she really meant was here was another example of someone leaving the house and not coming back. People just burned up out there.

EDGAR wheeled his black Mercedes-Benz along Northwest Marine Drive. Like a test-tube baby I was about to be reinserted into the womb. No more abortions, Matthew. I sat in the back feeling slightly sorry for myself while the white sandy beaches of Spanish Banks whizzed past on the right; the tide was so far out it appeared that the tankers anchored in the middle of English Bay were marooned. Looming in the distance was Lion's Gate Bridge, an enormous expansion bridge linking Stanley Park with the north shore. Watching the bridge fade as we circled along the road between the sea and the endowment lands, I wondered what they'd done with Louise. Had Nelson stuffed the big boa into a vat of formaldehyde?—a sort of constant remainder to all future "doctor's kids" who thought they had some preordained right to his rightful spot in medical school. Or had he sold Louise to a snakeskin merchant who peeled off her hide for ladies' bags and belts? Nelson might have used the money to buy his way into a medical school in Mexico or India. Or had Wong mailed Louise back to his folks in China? He might include a private message in Chinese: If I hadn't been looking at my lab partner's gun and throwing up in his briefcase, this creature would've eaten me.

We missed the law school the first time around. Edgar stopped the Mercedes and asked a student for directions. We were told to go back to the intersection of Northwest Marine and Chancellor. With the motor idling, a car hooted its horn at us from behind. I slumped down in the back seat. All we saw as we drove through the gravel entrance were three or four prefabricated buildings with green paint peeling from the sides.

Edgar pulled the Mercedes into the parking lot. In front of us was a surplus army barracks with signs posted—Faculty Parking Only. From the appearance of the building this law school was straight from *The Gulag Archipelago*. A military school for lawyers.

"I want you to stay in the car, Matthew."

He reached over onto the passenger's side and pulled out a little flag stand from the glove box.

"Okay," I said, still half-slumped down in the back seat.

"You don't know it now, but this is all for the best," Edgar said. He unfurled a small Haitian flag from the gold stand, and got out of the car. That was his shorthand way of saying that someday I'd thank him because I never caught on fire like "Wild" Bill or went missing-in-action like father.

I watched Edgar put the flag stand on the right fender of the car, and enter the army barracks. As soon as Edgar left, I loosened my tie. Jut as I stretched out, a girl came up to the car, and stared at the Haitian flag, and then stared at the Faculty Parking Only sign. She looked inside at me. I ignored her—or tried to—by looking at a large Edwardian mansion barely visible through the bushes and trees on the opposite side of the driveway. I thought this must be the command headquarters where the officers slept. But she leaned against the window and knocked on the glass with her knuckles. I rolled it down. She was eating a strawberry ice-cream cone. The ice cream was melting down the side of the cone and running between her fingers.

"I think you represent a very corrupt government," she said.

I took her for a person of Nelson's class and glared back at her with disdain. The ice cream was dripping against the side of Edgar's black Mercedes. It was no accident. A subtle form of protest; the sort of grudge factor most people feel when they see a seventeen-year-old seated in the back of a Mercedes.

"I know all about your corruption in Haiti," she continued. "I was a Political Science major. I know what you do to people down there." Her tongue curled around the edge of the cone like a cow licking a block of salt.

"What do we do?" I asked.

"You force people to live in mud huts. Give them food full of bugs and germs," she replied. "Of course, you'll deny it."

"And we shoot old people and anyone else who won't work," I said, smiling. Pulling back my jacket just far enough so she could see my Colt in the holster. She wasn't like Wong. She didn't even flinch; just nodded her head. I didn't want to come right out and tell her that Edgar always used the diplomatic stand and flag so he could park anywhere in the city without getting a ticket.

"I think you're a very evil person," she said.

I shrugged my shoulders and let my jacket fall back over the holstered Colt. She'd started to crunch into the cone, eyes glaring at me and Edgar's Mercedes. It didn't occur to me that this girl could be a law student. With a square face, short brown hair, and overweight, Joan Bildson was the oldest daughter of a Burnaby butcher. She'd gone to some grease-ball public school that catered to no-hopers. Then she took an Arts Degree and enrolled in law school because she wanted to be a voice for the working class. Joan was at least one decade ahead of her time. This was the 1950s, and no one was shouting for working class rights. Everything was supposed to turn out all right for everyone. Joan was one of the few people I knew then who believed that nothing ever turned out right for the no-hopers.

CHAPTER 3

DURING the war, Dean Scime's office had been an army officer's bedroom. Altogether about thirty officers dined in what later would become the law school library. The first and second floor showers remained after the minor renovations to the barracks. None of the professors used the showers, which might have meant academics have cleaner jobs than soldiers, or without any chance of a surprise inspection, they could get dirty and never get busted for it. The building was called Mary Bolton Hall. Not the sort of place where you'd stumble over a table of Nobel Prize winners.

The law school's less-than-executive quarters were a sensitive subject among the faculty. Edgar, as a gynecologist, had a reasonable idea of what went on inside the average Vancouver bedroom. But nothing in his professional experience had prepared him for Mary Bolton Hall. Edgar stood in the doorway of the Dean's bedroom-cum-office puffing on his cigarette, wondering if Matthew Burlock was going to receive the law in what looked like a working-class brothel.

Dean Scime immediately tried to put him at ease. The physical plant (as Dean Scime called Mary Bolton Hall) was the source of some embarrassment. Lawyers, even academic ones, aren't normally found plying their trade from someone else's former bedroom. He might've made a joke about the surroundings to put Edgar at ease—a "This is where we put the law to rest" sort of remark. Dean Scime took this series of connecting bedrooms and showers seriously enough to avoid any direct reference to the subject. To divert Edgar's attention he launched into a legal theory. Edgar, sitting across from the Dean, probably bridged his fingers and hooked his thumbs under his chin. This theory was called Scime's law.

The heart of the Dean's theory was based on an inverse relationship between the date a faculty is established and the amount of money a university will cough up for the physical plant to house them. In other words, you were kept out of the sitting room until you proved your worth in the bedroom, as Edgar once summarized it for me. Dean Scime sat at his desk for nearly fifteen minutes outlining the economic, social, and political consequences of his theory, rolling a piece of chalk between his fingers and getting it all over his suit. He thrust the chalk at Edgar to punctuate each point. A group of monks had camped for ten years in a forest near Oxford before they got their building. They ate roots and bark. That was a thirteenth-century authority for Dean Scime's theory.

Edgar could take no more.

"My son's got cancer," Edgar said, taking a handkerchief from his suit pocket.

Dean Scime recoiled. The chalk rolled across his desk and fell on the floor. His eyes narrowed as he watched Edgar blow his nose.

"Cancer," whispered the Dean.

"His one and only wish is to be a lawyer."

The Dean patted Edgar's arm.

This bare summary of Edgar's fraud only came out many years later. At that time Edgar had shoulder-length hair, wore Indian beads and a headband, and lay in a hospital bed. His eyes were sunken and his beard nearly white. He told me how I got into law school, and many other things. Peace and brotherhood. The obiter of the 1960s had overtaken Edgar near the end.

Dean Scime, who resembled Spencer Tracy, lifted a bottle of Scotch from his desk drawer and filled two finger-marked water glasses. He poured Edgar a drink and pushed the glass across his desk. Edgar wiped the rim with his handkerchief and threw back the two shots. He put the empty glass back on the Dean's desk.

"It's tough," said Dean Scime. He refilled Edgar's glass.

"I don't expect any special favors," Edgar said.

"How much time does your son—"

"Matthew," interjected Edgar.

"How much time does Matthew have left?"

"Six months. Maybe a year at most."

"I see." Dean Scime, following Edgar's example, threw back the Scotch and swallowed hard. His jowls shook. "Cancer," he repeated to himself.

Edgar sighed. Over Dean Scime's shoulder he watched two sea gulls chasing a Great White Bald Eagle. The eagle glided in a wide circle over the cliffs of Wreck Beach, eyes alert for baby gulls or gull eggs. The sea gulls dived at the eagle.

"Where is it—this cancer?"

"In his bones—blood—the liver's probably next."

"That bad?"

"It's fatal," replied Edgar, putting down his empty glass. The eagle had become a pin dot in the distance with the sea gulls still giving chase.

"Matthew would find law school very hard even in the perfect glow of health."

Edgar blew his nose again. Then he played his next and best card.

"He doesn't know," Edgar sobbed.

"Term's already started. And Matthew has no qualifications." Dean Scime was about to say something else, then broke off. He rolled another piece of chalk between the palms of his hands. He shifted around in his chair, and glanced at a photograph of Mrs. Scime and the two Scime children framed over the basin in the corner. It was the sort of picture that would have kept Louise in her cage and me on the road to medical school. "But under the circumstances, I will give Matthew a place."

My admission into law school was an act of compassion.

Like the kid everyone chips in ten dollars so he can see Disneyland before he rots away into a dollop of boiling protoplasm. During the first term, Dean Scime would stop me in the narrow corridors of Mary Bolton Hall and slap me on the shoulder. He seemed slightly disappointed that I looked so healthy, that part of my flesh didn't slough off in his chalky hand, and that he coughed much more than I did. There was always a little mist in his eyes. Deep down, he wanted to be at my side, when that final uncontrolled inflammation ignited and Edgar could hang me next to Ray in his study.

When Edgar himself was melting down with cancer he told me one more thing. As he left Dean Scime's office, he saw the eagle again. He hadn't disappeared after all. This time there was a lifeless baby sea gull in the eagle's beak, and the gulls had given up the pursuit. Towards the end Edgar was loaded to the gills with painkillers. He'd read everything Dr. Timothy O'Leary had written. He told me that opiates were as safe as sugar. I wasn't certain how much Edgar really remembered and what he'd later made up.

THREE weeks later, after Tort class with Dean Scime, Joan and I climbed down the steep, winding path to Wreck Beach. The path was a winding, well-trodden staircase of packed clay and mud twisted around tree stumps, rocks, and gullies. The descent cut through a forest of fir, alder, pine, and cedar; the sun breaking through the gaps like light filtering from small windows in a cathedral ceiling. From the top it was a three-hundred-foot drop to the beach below. Joan led the way down. She jumped, leaped, and darted in a zigzag pattern, kicking up a little cloud of dust. It was one of those things fat people do to show someone else how fit they are. I was out of breath halfway down and Joan had to wait at the bottom several minutes before I appeared. My legs were rubbery and my heart racing. So this was what it was really like for mother to step out of the house.

"You don't look well," she said. Only people with terminal cancer get fatigued running down the side of a mountain was the implication.

"Just out of shape," I replied.

At the bottom of the cliff, we turned right and crossed the sandy beach to the foot of a twenty-foot high concrete gun tower. After the World War II ended, the troops pulled out of the barracks above and abandoned the gun tower on the beach. The door had been pulled off. I followed Joan inside where the air was cold and damp. Beer and whiskey bottles were scattered along the floor. Under an observation window someone had built a fire and the wall had been scorched black. Joan shouted "hello" and a loud echo ricocheted back and forth against the walls. I imagined that her butcher father's house must have looked something like this. Joan obviously felt comfortable here.

In the afternoons, she'd come to this secret hiding place to do her assignments and eat lunch. As I poked around the empty bottles with a stick, Joan sat at a rough table fashioned from a log she's dragged in from the beach. My eyes were now accustomed to the half-darkness inside. She was smiling at me. I looked up at the ladder leading to the observation area above, and wondered if her mother was coming down to welcome me to the Bildsons' modest dwelling. I said very little and finally leaned against the damp wall. Maybe I should have let Louise eat Wong after all. In boarding school you learn to suppress your emotions. I watched Joan, sitting with her legs crossed, unwrap a large piece of cake. It was topped with a thick, pure-butter icing. She broke the cake in two parts with her hands. She looked at both pieces and handed me the smaller one.

I'd never met a girl like Joan.

In boarding school you form the idea that girls only float to the surface along with some special event like a concert. They appeared to come with season tickets.

I sat down across the log from Joan. She leaned forward

and kissed me on the lips. I smelled carrot cake on her breath. I'd been kissed on the lips in a concrete gun tower constructed to sink all the Japanese warships and submarines sent to capture Vancouver. She ruffled my hair with her free hand. Later I would kiss many more women. A filament of Joan's carrot-cake kiss that day on Wreck Beach would drift into my nose with each fresh set of lips for years after.

Joan had taken me into her confidence after I told her my grandfather had been a fireman killed in the line of duty. That wasn't exactly working-class credentials but it was good enough for Joan.

We'd come a long way since the day she'd seen me sitting in the back of Edgar's Mercedes. I thought she'd mistaken me for the Haitian Ambassador. Joan laughed, the fat part on the back of her arms shaking. Ambassador, she moaned with delight. Not a chance. She thought I was just a heavily armed Ambassador's kid. Her tone was the same as when Nelson had said I was just another doctor's kid. I was back, so I thought, about where I'd started my university career. Just a different kind of kid.

After we left the gun tower, we walked along the beach barefoot.

"Why did you kiss me?" I asked her, trying to skip a flat stone across the water. But it just dropped in and sank.

"I wanted to kiss someone who's dying," she replied, reaching down and picking up a flat rock. Hers skipped five times before it disappeared.

I felt humiliated and walked along ahead for a few steps. She threw another stone, and from the corner of my eye, I counted six skips. I sat down on the beach and stretched my feet to the edge of the water. Joan wiped her nose with the back of her hand as she stood over me.

"You're not really dying, are you?"

I stared ahead at the water, ignoring her. Edgar told me that Dean Scime was an old friend who'd squeezed me into law school. He'd sounded credible to me. I'd been accepted on the merits of my outstanding performance at boarding school. There was always one last place for a first-class mind. But Edgar's eyes were still puffy from crying, and I never knew him to cry with joy. I suspected there was some crime responsible for my admission. Now I had to face the truth from the lips of a butcher's daughter. Behind the base of my skull I felt a dull ache; one of mother's migraines had struck. I picked up a handful of sand and let it fall out between my fingers.

"Well, are you or aren't you?" she said, sitting down beside me.

"Who told you I was dying?" I asked, wondering just how far Edgar had gone.

"Dean Scime told me. It's supposed to be a secret." She emptied the sand from her shoes, and started to put them back on. "But I think it's bullshit."

"I'm not dying," I said, the spume washing over my toes.

"You don't know that you're dying, though."

"It's a lie."

"Don't worry, Burlock. I won't blackmail you. All you upper-class guys sink into monkey shit at the end of the day. Disappear without a trace. Just a little bubble of pus on a pile of monkey shit."

Joan didn't sound particularly annoyed or alarmed; she seemed, on the contrary, quite pleased with herself. Anger, ridicule, or scorn is unnecessary when disaster has dropped like a sledgehammer on the type of person who normally makes you feel inferior and stupid. Nelson had been very happy when it sank into his thick skull that I'd shot Louise through the eye. This merrymaking at my personal misfortune was becoming a recurrent theme in my life as a university student.

"Well, I don't know where Dean Scime got that idea," I said.

Joan finished tying her shoelaces; she leaned back on her hands. Her tongue darted over her lips, searching for some final trace of carrot-cake crumb. She kissed me with wet lips.

"The Haitian Ambassador told him," she whispered in my ear.

"I told you before. Edgar's not an Ambassador."

"Then who is Edgar?"

"He's my gynecologist."

"Dumb shit. Men don't have gynecologists."

"Well, I've had one since I was five."

She stood up quickly, a flash of anger in her eyes. "Oh, God. What bullshit. Maybe you are really dying. Little worms eating holes in your brains."

IN the class of '57 there were six women, including Joan Bildson, and forty-seven men, and one boy who didn't eventually die of cancer. Over the intervening years, four members of that class have been disbarred; three appointed to the bench (counting M. Burlock); five became Queen Counsels; one Commissioner of Labour; one Liberal MP. The rest drifted away like the early morning haze on an autumn day over Grouse Mountain.

No one could have predicted the success to be obtained by the members of our class during the first few weeks. They didn't look important or even sound sensible. For the men, life revolved around hockey, football, women, and beer. After I learned how Edgar managed to get me into law school I kept a low profile. I didn't know how many others knew about my "cancer." I wanted to avoid explaining anything to anyone. Probably it was my age that caused most of the other students to whisper as I passed. I told one or two guys who pressed the point that I'd been a science major and left the rest vague. I took up smoking cigarettes to look older. I spoke in a lower voice. I didn't shave for a week but nothing much happened except a little thin Chinese-like beard appeared on my chin.

Joan Bildson was different from the others. Maybe because she had, in a manner of speaking, taken me to her home. I opened up to her and trusted her. She looked after me; I brought out a strong mothering instinct in her; and was deeply sorry that my mother had married outside a fireman's social class. So we passed the days together, which caused a number of ugly rumors. Before tort class one morning, she took me aside in the student lounge.

"Bet you'll never guess what I found written in the women's washroom," she said.

"What?"

"Something about the Dean."

Joan knew how to get your attention.

"A picture?"

"No, an equation."

She squeezed her tort casebook against her chest. I assumed this was another dig about my failed science and medical career. I'd told her about Nelson, Wong, Louise—the entire story in the gun tower one afternoon.

"Someone wrote above the toilet—Ready?"

At the next table, Yates and Cook, two of our classmates, whispered and nodded in our direction. I turned my chair so my back faced them. Yates asked Cook if he thought I was getting any from Joan. They never said what they meant by "any" but I had a reasonably good idea. When I'd pass Yates in the hallway, he'd curl his index finger into an okay sign around his thumb and pump his other index finger through the hole. "Getting any, kid?" he'd asked. I dismissed Yates and Cook as perverted products of the public school system. Just two grease-balls who loved using the word tits.

"Just tell me," I said to Joan, glancing back at Yates who had his fingers in a lewd pumping motion.

"Above the toilet someone wrote: Scum plus Crime equals Scime." She giggled the way I imagined fat women did in bed when they were "getting any." I put both of my hands palm down on the table in clear view of Yates and Cook. I wasn't fooling around under the table. There was the proof.

"Well," said Joan.

"Well, what?" I asked, glancing at the headnote of a recent

House of Lords case. An eighteen-year-old youth (as Lord Simmonds called him) had killed a prostitute named Doreen Mary Redding.

"Who do you think wrote it?" asked Joan. She was drinking milk straight from a carton. A thin white moustache formed on her upper lip. I wanted to wipe it away but looked down at the case. I began to sweat. The eighteen-year-old youth had "the misfortune to be sexually impotent." He was trying to get any from a Doreen in a Leicester street. Oh, my God! He tried to hold her down with brute force, pinning her to the wall of a building. Then Doreen kicked him in the balls. He pulled out a knife and stabbed her twice; once for each ball, I'd guessed. When she fell to the street, Doreen was dead. Not the sort of case I'd repeat to mother. Another example of Wongness in the world.

"I did it," said Joan.

I looked up from the casebook, the spirit of Doreen seated before me. Unlike the reasonable man I was out of control. Before I knew what I'd done, I heard myself shout. I'd been reading the House of Lords judgment as if it had been written about Joan and me. I was personally involved. How do you convict an eighteen-year-old of murder after he'd been kicked in the balls and jeered at? The reason had to be the knife. I hated knives. They are so working class. The House of Lords must have thought along the same lines. They said the kid in Leicester hadn't acted like a reasonable man. Now if he'd shot her, obviously that would have been manslaughter. I was catching on fairly quickly as to how the system worked.

Yates and Cook had broken out into laughter when I shouted.

"You like that case," shouted Yates. He now teaches contracts at Queen's University.

"It made him jump right out of his diapers," Cook said, joining in. Five years ago Cook was disbarred for playing the stock market with money he'd "borrowed" from his client's trust fund account.

This was one reason Dean Scime didn't want kids in the

law school. It was like going to a three-year-long X-rated film. Gory violence, explicit sex with foreign objects and animals, robbers, rapists, murderers, and assorted cheats, frauds, and carelessly stupid, feeble, blind people. When you got warped enough from reading all these stories, then Dean Scime said you'd start to think like a lawyer.

"Let's get out of here," said Joan, polishing off her milk. The white moustache was more pronounced now. She pushed back her chair and stood up and threw the empty carton at Yates. "This belongs with the rest of the trash," she said.

"Watch your private parts," said Yates, as I rose with my books.

Lord Simmonds' judgment quoted the accused as saying that: "She kicked me in the privates." After several weeks of my limited association with Yates and Cook, I didn't believe some working class kid in Leicester would use those words. The police interrogation officer must've written down privates when the accused screamed that: "the crazy cunt kicked me in the balls."

Like Lord Simmonds I stared down at them with distaste. Confrontation was something they often demanded. I watched Yates light a Lucky Strike and throw the pack on the table. He folded his arms and leaned back on two legs on his chair. I went up to him. Joan, who stood to my right, gave Cook the finger.

"Yates." I put my books down on the table. "Your trouble is lack of proper schooling. Twelve years of studying in some sewer's warped you. It's given you turds for brains." This sounded more brave than it actually was; he could have broken me like a matchstick. But breaking a seventeen-year-old who was dying of cancer was even beyond his minimal moral code.

"Listen, piss ant," Cook said. Yates pushed him back in his chair.

"It's your sort who are always kicking or getting kicked in the genitals," I said, scooping up my books.

Yates started laughing as he put out his cigarette in Joan's milk carton. "Genitals? Christ, do you have genitals, Cook?" he said. He threw the milk carton at Joan but she ducked and it landed on the floor.

"No, but I've got two big balls," said Cook, rocking back in his chair.

"Too bad there's nothing between your legs," Joan shot back, and walked towards the door.

"Hey, she's pretty clever," said Yates.

Outside in the corridor, Joan put her arm around my shoulder. "It's all right, kid. You did just fine with those assholes." That wasn't the point. I'd lost control and allowed them to suck me into their little game. Always a mistake. When you're seventeen it's easy to become sexually humiliated and degraded. I knew exactly what went through the Leicester guy's mind as he pulled his knife. This hot taste fills your mouth. I understood better what must have gone through Lord Simmond's mind: no accident or misfortune that life throws at a gentleman is ever sufficient to throw him off course from his duty and destiny. He may suffer a temporary setback, or indeed a short-term loss, but his breeding teaches him that he can never, ever be defeated. That only happens to people like the guy in Leicester.

We put our books in a locker. Joan was getting hungry. The milk now dried on her upper lip like cement suggested we break for an early lunch. It sounded like an excellent idea. So Joan and I hiked down to Wreck Beach and ate sandwiches in the gun tower. That was to make me feel much better—at least for a while.

CHAPTER 4

IT was too cold to stay very long inside the gun tower and neither of us felt like burning a fire. After we finished eating, we walked below the cliffs and picked our way among a large boulder field which ran down to the edge of the sea. We hopped from boulder to boulder, landed in the sand, and then found footholds in a six-foot-high boulder. We both climbed up and from the top we watched a Canadian Pacific ferry crossing Georgia Strait on the way to Victoria. The sea was calm and we could see all the way over to Bowen Island. Back on the beach we removed our shoes, tied the laces together and put them around our necks. She walked in my footprints for a while, then she walked ahead and I followed in hers. We threaded our way along the beach until the gun tower disappeared behind us. I had my briefcase and inside two loaded guns. As we walked together, Joan nibbled on an apple she pulled from a brown bag. She breathed heavily as she walked and ate at the same time. I told her it wasn't good for her digestion; she said she needed to exercise while she ate, or she'd get too fat. Around the next bend we found a large log washed up on the beach and sat down in front of it.

Joan unwrapped a candy bar and took a bite. I shook my head as she offered it to me. "Both of those guys are pricks," she said. "Don't let them get to you, Matt."

I'd never heard a woman use words like prick and asshole before.

"I'm going into the water," I said, standing back up.

"Hey, wait up, Burlock," she said, sitting on her knees. We were on a long, lonely stretch of beach. A few sandpipers darted back and forth on the wet surface of the sand. Like Joan they never seemed to get tired of feeding. "Jesus Christ, will you wait a minute."

About twenty feet away I put the briefcase on a dry log. Then I slid onto the log, crossed my legs, and watched Joan leaving size-9 footprints in the cool, wet sand. She had chocolate on her mouth; it spoiled her pure, white moustache.

"I don't want to talk about them," I said.

I buttoned my sweater as she climbed up next to me. "You're right. Who wants to talk about assholes." She bent one leg up, rolled up her jean cuff, then rolled up the other one. All the other women in the law school wore dresses. Joan made a point of displaying what in those days were working-class symbols.

"It's no different in Science," I said with the air of an expert. "Guys like Yates and Cook are everywhere."

"Fucking right," she said.

I reached over and wiped off her mouth, rubbing the chocolate and dried milk on the side of the log. "Just in case you try and kiss me again," I said. It seemed to make her happy in a strange sort of way. Still, I couldn't figure her out. Women I'd been around didn't use words like fucking, wear jeans, and wear food on their face instead of makeup. Even mother, who'd been to New York to meet Brecht, had probably never heard those words. It was part of the Wongness that kept her a prisoner inside the house. This was 1954. Women had a different language from men then. People have forgotten that. It's understandable, women since 1968 having said "fuck" more times than all men and women who ever lived before.

Joan told me about Yates. They'd been classmates at Burnaby Grease ball High School. His father had gone broke selling lightning rods in Manitoba. He then picked up the family and moved to British Columbia to make a fresh start. Yates' father worked in the shoe shop two doors down the street from Bildson's butcher shop. The shoe shop had been owned by a Japanese family but the Government put them in concentration camps during the war. This allowed assholes like Yates' father to get the shop for next to nothing. After the war, the old man wouldn't even give Mr. Tanaka, the former owner, a job repairing shoes. The whole family were racist assholes, according to Joan.

Yates was climbing his way out. His father had taken his step up by standing on the heads of a poor, helpless Japanese family. Yates himself was about to follow suit. Joan was acquiring weapons to take back to the streets of Burnaby. She hated people like Yates more than the Haitian Ambassador. But social consciousness was like nuclear fission in the 1950s. No one was exactly certain how it worked and who was responsible for turning it into something useful. Everyone but Joan. She had extrasensory perception; she quickly spotted the useless opinions people hid the truth behind, and attacked with precision and with the maximum amount of destruction. She was shrewd in the ways that people oppressed one another.

Our first week of class Dean Scime assigned the class a famous negligence case decided by the House of Lords in the 1930s. This wasn't an impotent guy kicked in the balls by a prostitute, but a Scottish woman who accidently swallowed a slug from her bottle of ginger beer. She'd been out on the town with her married boyfriend. Fate struck and she was carried off to hospital throwing up and very pale. The case was reasonably clear: if you make ginger beer then you must be careful to prevent slugs or other disgusting things from getting inside. If there was any surprise, it must've been allright before the 1930s to let slugs, mice, and snakes slip into your ginger beer and make you sick without the beermaker having to pay damages.

Dean Scime obviously liked this case very much. We spent days on the slug-in-the-ginger-beer. The last day on the subject, he introduced a Canadian sequel to the British case. An old woman, someone who'd be called a bag lady now, read through a pile of newspapers she'd collected and discovered a news item on the large damage award this Scottish woman had received for drinking ginger beer with a slug in it. Some light flashed on inside the old woman's head. It was in the early 1930s when the depression had struck. Banks all over North America had folded. People lined up at soup kitchens. The jobless slept in parks, ate out of garbage cans, and rode freight trains across the country in search of work. There was little to fall back on: no unemployment insurance, social welfare, food stamps. It was every man, woman, and child for themselves. Darwin economics.

Irene Anglin boarded a train at the Main Street station in Vancouver. She didn't have a ticket, and the conductor put her off at Calgary, feeling sorry, he didn't phone the police or have her charged. With a panhandled dime she bought a bottle of Coca-Cola, retreated to a back alley, opened the bottle. She set it on a window ledge. Then looking around to make certain she was alone, she took a jar from her handbag and removed a slug. She smiled and dropped it into the coke bottle, and made her way back to the street. She took several long hard drinks from the bottle. Quietly she returned to the shop where she'd bought the coke, screamed and collapsed on the floor.

A Calgary law firm settled her case with the local bottler of Coca-Cola for nearly eight hundred dollars. After fees and disbursements the widow left Calgary with nearly three hundred dollars, a small fortune in those days. Her next stop was Regina. The bottlers in that city made a similar settlement after Irene drank a bottle of their finest, laced with a British Columbia slug. The old widow was making a decent living for the first time since the death of her husband. On to Winnipeg and the bottlers of ginger ale. There Irene Anglin faced a problem after drinking her third and final bottle of soda pop with a slug. Dr. Pepper and ginger ale were owned by a tycoon named James Morgan. It was 1937 and the old bag lady started to cry at the police station. Mr. Morgan saw her briefly in the police station interrogation room. She'd signed a full confession. The police had an open-and-shut case against the Vancouver slug lady.

But Morgan declined to have the police prosecute. The kingpin of Canadian bottlers stuffed a five-dollar bill into the old lady's hand (the Winnipeg police having confiscated about five hundred in cash from her bag) and saw that she was put on a train back to Vancouver. Dean Scime told it as a funny story, how laymen get all confused about the nature and the purpose of law. Joan didn't quite see it that way. She rose from her chair, her cheeks febrile. This was nothing short of absolute proof of how the big money men of Canada exploited the working classes. For five minutes she talked about how the government had never done anything for the working people of Canada except to screw them and throw them into concentration camps and prisons. Very strong stuff from a first-year woman law student in 1954. Dean Scime had become Scum plus Crime. She made a special trip down to the courthouse in Vancouver and wrote her little equation on the walls of both the women's and men's toilets.

All Dean Scime could think of saying was not directed at Joan but at me. "Are you feeling all right, Matthew?"

"Just fine, sir," I replied.

"The rough-and-tumble of law school can be tiring," he said, glancing at Joan. "With Miss Bildson's permission, maybe Mister Burlock might explain our next case."

His voice crackled like someone whose private scandal had been made public. It was safe to call on a harmless kid who was Joan's friend. She might cool down. I gave what amounted to, by any standards, the most confused, inaccurate description of the following case. Yates whispered over my shoulder, "Hey, what page you on—or what are you on?"

My concentration had been destroyed. After the class I asked Dean Scime to show me his newspaper-clipping file about the old widow. I went back to his office. In the closet where officers once stored their uniforms, Dean Scime pulled out a filing-cabinet drawer. He handed me the file and said I could take it away for the day. The conclusion was inescapable as I read through the press reports: Irene Anglin was Wild Bill's widow. A reference to Wild Bill appeared in one of the clips. The old bag lady whom Joan was willing to defend as a victim of the capitalist class was my grandmother.

CHAPTER 5

EDGAR and mother had kept many secrets about the family but this was quite something else. Everyone in Mother's life who ever left the house got burned up, went missing-in-action, drank slugs in their soda pop, or killed expensive boas. I had the files spread out on a blanket that Joan had brought down to the beach. We read the clippings together; she even stopped eating. A picture began to emerge about my grandparents. In 1938, the year Edgar married mother, my grandmother was gulping down slugs for money. Why hadn't someone in the family looked after her? Wild Bill's widow packed into a train, photographed by the press, branded an elderly desperado. This lonely, forgotten bag lady in her rumpled dress had been denied any official recognition by the Burlocks. I was shattered. There are certain things parents shouldn't hide from their children: adoption, deadly disease, and . . . family connections—all family connections; even the ones rooted in the common, simple folk.

I was desolate and told Joan how disgusted I was about the shabby way my family had acted. Wild Bill's widow sleeping on park benches. Her dirty underclothes hanging below her dress. Hair uncombed and windblown. Shoes scuffed and holes in the soles. Joan tried to calm me down. A grandfather who was a fireman was one thing; but a genuine bag lady for a grandmother even out-working-classed Joan. She was impressed. I didn't see it the same way. I told her I wished Edgar really had cancer—something a seventeen-year-old regrets years later standing in front of the deathbed of a man and watching the cancer devour him before your eyes.

For Joan, I was full of surprises—an enigma—the mystery kid in the back of a Mercedes whose grandmother ate slugs for a living.

Sitting beside me on the blanket, Joan put her fleshy arm around my shoulder, squeezing lightly like a butcher examining a piece of Kobe beef. "Who are you, Burlock?" I avoided eye contact. "Where did you really come from? And where in the hell do you belong?"

"Don't ask me," I said, putting the newspaper clippings back in Dean Scime's file. I looked out at the sea. There was a fishing boat about half a mile out. It was too far away to see the men fishing. All I could think about were Wild Bill and Irene out there somewhere, smiling that I'd finally found out some basic facts about their existence. Like the fishermen, I couldn't see what I was really fishing after. There had to be something else below the surface. I just needed the right bait and some patience.

"You can't run away from this, Matthew."

She ruffled my hair, and with the other had pulled a beef and tomato sandwich from her handbag. There was a minimum of half a pound of sliced roast beef between two pieces of white bread and maybe one large tomato. She took a healthy bite.

"Ah, it's not your fault. You're just a funny kid." She talked with her mouth full, stopping only to swallow and pull back the bread to check at the amount of beef left inside. "Dean Scime's told that stupid fucking story about your grandmother—what an asshole." I glanced at her. Seeds from the tomato were caught between her front teeth.

"She died when I was two," I said.

"Don't get into a blue funk."

"It's not just that," I said, watching her jaws pumping up and down and bits of bread falling on her chest. The sea gulls could live on the droppings she left behind.

"Well, what is it? No, bullshit. Out with it."

"It's everything. My grandmother eating slugs for bucks. An impotent eighteen-year-old gets kicked in the balls in Leicester. My not dying of cancer. Edgar's obsession with Koestler; mother's obsession with Brecht. Life is one big Wong."

She raised the sandwich towards my mouth but I shook my head. The fishing boat had pulled up anchor and was moving on. Try another place or another day. Sometimes you just give up and know that you're not going to catch what you came for. Joan licked each of her fingers. The sandwich, except for some minor debris on Joan's clothes, was gone. Leaning forward, she wiped her hands on the log. "Do you want to fuck?" she asked. "It might make you feel better."

I turned towards her, touched her hand. She smiled and little specks of beef and tomato seed were wedged in her teeth. No wonder the eighteen-year-old in Leicester had become impotent. I was breathing through my mouth. The garlic in the mustard was overpowering. She rested her hand on my leg and gave it a light squeeze.

"This is a nude beach, Matthew. You don't have to be shy."

If I had one single wish at that moment, it was not to see Joan Bildson naked on Wreck Beach. I wanted more clothes on her body, not less. With everything else on my mind, I didn't want to stare at folds of fat hanging like Venetian blinds down her belly; dimples rippling like rail stake holes on her thighs; or breasts sagging like hocks on an old mare.

"I'm a virgin," I said.

"Oh," she sighed, taking an apple from her handbag. She rubbed it along the side of her jeans. As she sat back on the blanket, we watched two sailboats about two miles out of English Bay. The wind had caught the sails, and boats were heading westwards towards the Gulf Islands and the open sea.

Their occupants might have been friends of Edgar's. That was the sort of person who sailed midweek in September; rich people, who felt safe on the open sea; no bag ladies to contend with—just the fresh sea air. Potter had taught me a great deal about such people.

"What are you thinking about, Burlock?"

"I was thinking about Potter."

"Not another gynecologist?"

"A virgin only needs one."

"So who's this Potter," she said after a moment, tossing the apple core into the sea.

From the tone of her voice I could tell she thought Potter might be a girlfriend. And that the real reason I didn't want to make love on the beach was that I was saving myself for her. Probably some upper-class snob who didn't eat garlic mustard on her beef sandwich. I let her wait a few moments for an answer, then I opened my breifcase and took out my Colt .45 (the one I used to dispatch Louise with) and a Colt .44. The last gun was in mint condition and well oiled. Joan belched and looked very much afraid. She had Wong's eyes at that moment, slanted with fear.

"You've seen this one before," I said, holding up the Colt .45.

"Where?"

"In the back of Edgar's Mercedes. Don't you remember?"

"I thought it was a toy."

The real guns were totally unexpected, she told me much later. All that term I'd been carting around an arsenal of heavy weapons, and hadn't said a word about them. Yet another surprise for Joan, and one she had not anticipated. I aimed the Colt and fired, breaking a Coca-Cola bottle about fifty feet away. I thought she was going to throw up but she ducked her head and covered her ears. I fired another shot, shattering another pop bottle. That one was also for Irene.

"Jesus fucking Christ," she said, her lips trembling. I'd never seen her frightened before, and never quite understood why people were afraid of something as straightforward as a gun.

"You asked about Potter," I said, switching guns.

"Are you going to do it again?"

I squeezed off another shot, this time from the .44, fracturing the neck of the Coca-Cola bottle into tiny atoms.

"You're a fucking crack shot." She slowly raised her head, as I put the .44 back in my case.

"Potter was my housemaster at school," I said, cocking the .45 and surveying my line of vision for another target.

"I don't think I'll ever figure you out, Burlock."

"During the great war, Potter was an artilleryman." I slowly squeezed off a final round. The bottom of the second bottle exploded. It was as if the bottled ginger beer had never existed.

CHAPTER 6

MRS. Potter had gone to a free lecture at the Colonial Theatre on Granville Street. The *Vancouver Sun* ran a photograph of the minister and the title of his free lecture: *Why Doesn't God Stop the War?* The title was printed in a bold caption. Potter didn't believe in newspapers or God. It was the same year Humphrey Bogart got the Oscar for *Casablanca*. Bogart's photograph was on the same page as the minister's. Why didn't God help Bogie get safely out of Casablanca? If God couldn't handle a scriptwriter how was he going to contend with Hitler?

It was a Monday night, February 28, 1944. The Fifth Army was catching hell at Anzio; bitter patrol fighting was going on all along the beachhead perimeter. Nazi tanks some six thousand miles away from Alpha House were inflicting heavy casualties on the allies. By seven, I knew that a casualty was one of our soldiers blown to hell and gone by a German. While we sat around the radio with Potter, his wife was down at the Colonial Theatre with another housemaster's wife trying to find out what God was going to do about the German tanks around Anzio. In Alpha House, Potter and about ten private school boarders sat on the floor in a semicircle listening to Groucho Marx on KIRO radio.

Huddled with the other children in my pajamas and slippers, I edged closer to the fireplace to keep my feet and hands warm. Potter sat in his overstuffed chair opposite the radio, legs crossed, in his smoking jacket, with gray jets of smoke rising from his pipe. When I looked up at him, these steel-blue eyes were fixed on the flame engulfing the logs in the fireplace. It was a rule that we remain silent for the entire half-hour during a radio program. I wasn't quite seven and the silence seemed to last for eternity. We'd fidget sometimes, only to find Potter's steely blue eyes fixed on one of us. Loneliness was the main problem; we each had close friends—that was important—and we all had Potter. But Potter never became friendly in a paternal fashion with any of the boys; neither did he fraternize much with the other housemasters or teachers. This was the classic English pattern for making a gentleman. We were taught self-reliance, responsibility, and duty. Lord Simmonds wouldn't find us slashing up a prostitute in Leicester. Despite the distance Potter kept, I always sensed he had an eye out for me.

My memory of that evening is particularly vivid: Potter leaning over to put on a fresh log, listening to Groucho Marx on the radio, watching the clock on the mantle. Like an old, forgotten roll of film from your subconscious. Each small frame is a single exposure of a highly detailed picture from the eyes of yourself as you photographed the world with seven-year-old eyes. Some of the boys laughed at Groucho Marx's jokes. I didn't understand many of them. I was more interested in the RCA Victor radio housed in a large walnut case. Larger than myself, the front dial was a circle like the face of a clock and illuminated from behind with a green bulb. Groucho Marx lived inside the case. I didn't understand how that could be or, if he didn't, how his voice got into the radio. Ignorance in science is normally one of the requirements for being a gentleman, so there was a certain chill in a master's voice if you started asking mechanical or technical questions. I tried to figure out the radio by myself.

In the center of my universe was Potter; steadfast, civilized, direct, and with proper English schooling, he was our role model. How all gentlemen should aspire to behave. But Potter was different from the other housemasters and teachers. As if every time you snapped his picture, there was a shadow covering the background. Men like Potter had "backgrounds" and my private school dispensed with a thorough investigation of applicants for the housemasters' post. Gentlemen suffered private misfortune. During the war a school took what gentlemen it could find and left the backgrounds in the shadows. Most men served in the armed forces. Some were pinned down at the exact moment at Anzio.

After the Groucho Marx program, Potter inspected our sleeping quarters and asked if we'd said our prayers. We prayed for the whole shopping list: the King, Mr. Churchill, Mr. Roosevelt, and Mr. King. This was the order suggested by Potter. From an English Gentleman's point of view, the Canadian Prime Minister rode in a distant last on the prayer sweepstakes. How could little Canada end the war?

Why doesn't God stop the war?

Mrs. Potter seemed disappointed after the free lecture at the Colonial Theatre. I heard her talking to Potter as I was thinking of dropping Mr. King from my prayer list altogether. A door closed and I couldn't make out what they were saying. In the dark, I listened to another boy pray and compared his technique to mine.

Did I pray for Potter that night? In truth, I don't remember. Although, some nights I did.

The room was dark when I awoke. The other boys were sleeping. It was a sudden start. Eyes wide open, sitting up in bed, and gripped with complete terror; a terror so lavish that it continued to rampage around my bed as I sat clutching a pillow to my chest. I could smell fire and feel heat on my hands. In this dream, Wild Bill Anglin, head cocked to the right, arms held out like Christ on the cross, stood aflame at the end of my bed, looking down at me with expressionless eyes. I prayed for God to send Wild Bill back where he came from. My heart pounded in my throat and ears. A small boy's nightmare lurks in the dark corners of the bedroom after his eyes open. In the world of nearly seven, Groucho Marx slept inside the RCA Victor; Edgar and Mother slept through the night, and Ray slept in Edgar's study twenty-four hours a day; the entire world was asleep and you were completely alone.

I was scared and immobile, listening to the other boys snore in the beds next to mine. Whether I closed or opened my eyes, Wild Bill, a dazzling, radiant burning torch was watching over me. Finally, I tiptoed out of the room. How could the other boys lie there breathing heavily with all those bright flames showering over their beds? Each step towards the door, I thought that one of those heavy breathers would explode into flames, another novice gentleman reduced to cinders and ash. Wild Bill remained at the end of my bed, as I closed the door behind me. The hallway light was on, and for the first time I knew that I was safe. That's when I began crying. Tears streaming down my face I walked down the corridor. Blubbering away, I couldn't stop myself. Hadn't I almost been burned alive? All my friends were still in danger. If I went back, I might catch on fire; if I went to Potter, I would be disgraced. I pushed forward, peeking around the entrance of the sitting room.

Potter was alone in his chair, pipe clenched between his teeth. The fireplace was hissing with the last red embers of the evening. He was listening to Edward R. Murrow who was reporting on the war from London. I stepped through the entrance. My feet were cold. I'd left my slippers at the foot of my bed where Wild Bill was standing. Edward R. Murrow talked about Hitler's secret weapon—robot tanks—radio-controlled tanks loaded to the turrets with high explosives. The Nazis had dispatched hundreds of the super-powerful tanks against the allied lines bogged down on Anzio Beach. Why didn't Mrs. Potter's God stop robot tanks? Why didn't she order them to get Wild Bill instead? I didn't care about Anzio Beach or the Nazis and their tanks. I only wanted to be safe.

"Robot tanks," murmured Potter. "What rubbish."

Standing on the edge of the carpet, one foot warming the other, I burst into tears again. My entire world was collapsing on top of me. Wild Bill in flames, robot tanks, all these men inside the radio, and Potter talking back to them when everyone else was out of the room. I sobbed; that kind of small child's shuddering sob, full of desolation and fear; a sob that takes their very breath away and threatens to suffocate them. Potter shifted in his chair, removed his pipe and looked at the door. I was squeezing a pillow between my arms, the tears falling from my cheeks and onto the pillowcase.

"And what do we have here?" asked Potter. He motioned with his pipe and I ran over and put my arms around his neck and held on tightly. He patted my back.

"What is it, lad? A bad dream?"

I nodded my head against his chest. I knew that adults told you the things that woke you were nightmares. I thought of them as little horses falling over trip wires and tumbling over a cliff. Nonsense, of course, but it was the only way I could understand what they meant. By definition, Wild Bill was not a nightmare; he was really burning and frying before my very eyes. Potter was more relaxed than I had ever seen him. He didn't push me away. One arm around me, his head tilted to the side, he resumed smoking his pipe and listening to the radio. Probably he thought I'd fall asleep and he'd carry me back to my bed. But I was wide awake. One ear pressed against his chest, I listened to his heart and with the other to Edward

R. Murrow. He was reporting that Princess Elizabeth and General Sir Bernard Montgomery attended the international soccer match at Wembly Stadium. Peeking through one eye, I saw Potter nod his head as if he knew these people.

"Were there robot tanks at the match, sir?" I asked.

Potter laughed, reached over and struck the bowl of his pipe against a large, black ashtray. "There aren't robot tanks, lad. It's propaganda to explain why the Fifth Army's stranded on Anzio Beach."

I didn't have the vaguest idea what propaganda meant and suspected it was another kind of nightmare. Maybe Wild Bill was propaganda. This thought propelled a new round of sobs. Potter shifted his weight and reached into his pocket for a handkerchief.

"You're a funny little chappy, Burlock." He wiped my face. His wool sweater was wet from my crying; it was scratchy and made my nose itch.

"I saw a man on fire," I said, pulling my head away from his chest and looking into his eyes.

"A man, was it?" he said, taking a different pipe from the black ashtray and filling it with tobacco from a leather pouch on the table. "And this man was in the bedroom?"

"Yes, sir." I watched him crimp the tobacco down with the tip of his thumb and stuff more into the bowl. "He was dying, but not really dying." I tried to explain but didn't have the words for what I'd seen.

"Oh?"

"I saw it. Really, sir."

"And does this man on fire have a name?"

"Yes, sir."

"Well, out with it." He struck a match and the smell of sulphur filled my nose. It was Wild Bill's smell. I waited until he lit his pipe.

"Wild Bill," I said.

"A burning man named Wild Bill?"

I nodded, breathing in the smoke from Potter's pipe. "Wild

Bill Anglin. I came to school so I wouldn't burn up like Wild Bill."

For the first time I saw emotion in Potter's eyes; they swelled and the pupils grew large. He looked stunned. "Wild Bill Anglin," he repeated slowly, putting the smoldering pipe into the ashtray. His voice sounded strange. The name had stripped off a mask from Potter's face. I hadn't seen this face before: a face animated with awe and danger. Maybe he'd seen Wild Bill burning after all? Nothing disturbs a child more than seeing fear on the face of an adult. If they're scared, then it must be really bad and no one is safe. I got scared all over again. Where could I run to next? I thought Potter had never been frightened ever. I was having serious second thoughts. My eyes became moist again.

"How do you know that name?" Potter asked, his hands firmly clasping my shoulders. He didn't sound like a man training future gentlemen any longer. Something had been jarred loose. I'd caught him by surprise. And surprise is the only power that children have over adults. I started to like this transformed Potter, and must have begun to look slightly cocky. I wasn't just little dirty-nosed Burlock who'd been caned for accidentally wetting the bed twice in one week. Instead, Potter had seated on his lap a less than seven-year-old shaman; a little chap with no experience of life but through some power of perception or enlarged consciousness had witnessed the burning of Wild Bill Anglin. A child senses when the balance of power shifts with an adult. I wiped my nose on my sleeve and climbed down from Potter's lap.

"I want another log on the fire," I said, stepping over and dragging a log from the bin.

"Go on, Matthew." For the first time he hadn't called me Burlock. I tilted a piece of alder on its top and let it fall into the fireplace. Half the log stuck out of the fireplace. From behind me, Potter removed the poker and shifted the log so that it rested securely on the remaining embers. He paced in front of the fireplace for a few moments while I sat cross-legged watching the smoke start to rise.

"That name—"

"Wild Bill Anglin's my grandfather," I answered, before Potter finished his question.

He had a funny little smile on his face like he'd remembered something that amused him. "He was a very great man." I looked over my shoulder. Potter was staring at the fireplace like I'd seen him earlier in the evening. Lost in thought, his eyes not quite focused.

"He was a fireman," I said. "He got killed in a fire."

"He died in a fire, Matthew," Potter corrected me. "Not 'got killed' in a fire."

"Wild Bill didn't study hard in a proper school. He probably said 'got' all the time."

"Who told you that?"

"Mummy," I replied, fingering the end of the poker.

Potter resumed sucking his pipe. It helped the thinking process; when he got stuck, the columns of smoke became thick and black. He switched off the radio. I watched him standing before the fading green dial. He'd put Groucho Marx and Edward R. Murrow to sleep. As he turned, his face looked troubled.

"Wild Bill Anglin was a clever man. Don't ever forget that, Burlock."

"Yes, sir."

"A great man. Understand?"

"Yes, sir."

Who was I to believe now? My housemaster had contradicted a major family myth which Edgar and mother had told many times. Potter sensed my problem, and I guess decided he had no choice but to take me into his confidence. Since I was about seven I didn't understand much of anything, and he wasn't about to stand towering above me and enter into any meaningful dialogue.

"One day you must learn about the Auto Ordnance Corporation of Bridgeport, Connecticut," he said. This made about as much sense at the time as one of Groucho Marx's jokes. I didn't know what to say.

"Yes, sir," I said.

Then we went down into the basement of Alpha House. The basement had the smell of an abandoned gun tower; the damp smell of concrete, a musky outdoors scent. From the first we'd been told by Potter that the basement was strictly off-limits. We were permanently, absolutely, and forever barred from ever stepping foot down there. Anyone who disobeyed would get the strap; hard rations; and maybe kicked out of school. The older kids made up stories about torture chambers and monsters to give the younger ones nightmares. The worst threat was for an older kid to say he was going to tell Potter he saw you pissing under the basement stairs. The basement was a symbol of all that could be and was wrong with life for a seven-year-old separated from his parents. It was the place where Wongness was kept chained.

Potter had to literally carry me down the stairs. All the dead bodies, monsters, rats, and bears in the world lived down there. And I had the feeling that Wild Bill hung around down there when he wasn't burning on a cross at the foot of my bed. I was trembling and speechless as we descended the stairs. I kept my eyes tightly closed and tried to force myself into sleep. At the bottom of the stairs, Potter reached up and turned on a light that hung suspended from the ceiling. I peeked out. The floors were concrete; and there were damp spots on the walls. Then I opened both eyes. No nightmares lurking anywhere. The naked lightbulb cast light across the room. Along the side of the walls were tiny windows with drawn curtains. Boxes and crates were stacked against one wall right to the ceiling. To the right were rows of bottles stacked on wooden shelves. This was Potter's collection of fine wines and port. We walked around an oil-fired central-heating furnace. Along the far wall was another light. Potter reached up and switched it on. A few feet away from the furnace was a table and two wooden chairs with the red paint peeling on the seats. Potter put me down. I looked around and under everything. Nothing jumped out or tried to eat me alive. My fear under control, I felt my feet freezing on the concrete floor.

"Sit down, Matthew," he said. Pulling off his woolly jumper, he placed it around my shoulders. It was still warm from his body. I tucked the sleeves around my feet. Then he took a key from his pocket and knelt down beside one of the stacked boxes. On the side, in red lettering, a name had been stencilled on the front. It read: Auto Ordnance Corporation. He pulled a brass lock free and carefully placed it on the table. Ruffling my hair, he glanced down at me with a big grin. In his undershirt, Potter knelt down and began removing guns from the box and placing them on the floor next to him. I had no idea what was going on. I'd gone from the frying pan right into the fire.

Potter looked over the weapons and selected two guns. He rose from the floor and put them with the barrels facing out in front of me on the table. Then he pulled the second red chair next to mine and sat down. I remember the pistol but was afraid to touch it. The second weapon was much larger—like a rifle—but not really a rifle. Potter took the pistol, turned it over, examined the barrel and the chamber. It was fully loaded. Now I could smell the gun oil.

"Go ahead, Matthew. You can hold it," Potter said, the pistol resting in the palm of his extended hand.

I put my hand around the gun. It was too heavy and I needed to use both hands. There was a cold, metal feel in my hands. I began to shiver. I must have looked slightly stupid, sitting on my knees in the red chair, with tear-stained cheeks, Potter's sweater draped around my shoulders, holding a fully loaded gun.

"It's a 1903 Browning. Belgian Fabrique Nationale d'Armes de Guerre made it." Just the sort of information every seven-year-old is dying to learn. But to Potter every gun was only as good as its manufacturer. He knew the name, model year, and ammunition specifications for every gun made since 1853. Other trivia included: the inventor, copyright holder, licensee, manufacturer, distributor, and ballistic reports. Those must have been the sort of things he thought about when all the boys were circled around the fireplace listening to the radio.

He stared off into space, thinking about the history of some gun.

"A boy not much older than you started a war with the gun you're holding," Potter said, tapping the table edge with a drum-roll-like sound.

I didn't have any idea what he was talking about. I just looked sleepy and very stupid. "Did someone die?" I asked, knowing he was waiting for some response.

"This boy killed the Archduke of Austria and his wife."

"Why, sir?"

Potter smiled; he was glad to have even a seven-year-old to talk about the history of his gun. "He was a political assassin. That's someone who kills kings and politicians."

"What was his name?"

"Princip. Gavrilo Princip."

"Did he live in Alpha House?"

That was the first time I'd ever heard Potter laugh. "No, not in Alpha House. It happened a very long time ago. June 28th, 1914. This is the gun he used. Understand, Matthew. Not a gun like this one. But this very one."

My mouth was wide open and a trail of slobber was running down my chin. I put the gun on the table. Potter wiped my chin. "Do you follow me, Matthew?"

"Yes, sir," I replied, looking up from the gun. I was uncertain what all of this meant and what it had to do with me. But I was vaguely aware that Wild Bill was somehow an important part of why Potter had taken me into the basement and started showing me guns.

"Gavrilo Princip started a war with that gun. Millions died because of this weapon." He picked it up and checked the chamber and firing pin again.

"Like Flash Gordon," I said.

That made Potter laugh again. I liked it when he laughed; it made me feel safe. I would be all right so long as he kept laughing. But I wasn't trying to be funny. It just came out that way. Like the other boys in Alpha House, I read the funny pages in the newspaper. All I knew about pistols had been derived from the Flash Gordon cartoon series. As far as I know, Edgar never owned a gun; mother wouldn't have allowed it. So my education on guns up to that point was from the highly muscular and half-naked Flash Gordon and his ray-flame gun. One burst from the ray-flame gun sent Flash's enemy, Krom, into retreat. Drawing from that experience, I surmised that Princip must have looked and dressed like Flash Gordon. He blasted away a couple of characters like Krom; then everyone started shooting at everyone else.

"Flash Gordon," repeated Potter. "If only John Moses Browning could have been here."

"Why don't you call him?"

"He's dead. Dead almost twenty years." Potter's tone was more serious; he was thinking about something other than what he'd been talking about. I saw adults do this all the time. Their minds going one direction and their tongues in the opposite way. Mother was the absolute master of playing track one and listening to track two.

"Do you dream about John Moses?"

The question caught Potter off guard. Since our encounter began with a nightmare about Wild Bill it seemed natural to me that Potter dreamed about John Moses.

"Yes, sometimes," he admitted, making a fist around the Browning. He had that look of awe; again, I was that shaman creature who descended from Wild Bill Anglin, and knew what other people dreamed. Potter had lots of dreams about John Moses and other gun people he'd known, helped, or worked for, who were, for the most part, dead. People like Colonel John Thompson, for example. And he also had dreams about Wild Bill.

Potter carefully replaced the Browning in the box and turned to the larger riflelike weapon on the table. I'd never seen anything as fantastic as this gun in Flash Gordon.

"This is a submachine gun, Matthew."

"Yes, sir. It looks heavy."

[61]

"It's all right. Hold it, if you like."

Potter stood behind me, with arms looped down helping me to hold up the gun. I was grunting a little under the strain and squirmed to get comfortable in the chair. I looked up and over my shoulder and Potter winked.

"That's it. You're holding a prototype weapon, Matthew. The only one like it in the world."

I decided that John Moses' pistol was more my size. I understood why Princip preferred it to a submachine gun.

"You all right?" Potter asked. I nodded with a long sigh. "Just hold it. I want to show you something else."

When he stood upright, the submachine gun caught me off balance. I slammed forward on the table, my chair falling out from under me. Two of my fingers squeezed the trigger in the crash. It was all over in a second. An instant of violent, rapid, deadly bursts, and then absolute silence. The impact knocked me back and Potter caught me before I hit the concrete floor. The submachine gun, still smoking, was on the floor. I wasn't certain what had happened. I was in a state of panic and confusion. Potter was laughing so I knew he wasn't mad at what had happened. He propped me up with his hands tucked under each of my arms. I surveyed the damage. Across the room, where Potter's wine and port was stored, I saw shattered glass and a blood-red pool of wine forming on the floor. I looked back at Potter. He was still smiling.

"You're a funny little chap, Matthew Burlock."

I thought the entire house would be buzzing from the explosion. I listened hard for some movement upstairs. But there wasn't a sound except the wine leaking on the floor. Potter had soundproofed the basement. No one had, or could have, heard the sound from the submachine gun. Somewhere thousands of miles away on Anzio Beach armies of men were hearing that sound every minute of the day and night. But it was absolutely quiet in the basement of Alpha House. The only casualties were a few bottles of Bordeaux.

The silence was broken by Mrs. Potter at the top of the stairs. "Ian, are you down there?"

"Yes, my love," Potter shouted in reply. He sat me in the chair. I strained to see her around the furnace as she climbed halfway down the stairs. Potter tapped me on the shoulder and put a single finger to his lips.

"What are you doing downstairs this time of night?"

"Just checking out inventory. I'll be up in a few minutes."

CHAPTER 7

THE summer that North Korean armies invaded the South I was about to turn thirteen. This was my second war while a resident of Alpha House. A smile spread across Potter's face as we heard about the invasion on the radio evening news. God hadn't stopped the war very long. The Wongness in the world had slipped out of sight for nearly five years. This was just long enough to permit Auto Ordnance Corporation to declare dividends and replenish their inventory.

Edgar wanted me to spend the summer holiday in Montreal with his sister Clare. Aunt Clare was an Associate Professor in the History Department at McGill University. Her husband, Uncle Jean, was a saxophonist in a jazz band that went on tours throughout Quebec. The idea was to improve my French; or more precisely, to teach me French. Under the surface was another reason that Edgar never expressly articulated. Perhaps he wanted Aunt Clare to be the responsible agent for my transition from boyhood to manhood. The trip to Montreal was part of some ritual, filled with the same mythology and magic as the primitive tribe sending a boy into the bush to kill a wild boar. Mother, not surprisingly, was against Edgar's plan. Uncle Jean was a bohemian type. He was just the kind of person your son could end up missing-in-action with. For weeks they had debates over the dinner table about the Montreal trip.

The Korean War resolved the family conflict. I was to stay on at Alpha House for the summer. With everyone speculating that World War III was about to break out, it seemed sensible to readjust the plans for Montreal. Edgar kept harping about my lack of French. A doctor needed to speak other languages. Maybe Edgar had a lot of French patients with womb problems, although I never heard him speak French or any other language but English. Nevertheless, my language training became an article of faith with him.

Edgar had other reasons for sending me to Montreal. Neither he nor mother wanted me underfoot around the house all summer. Mother would have to hold down her brandy intake; Edgar might have to make some time for me at home. The important thing was a respectable place to send me for temporary exile until school resumed in the autumn. I asked permission to spend the summer at Alpha House. Potter had studied languages at Oxford, I'd argued. In 1916 he went down from St. John's College, Oxford with a good second-class degree. He would make an excellent French teacher. Mother appeared to favor the solution but neither of them would commit to the idea without further private discussions.

After dinner, I'd gone to bed listening to the radio. The news carried a number of reports about the hostilities in Korea. I dreamed that Potter and I were in Korea, each armed with a submachine gun. It was hot and airless, the terrain desolate and mountainous. We found some shade in a small clump of trees and stretched out, with Potter opening a canteen, drinking, and then passing it to me. I wiped the dirt off my mouth and drank. As my eyes rose up to the neck of the canteen, I noticed the insignia of his helmet which read in small red letters: Auto Ordnance Corporation. Behind Potter was a jeep with the same writing on the door. After I screwed the lid back on the canteen, Potter pulled a sealed envelope from his pocket and tore it open. He pulled out some papers and a map. He spread the map out on the ground between us.

"Our first delivery is here," he said, pointing at a red sector on the map.

"The North Koreans?" I asked.

"And tonight another shipment to the South Koreans."

"But whose side are we on?"

Potter started his explanation in French. I didn't understand more than a few words. But he kept on speaking French, gesticulating with his hands, pointing at the map and reading from the orders. I told him that I couldn't follow what he was saying. Potter replied, *"Oui,"* and continued as I sat there shaking my head. He saw my expression, clasped his hands together and shifted into Latin. I lay back on the ground, staring up at the trees while Potter talked to himself. Above and behind him in a tree, I saw Wild Bill in his fireman's uniform perched on a limb. After a few moments, Potter was discussing the orders and map with Wild Bill. They both spoke Latin and walked over to the jeep and opened a crate of sub-machine guns. A queue formed behind the jeep, and a soldier approached Potter, who gave him a gun; he then walked over to Wild Bill who gave him ammunition. Suddenly everyone was shooting and people were bleeding, falling to the ground, over the jeep, some dead, others crying and moaning. But Potter and Wild Bill kept on working, speaking in Latin and ignoring what was going on around them.

I started to shout. When I sat up in bed there was static on the radio. The room was dark but I could see the form of mother sitting on the foot of my bed. She was in her dressing gown, her hair pulled back and holding a glass of brandy. I could smell it on her breath. I sat very still for several moments. I wasn't certain if I was awake.

"What time is it?" I asked.

"About two o'clock."

"How long have you been sitting there?"

"Maybe an hour. Maybe longer." She drank from her glass.

"You scared me for a moment." I didn't want to tell her that in my dream I'd just about gone missing-in-action with Potter and Wild Bill.

"You were dreaming," she said. I watched her fill her glass from a bottle she lifted from the floor. A good drinker can see in the dark for a bottle. And mother was, if anything, a very good drinker.

"Just about Ray," I replied. When I was smaller I sometimes had dreams about Edgar's skeleton walking into my bedroom and crawling into bed with me. As I became older, if I had a bad dream, I blamed Ray. It became one of those family joke kind of things.

"We've decided you can spend the summer at Alpha House. Edgar phoned Potter tonight and made the necessary arrangements."

"That's just great," I shouted. "Can I go tomorrow?"

"If you like." Though I couldn't clearly see her face, I could tell that she was looking down at her glass or bottle. Her voice had become small and sad. I wondered if something was wrong. She might be sick.

"You're at the age where we should have a talk."

Mother never spoke to me in a motherly voice; not that she spoke harshly or indifferently in my presence. Instead she addressed me very much like an adult. It apparently didn't occur to her that I lacked vital information on most subjects and had virtually no experience as well. I assumed that she was basically talking to herself and I was an innocent bystander. Often it was like Potter speaking to me in French and then in Latin in the dream. That night was to prove no different from the other occasions she actually talked to me. I didn't follow the complexity of the ideas she expressed but I stored the words in my memory; words which would have more meaning as the years passed.

Mother asked if I ever noticed that Edgar and she read very different kinds of books. Now that I'd been around the house often enough to observe their reading preference, I noticed that both were readers. So I gave her an affirmative reply. They read in isolation as well. Had I noticed that? Since they appeared to do very little together, that was easy to answer. She seemed assured and drank from her glass. She paused for nearly a minute, choosing her words with care and rolling the brandy across the tip of her tongue, oiling it for the speech she'd prepared for me.

Serious writers are concerned only with betrayal and treachery, which are the same thing. Where they differ is on the human condition when subjected to betrayal. Edgar, for instance, like many others, subscribed to Rubashov as the archetype for expressing this human condition. She, on the other hand, to Macheath, Brecht's principal character in *The Threepenny Opera*. We can betray ourselves and we can betray others. And we can be betrayed by nature, political, economic, and social systems as well. The fuel for the engine of betrayal always has been lying. Without lies you can't really betray anyone or anything.

Both Rubashov and Macheath were expert liars and made substantial personal profits for their efforts. Both writers sent a prince to deal with these liars. The prince Edgar's writer sent to deal with Rubashov carried an order of execution in his pocket. The entire book about Rubashov was just one long, drawn-out saga about how people who betray must ultimately desire self-annihilation, and are drawn to self-sacrifice in the name of this prince. But the play about Macheath has another kind of prince. Like the prince in Cinderella, the end is guaranteed to bring forgiveness, rescue, and freedom. The Rubashovs kill themselves or incite the prince to do it for them. The Macheaths believe that the prince also betrays, so it's stupid to kill yourself for one; they understand that to be a prince is itself based on some distant betrayal. Edgar thinks that it's a weak prince who pardons those who betray. But it's a clever prince who grants the pardon. Why? Because the clever prince always has the option of pardoning himself in the future. That can't happen in Edgar's world. No one's pardoned; everyone must die.

She didn't ask if I understood any of these alcoholic ravings or if I had any questions. Her bottle in one hand, glass in the other, she rose from the bed, walked around to the side of my bed, and turned off the radio which was still playing static. I smelled the brandy on her breath as she leaned down. She was about to kiss me, then stopped and walked out of my bedroom, closing the door behind her. I lay back, hands behind my head, for a long time. The entire explanation sounded like she'd read it somewhere or had learned it from someone else. I had the idea that perhaps there was something behind the words which she intended to leave vague and in the air. By the time I reached law school I'd concluded that betrayal was central to the Wongness I was discovering in the world. By then I'd learned from Potter that both kinds of princes relied very heavily on the Auto Ordnance Corporation like a medical kit every time a frenzy of Wongness led to mass killing.

CHAPTER 8

FIVE days after I arrived at Alpha House for the summer holiday, President Truman ordered American troops into South Korea. There had been a procession of cars at the house all day with parents coming up to the door and collecting their sons. Shaking hands with Potter, passing small talk about the school, the war, and gardening, and carrying suitcases to the open car boot. By five o'clock only Carleton was left sitting on the porch waiting for his father. Carleton, who was ten, had a silly crooked smile, a number of small warts on his face, and a crew cut. As his father's new Ford stopped at the curb, Carleton raced down the stairs with his suitcase and pulled open the door. Potter and I stood on the sidewalk in front of the house. Carleton's father, who looked like an older version of Carleton who shaved, stepped out of the car and chatted with Potter. Carleton rolled down the window to listen. Finally, the Ford pulled away with Carleton leaning over the back seat, waving good-bye to Potter.

School was over for another year. I let out a long sigh and looked up at Potter who had turned back from the street. He patted me on the shoulder; the real learning which was interrupted during the school year was about to begin in earnest. A stillness washed around us. Like statuary we stood on the green verge watching Carleton's car disappear down the street lined with horse chestnut trees. We were lost in that sudden silence. Alpha House was empty: no laughter, chasing around the garden, the sound of schoolboys at play. It was as if all the bright stars had fallen from a corner of the sky leaving a huge, blank space inviting us to step into the void. Like Rick standing on the runway as the propellers started on the last plane from Casablanca, we knew something was about to happen that we could never call back.

Mrs. Potter stepped out on the porch. She must have been watching us stare down the street for a while. "Why don't you two take a walk and have a chat," she said. The first fragment of conversation to echo through our new, silent universe. "I'll have tea ready when you get back."

Potter turned back towards the house, shading the sun from his face with a raised hand. "Splendid idea," he said. She waved us off as we started down the street.

I knew that Potter was armed. He was packing a Webley-Fosbery 1902 automatic pistol. It was one of his sentimental favorites. Colonel G. Vincent Fosbery, the inventor, was Potter's uncle and had introduced him to John Moses Browning.

"I thought we might take a stroll through the Endowment Lands," Potter said, as I walked along his side.

"First-rate idea, sir," I said, patting the Colt .45 under my jacket.

Two blocks to the west of Alpha House were the Endowment Lands. Twelve hundred acres of virgin forest: Douglas firs, cedars, pines, dense undergrowth, blackberry bushes, wildflowers, and large wild ferns. The trees grew so tightly together that the sun didn't filter down to the trails; some of the trunks were carpeted with a rich, thick green moss and ivy. We crossed Camosun Street, climbed up a small embankment from the road, and pushed back the gate of tangled vines and scrub brush. Inside was a small trail heading due west. I knew this trail well. For nearly six years, Potter and I had taken hikes along the trail that led deep into the untouched wilderness. Often from the trail, a narrow clearing led to a stream where we'd see deer, raccoons, squirrels, hawks, eagles, and egrets. The terrain was teeming with their sounds as we crisscrossed the path over streams, around hills, down gullies, and across tiny meadows covered with tall grass and white-and-yellow wildflowers.

Alpha House, Anzio Beach, Berlin, London, Ottawa, Seoul, and the Auto Ordnance Corporation were row houses on the same distant street, sharing common walls, stairs, gardens, and paths; but the street was on some other planet where the water was polluted, the air smelling of smoke, and filled with the noise of machines. We hiked about two miles before stopping beside a stream. Three years before, Potter helped me make a small wooden footbridge. We left the bridge hidden under a large cedar where we'd camouflaged it with underbrush. We pulled the bridge out and positioned it across the stream and walked across to a small clearing.

Potter called this place John Moses' Clearing. He showed it to me the Spring the Allies were fighting from house to house in Berlin. In a way, Potter's approach to me was little different from mother's. He talked, as if to the trees on the edge of the clearing, or to himself, about the Auto Ordnance Corporation. Over the years I began to place the puzzle together but, at twelve, still had only a rough idea what all the pieces meant once assembled.

But I knew this much: Potter was an extraordinary man. Perhaps he just seemed that way to a schoolboy who was impressionable, or the stories were part of the magic of the forest setting, or the many guns he skillfully handled set him apart. On each excursion, Potter carried a different type of weapon, concealed on his person or in a case, and once we reached John Moses' Clearing he'd surprise me with guns ranging from a Scottish flintlock pistol to a Webley & Scott Mark 1 automatic. As he handed me the latest pistol, that was his signal to describe the weapon and ultimately how it had figured into the fortune or misfortune of Auto Ordnance Corporation. One story always stood out above the others: how he began to work for John Moses Browning.

CHAPTER 9

THE first time Potter met John Moses Browning, a sixty-year-old American from Ogden, Utah, Browning was sitting in the garden of Colonel G. Vincent Fosbery's small country estate near Guildford. It was the summer of 1915 and the roses in Uncle Foss' garden were in full bloom. The rolling green hills stretched to the horizon behind the house. Potter had come down to the estate at the end of Hilary term. He'd taken the train from Oxford into Paddington Station and left Victoria Station for Guildford. He was seventeen that summer, and already spoke German, French, and Italian with fluency. John Moses spoke only American. Potter had closed the gate, walked into the garden and saw the two men seated at a table. Their backs were turned toward him. He stood for a moment, listening to them talk. But he was too far back to make out what was being said. Potter knew that Browning was the man whose pistol had started the war. He expected John Moses to be a tall, worldly, and wise man, with the appearance of a king and intellect of an Oxford don.

But John Moses Browning was street-smart and street rough. As Potter approached the table, Browning caught sight of him and motioned him to hurry. Like most Americans, Browning expected everyone to run.

"Your uncle says you're a bright boy," were the first words Browning spoke to him. Dressed in a brown suit, a gold chain hanging from his vest, John Moses sat in a garden chair with his legs stretched out. "He says you speak a lot of languages."

"I speak several," said Potter.

"Several?"

"Not counting Latin and Greek."

Uncle Foss watched John Moses interrogate his nephew with bemused restraint, filling the sherry glasses. After all, Potter had been trained as a gentleman his whole life, had kept to the company of gentlemen, and into that impassable isolation had sprung an American gun inventor and merchant.

"I ain't thinkin' of sellin' guns to the Latins and Greeks, boy," said John Moses, lifting his sherry and drinking it like beer. That raw, leathery cowboy face broke into a smile, the smile of an old ranch hand. "To move cattle, you only need to know one language well." Browning removed a pistol from the holster inside his coat and laid it on the table. He poured himself another sherry. Uncle Foss arched an eyebrow at Potter as he stared down at the gun.

John Moses was much more than a cowboy from Ogden; he was that brilliant, inventive, determined and powerful, Howard-Hughes type of American. A flamboyant, curious, tireless, and inspired exile who travelled across Europe living in London, Paris, Rome, Berlin, and Moscow. Always on the move, he could no longer go back home. He was driving cattle herds over large regions, picking up hired hands here and there for special jobs.

He came with a job for Potter. The presence of John Moses in Uncle Foss' garden wasn't an accident; it had been prearranged because Potter roomed at Oxford with an Italian named Gennaro Revelli. Gennaro's father was a hard-driving and drinking Italian colonel, with two mistresses in Turin and a gun factory called Villa Perosa. The factory was near Pinerola.

The Colonel, according to John Moses' intelligence sources, had been neglecting both mistresses and the bottle while perfecting a submachine gun that purportedly fired at the incredible rate of 3,000 rounds per minute.

If such a weapon existed, the consequences would be staggering. Existing weapons would be like writing books with a quill pen while the Colonel's submachine was like doing the same thing on a computer. John Moses would be left behind in the dust as someone else drove the cattle herds. Even a more disturbing possibility might occur. A light, individual submachine gun would transform every man in the trenches into an instrument of destruction beyond anyone's imagination. Every private would possess the capacity to mow down trees, men, women, children, animals, and buildings. The race was on in America and Europe to be the first to make this technological breakthrough. There were strategic, political, and selfish personal reasons as well.

The selfish personal reasons were not necessarily the same for Uncle Foss and John Moses. As the man behind Fabrique Nationale, John Moses' interest in the Revelli submachine was strictly commercial; a businessman, smelling a major technological breakthrough, worries about his cartel and monopoly. Uncle Foss, though a gun inventor, was not a gunman like John Moses. He was a British officer and gentleman; his family had occupied the same tract of land, gone to the same parish church, Eton or Harrow, belonged to the same London clubs, for about three hundred years. His claim to privilege had been drawn from a different well than John Moses'. From the inner depth of his English soul, Uncle Foss felt a chill pass; the bitter, cold wind was the thought of armies with working-class recruits equipped with the Revelli submachine gun.

Everything would be changed. Empire, rank, privilege and property would be at risk. The privileged classes would no longer possess the monopoly over the essential tools of betrayal. In 1915 it was still standard practice for officers to hand out fifteen rounds per man: fifteen shots rationed to men who were forced out of the trenches and into no-man's-land. The entire philosophy was simply one of defense. The prince of execution and the prince of pardon limited or contained the opportunity for betrayal by keeping the common man's weapons defensive in nature. Over the centuries there had been a conspiracy among all princes to retain their privilege, power, and empires by carefully controlling the tools that in the hands of their subjects might one day be pointed at them.

No soldier had a higher duty than to provide an impenetrable wall around his superior. The relationship was clear. Protect us and you receive your fifteen-round ration. Betray us and even with fifteen rounds you will not succeed. Revelli toiling away in his workshop was about to shift irrevocably the basis of that relationship and threaten the underlying structure upon which it was based.

For their own reasons, Uncle Foss and John Moses wanted the Revelli submachine gun. They'd formed an alliance, as is often the case with the Americans and English, for a joint operation to achieve very different goals. Had Revelli invented the first functional light submachine gun, then Uncle Foss was quietly convinced (he had contacts high in the War Office) that the weapon could be banned by international treaty. All the princes would agree to such a ban. John Moses' purpose was to divert resources to the immediate manufacture and distribution of such a weapon before the Europeans could effectively act. It would be a horse race and both were gambling men; besides, neither had much option but to deal with one another. John Moses would sooner or later break Revelli's security and steal the gun. And without his help, Uncle Foss knew that his nephew would stand little chance in reaching or coming back from Italy alive. They were in a standoff. But they had they agreed to combine resources, each keeping an eye on the other, each hoping to shift the other from their respective positions about the use of the Revelli gun.

In early July, 1915, as the Webley-Fosbery self-cocking pistol (Uncle Foss was co-inventor) was jamming in the mud, dust, and shit along the Western Front, Potter arrived at the Turin train station. He was met by his Oxford roommate, Gennaro Revelli. They exchanged handshakes. On the station platform the two boys looked over each other for the first time outside of St. John's College. Gennaro seemed more foreign; his hair slicked back, shining in the sun, and he was growing a moustache. In Gennaro's eyes, this Englishman must have looked very tired, pale, and shopworn. His Italian, as Gennaro remembered it, seemed much better in Oxford than on the station platform. The main change would have gone unnoticed. Potter was now on the payroll and under the protection of Fabrique Nationale and John Moses.

There were many questions Potter asked himself those first few days. Exactly what was he doing in Italy during the middle of this war? Was he a spy? Was he in any real danger? Towards the end of the week, Gennaro and Potter had pretty much readjusted to one another and made the rounds of Turin mainly on foot. Potter met a number of Gennaro's friends and family, drank wine in local cafés, and read Italian newspapers. Most of the nagging questions faded and he began to believe that he had come on a genuine holiday. This leisurely touring ended on the following Monday, when Gennaro drove Potter out to his father's factory.

Colonel Revelli gestured to Gennaro and Potter who were at the opposite end of the factory floor. Gennaro waved back and motioned for Potter to follow him. They wove through the workbenches. Several dozen employees were busily working on parts for guns; others were assembling weapons, cleaning and polishing; and still others worked at the end of a conveyor belt, removing the finished weapons and packing them into crates. This was what John Moses and Uncle Foss had wanted to know. He made mental notes as they passed down the lines. Once inside Colonel Revelli's office, Gennaro's father warmly embraced Potter. Gennaro's friend is my son. That was his attitude, no doubt formed by Gennaro's overabundant praise for his roommate's family position in England.

Colonel Revelli unveiled a Mitriaglice Leggera Villar Perosa M15 which had been mounted on his desk. This was the first submachine gun invented. The Colonel and his son beamed with pride as Potter approached the desk and examined the weapon. Unlike a rifle there wasn't a stock; there was absolutely no wood on any part of the weapon; and there were twin steel barrels that rested on a tripod. The Colonel reached over and pulled back the bolt. In Italian he asked Potter if he'd like the pleasure of pulling the trigger. Potter squeezed and the bolt sprang forward with a loud clunk. Potter looked up at the Colonel, and then over at Gennaro. Wasn't there some sort of mistake. This was supposed to be a grand secret. Instead, the inventor provides a factory tour and a close-up inspection of the weapon. It didn't stop there. The Colonel's eyes fired with pride, kissed his fingers and touched the twin barrels. It's for you. Just like that, Revelli gave Potter the submachine gun.

Didn't the Colonel know that he'd invented the world's first submachine gun, and that John Moses and Uncle Foss had been plotting to get one? Colonel Revelli saw his inspection in a very different light. For him the achievement wasn't going to shatter the world. As a military man, his submachine gun would make it slightly easier to gun down airplanes and stop armored vehicles. After all, it weighed fifteen pounds; it wasn't the sort of thing you could run sprints with and not be the worse for wear. Revelli hadn't the slightest intention of equipping the common infantrymen with his submachine. As he pointed out, the submachine was fixed to a tripod; it was meant to be placed on the ground or a vehicle and fired. Anyone who'd suggested that the tripods should be ripped off, shoving on a wooden stock and handing them out to the ordinary soldier would have to be mad. The British and the Italians had one unified, well-mannered idea about how and who should fight wars and with what kinds of weapons. There was no doubt about that. Uncle Foss had, perhaps, under John

Moses' influence, confused the Italians' perception of these matters with the Americans'.

There was a heavy scent of betrayal in all of this. And the smell came from the door of Belgian Fabrique Nationale d'Armes de Guerre.

Potter was told that the Revelli M15 had gone into limited production at the Villar Perosa. No one had any intention of launching a full-scale production of the weapons. Just a few for the Italian army to hammer away at airplanes. The gift of the gun was a sign of respect to Uncle Foss, another European gun inventor. No plots or designs to rearrange modern warfare; no attempt to hide the submachine; and no fear that, taken back to England, it would have any consequence other than forming a friendship between two Oxford classmates. Sometimes the world is very straightforward and simple.

BEFORE my thirteenth birthday had passed at Alpha House, I knew the basic outline of Potter's early life. Uncle Foss had invented a very unreliable handgun. Uncle Foss knew John Moses Browning and had sought his advice on perfecting the flaws in the Webley-Fosbery. John Moses left the United States suddenly some years before. There was some mystery over his departure and why he never seemed to return. His Browning pistol started a war. Now he wanted very badly to make a new, different type of gun. He thought that Colonel Revelli had beat him to the punch but that was based on some faulty intelligence information. Alternatively, John Moses might have known the truth about the Revelli setup before he sent Potter off to Turin. He was after something more than the Revelli submachine gun.

There were so many hidden agenda that it became virtually impossible to know what the true intentions of anyone were or came to be. Potter later became aware, for example, of a debt that John Moses owed to Colonel Thompson in the United

States. It was more than possible that getting possession of an actual Revelli was John Moses' way of repaying the debt.

A fifteen-pound submachine for shooting down airplanes and troop carriers, a seventeen-year-old boy fresh from Oxford, and Wild Bill Anglin filtered through the conversation in the meadow clearing. Potter dribbled out pieces of one story, then another, his mind darting here and there, like someone who not only knew the way but all of the little side roads. By the time the Korean War had begun, I was beginning to form an idea of the map he was drawing. But like the map in my dream, a lot was still in a language I didn't fully comprehend.

We never talked about Potter's adventures or guns inside Alpha House. The discussions were clearly off-limits. Even when we went into the basement and examined Potter's gun collections, the conversations were about specifications and other facts. The opinions and speculations were things of the forest meadow. As I became older, Potter watched me more closely as he told the stories, and was more inclined to edit or to lapse into vagueness; this happened, it seemed to me, the closer he came to some essential, painful truth that he didn't want to disclose.

One incident sticks in my mind as an example of his drop-and-run approach. We were sitting together in the clearing. Mrs. Potter had packed us some oranges. I was peeling mine on the grass, listening to Potter. I threw a piece to a squirrel. My mind was probably wandering from a story I'd heard bits and pieces of before. Potter saw this and must have been slightly upset.

"Burlock."

I looked over at him. He drew himself closer to me.

"Out of World War I there were only five people fighting the real war. Uncle Foss. Colonel Revelli. Colonel Thompson. And we can't leave out John Moses." Then he paused, seeing he had his full attention. "And the fifth man, Wild Bill Anglin."

Edgar avoided the subject of sex with me until 1968; by

then I was in my thirties. Maybe the garage mechanic's son never understands engines until relatively late in life as well. When Edgar first addressed the question of sex, his lips were cracked and blistered. He had one of those little plastic bracelets around his right wrist and several tubes running under the sheets of his hospital bed.

"My experience was mainly clinical," said Edgar, as I sat next to him.

I struggled to fight back the tears. "Most kids find out soon enough on their own," I replied.

His head turned on the pillow, he winked and flashed the peace sign; the bracelet sliding almost to his elbow on a forearm that had largely withered away.

I didn't tell the truth to Edgar. I merely followed the standard convention of comforting a person who's dying. Edgar's cancer not only efficiently reorganized his cells but unlocked thousands of memories shut inside; little bubbles rising to the surface, carrying some new payload from the distant past. There wasn't a medical cure for the cancer; and Edgar's memories were beyond anything remotely connected with medical science.

Perhaps I underestimated the degree of Edgar's change during the late sixties. The real story of my sex education might have amused him. But it would have led to many other complications.

WHEN I was fifteen Potter told me about his first woman. On that day, we walked beyond John Moses' Clearing, way deeper in the forest than I'd ever ventured with him before. After two hours we crossed a road, and, the forest behind us, we walked along the cliffs overlooking the sea. Potter had packed a 1915 Beretta under his coat. He passed it over to me for inspection. Like Uncle Foss' Webley-Fosbery, the 1915 Beretta had the reputation for sudden explosion in the face of its user. I checked the chamber and pulled out the clip; it was, of course, loaded.

"A simple blow-back action," I said, shifting it from my right to my left hand.

"That's it, get the feel of it."

It had the look of a Colt .45 but the hammer of the Beretta was concealed; the line was smooth, controlled, even tailored. I ran my fingers over the barrel.

"What do you think?"

"Same feel as the 1903 Browning," I replied, extending my arm forward, drawing a bead towards the sea with my right eye.

Potter liked the reference to the Browning. His hand ruffled my hair. The same reaction I'd received at seven when the 1903 Browning had been the first pistol I'd ever seen or held. We both remembered the incident.

Potter led the way down a path that descended towards the beach below. I was tired from our wandering through the forest. But Potter appeared as fresh as when we started. Clutching the Beretta, my legs aching, I stayed several feet behind. He stopped as the trail widened to form a small ridge. A hand raised over his eyes, Potter stood for a moment like a mariner on the crow's nest canvassing the weather forming on the horizon. We'd climbed about fifty feet down from the side of the road. And from our vantage point the sea arced in a 180 degree semicircle around us; bursting with reflected sunlight, calm and smooth as the hammerless line of the Beretta. A tug, pulling a large log-boom, steamed towards us from the North. Sheltered against a light wind, our backs to the cliff, we sat huddled together watching the tug wind down the coastline, like a solitary sperm with a long, undulating tail slowly swimming homeward. We watched transfixed. After some time, Potter began telling me a new story; one designed to bring home the role of Fabrique Nationale in his own sexual development.

The summer of 1915 Potter lost his virginity in Turin. The summer had in store many firsts: first job; acquiring the first submachine for Fabrique Nationale; enjoying his first trip out of England; and crossing Europe during the First World War by train. And Lollia was his first woman.

She was twenty-eight, and one of Colonel Revelli's two mistresses. Full lips, long dark hair were set off by brilliant emerald eyes; the eyes the color of the Mediterranean Sea reflecting the hot July afternoon sun. Her family lived in Turin, and her father worked in Revelli's factory making gun barrels. Revelli had taught her the social graces; the sensitivity, the shy charming manner, and intoxicating smile suggested a woman who was wellborn.

Lollia had been Colonel Revelli's mistress since she was sixteen. Potter would have thought differently of her then. The walk, touch, smile, and laugh of a sixteen-year-old girl is something tangible and accessible to a seventeen-year-old boy. They occupy a territory of shared experience, doubts, and dreams. By twenty-eight, the dragline has pulled long enough to form the tiny wrinkles and lines accompanying the smile and laugh. The self-consciousness is gone, along with the spontaneity and the tears easily formed by a lover's glance or touch. The form of Lollia might have been Potter's dream of a woman but the substance of such a woman made him feel immature and silly.

Potter talked about Lollia until the stars sparkled above the black sea dotted with lights from the occasional ship in the distance. Something snapped in him; he couldn't help himself, circling back to events, assembling the people, the streets and rooms of Turin like a lawyer arguing through the facts of a case with his junior.

I sat listening, pointing the Beretta at first one star, and then another. If I could shoot one out of the sky, it would smash into the sea; jog another memory from Potter, one he kept closing in on and then backing away. I wanted to turn the entire sky black like the interior of a deep sleep, where Potter's dream, would materialize and I could follow him through the streets of Turin.

CHAPTER 10

AFTER the factory tour at Villar Perosa, Gennaro and Potter visited Turin's most holy relic: the Shroud of Turin. According to legend, the actual shroud was locked inside the stone sarcophagus. For Gennaro this was no legend; it was fact. The genuine cloth used to wrap Jesus' body was inside. The image of that man, or God, seared into the shroud was as real as the Revelli M15 submachine gun. They studied a replica of the shroud on the wall near the sarcophagus. Potter looked up at the image of a man, his arms spread-eagled, his legs together, head tilted to one side. The most important relic of historical betrayal in front of him, he turned to Gennaro.

"It could be a sham," he said.

"No," replied his friend, looking over at the sarcophagus. "Some things we must take on faith."

Potter thought about John Moses Browning, wondering if that American had ever taken anything in life on faith. And whether Potter himself had left England for Italy solely as a matter of faith in Uncle Foss and the things his family stood for. The gift of the submachine gun from Colonel Revelli was another genuine act of good faith. This tattered garment, however, for Potter represented a leap of faith right to the edge of mysticism.

"The bones of dead saints fill the monasteries. There are more bones than saints. That's the problem," he said.

Gennaro immediately took up the challenge. "Who is to

say that Edward the Third's bones are really buried in Westminster? Maybe someone clever forged his effigy?"

"That's not quite the same."

"Because English faith doesn't travel well abroad?"

"I only raised the possibility. That's all."

"And I raise the possibility that the royal effigies of Queen Elizabeth the First, King William the Third, and Queen Mary the Second were bogus. Their bones have rotted away centuries ago. Maybe in Italy."

By the end, they compromised. The English Church and the Catholic Church should be trusted not to betray the faith they preach. Faith based on betrayal is no faith at all, and if the churches, of all institutions, can't be counted on to be the one instrument that doesn't betray, then the Shroud of Turin wasn't real and Edward the Third's bones didn't rest in Westminster. The friendship restored, they left the church. With Gennaro a half step behind Potter on the stone steps, a thought flashed through Potter's mind and he turned back towards Gennaro.

"Just one more question. Why wasn't the shroud mentioned in the bible?"

That, of course, wasn't one question; it was reopening the core of the debate once again. Gennaro, rolling his eyes, retorted, "The English are better suited to paganism. That they can understand."

Before Potter could respond, he collided with Lollia. As she walked up the stone steps, Potter stumbled into her and tripped, lost his balance, and fell back into Gennaro who broke his fall. She crossed herself, silently nodding at Potter. Then she saw Gennaro. He recognized his father's mistress. He smiled at her as Potter got back on his feet, looking sheepish.

"As I was telling my friend, faith is having a friend behind you to catch you when you fall," Gennaro said.

"Terribly sorry, how stupid of me," sputtered Potter. So this was the real idea. A man had a wife, at least one mistress, and believed in the Shroud. Colonel Revelli didn't hide the parts of his life that an Englishman would clothe with complete discretion and secrecy. Gennaro, indeed the entire Revelli family, knew of Lollia, and the Colonel's other mistress. But the overriding faith that the family was immutable made these activities less than betrayal. To have questioned the morality of the arrangements would have made as much sense as to call into question the morality of making guns to fight a war. They were merely obligations carried out with a sense of duty and honor.

Lollia was on her way to mass. She attended mass daily. Even the church granted her dispensation to fulfill her obligation to the Colonel, and in turn, like Gennaro and his father, she believed in the authenticity of the Shroud. She travelled nearly forty minutes by bus to pray in the presence of the Shroud and give her confession. She confessed her sin with Colonal Revelli; and Colonel Revelli confessed his sin of making guns that killed people. They both believed that the Shroud allowed the priest to intercede on their behalf with the dead. Many people were dying in the war, and with them the faith that had held Europe together.

There was more than simple faith on each side of the equation; it was blind faith. Blind faith of the priest that the absolution will restore the faithful in the eyes of God; blind faith by the confessor that the priest has such power. Blind faith that the process can be repeated over and over on a daily basis. At the heart of this faith was betrayal. The image of the man on the cloth betrayed by a friend. Without the disgrace of the betrayal there could be no martyr for the betrayed. The duality of faith rested on this relationship. Only if everyone was God would disgrace and martyrdom become irrelevant.

Lollia and Colonel Revelli understood the equilibrium between faith and betrayal. Her lover manufactured pistols, rifles, and submachine guns; his technology turned men, women, and children throughout Europe into pieces of torn flesh and blood. Like the priest turning bread and water into the flesh and blood of Christ. She slept with a kind of priest. But not for two months; not since he devoted himself exclusively to perfecting the M15. When he returned to her bedroom she found him changed. The night became a high wall enclosing each on the opposite side. They struggled to find each other through lovemaking. Afterwards he would sleep. Then, in the dead of night, howling like a wolf in a leg trap, he cried out, and she calmed him, stroking his head. She whispered to him not to be afraid. He would rest more easily in her arms for a while. The war had aged him, she thought. He had begun using her bedroom as a confessional. The mistress transformed into a priestess. With so much forgiveness to ask, the Church was no longer a sufficient outlet.

Potter, while only seventeen, sensed something extraordinary about this woman on the church steps. The emotion in the eyes were something he'd rarely seen in an Englishwoman. And her dark, large eyes directly met his gaze until he felt himself blush and glance back at Gennaro.

"He's not himself today," said Gennaro. He kissed Lollia on both cheeks. Potter cleared his throat. "Of course, this is Potter, a friend of mine from England." Potter extended his hand to Lollia.

"Father was very taken by Potter," Gennaro continued, after a silence which Potter didn't fill. "We were at the factory yesterday. Guess what father did?"

"He gave you both a personal tour."

"No, no. He gave Potter one of the new guns. The one father has been working on."

Potter's eyes remained fixed on Lollia throughout the conversation. He felt a sense of urgency about this woman; the sense of faith that Gennaro had spoken about inside the church, the blind faith that takes people on pilgrimages, holy wars, and to worship the Shroud.

"Potter," said Gennaro, but Potter appeared not to hear him. "Potter, I said Lollia's brother is studying to enter the priesthood in Rome."

"You must be very pleased for him," Potter replied.

"Be careful of this one, Lollia. He thinks our Shroud is a fraud."

Lollia crossed herself. "I didn't say that, really," he stammered. The words had left him a mute, confused foreigner. The luxury of her presence surrounded him totally. Gennaro noticed that his friend was overwhelmed by Lollia and this amused him greatly. After all, Lollia was just Lollia. Her father labored in his father's factory; and his father was paying the cost of her brother's priesthood education. He glanced over at the clock tower opposite the church.

"Sorry, but I've got to run. Maybe you could persuade Potter here to believe in the Shroud." Gennaro slipped away with an excuse that was no excuse. Potter didn't try to follow after him. From the steps they watched Gennaro dart across the street, and from the other side, he waved good-bye and disappeared into the crowd. They stood side by side, the sun in their faces. An awkward moment of silence passed. A seventeen-year-old Oxford student and the mistress of an Italian arms manufacturer turned to one another. She reached out and took Potter's hand.

Was she really going to convince him about the contents concealed inside the stone chest?

They started walking up the stairs. Her eyes half-lidded as if in prayer and her head covered, she stopped before the church door. Her prayer appeared to have ended. She pulled the shawl from her head.

"I think we should leave the Shroud for another day," she said.

"What would you like to do?"

"I'd like to see the gun."

"The gun?"

"The one given to you by Gennaro's father." She squeezed Potter's fingers in the palm of her hand. "Please," she whispered.

They rode in the back of a taxi to Potter's hotel. She spoke of her brother's training for the priesthood. How important this was to the family. That in Italy, to have a son become a priest is to gain favor in the eyes of God; every member of the family will do what is necessary to accomplish this goal. And what was a priest, thought Potter. But a man devoted to keeping alive the memory of an executed criminal for those who believed in Him as the living God. The picture of this man was imprinted on the Shroud. Or so it was said. It was as if the cloth had been dipped into a vast primordial soup and the blueprint of a man's soul formed as one grand cosmic stain.

At the hotel, Lollia waited in the lobby, and Potter took the lift to his room on the second floor. Inside his room he packed the Revelli submachine gun into a leather carrying case. She explained when he came back down that she wanted to see the gun in the privacy of her own room. The owner of the hotel had a big mouth. If she accompanied Potter to his room, it would be all over Turin the next day. So they took a bus to the outskirts of Turin. It was nearly empty halfway out of the city. They sat near the back, Potter holding the leather case on his lap. Near the south edge of the city, they got off the bus and walked down a cobblestone street lined with old stone houses. Potter shifted the case, stopping to look at flower boxes in the windows along the way. Sets of eyes met them from the windows. Lollia didn't acknowledge them and walked several steps ahead of Potter.

Once inside Lollia's house, she put the keys in her handbag and tossed it on a table in the entrance way. The main room was plainly furnished and decorated and didn't have a lived-in look; it was more like the waiting room in an English provincial doctor's surgery. She took his hand and led him up a flight of stairs to a small landing. She opened the door and walked in. Lollia's bedroom was completely white. Curtains, bedcovers, carpets, walls. It was as if the stone chest in the church had been opened and all of this was carefully preserved inside. She closed the bedroom door and disappeared behind a screen near a closet.

"Please set up the gun," she said from behind the screen.

Potter could see her eyes over the screen; they seemed to be smiling.

"Where?"

"Over there, near the window."

He carried the leather case over to the window, and peeked through the curtains. The sun was setting, and the last rays streaked through catching his face. He could hear her undressing behind the screen, as he knelt down and opened the case. He began to assemble the gun, first putting the tripod together.

"Would you like a drink?" she asked, once again standing on her toes and looking over the screen.

"Lovely idea."

"There's wine on the table behind you. Pour yourself a glass."

"And what would you like to drink?"

"A glass of wine."

Potter felt a little stupid. Why had he asked what she'd like to drink when the only bottle on the table contained red wine. He finished screwing on the twin barrels, pulled back the bolt, pressed the trigger. Click. He rose and walked to the table, removed the cork from the bottle, and filled two glasses. He imagined that Colonel Revelli had stood in that spot many times; perhaps using the same glasses.

"Is the gun ready?" she asked.

"I've assembled it, if that's what you mean."

She came out from behind the screen in a silk dressing gown, and walked immediately over to the gun. Potter handed her a glass of wine, somewhat disappointed that he was no longer the sole object of her attention. She knelt down and inhaled the air around the gun.

"It smells like my father," she said, laughing. She touched the glass to her lips and drank.

"He works at the factory?"

"For over thirty-five years. Now tell me, what will you do with this gun? Shoot ducks in Oxford?"

"Actually, it's a gift for my Uncle in England."

"Colonel Fosbery."

This surprised Potter immensely. Obviously, Revelli talked of shop as well as of love in this bedroom. Why would he have told her about my Uncle Foss, he wondered, sipping his wine. Was she his mistress, business partner, or someone else's partner? Italians were proving themselves to be a complex people to understand.

"And what will your uncle do with the gun? Maybe have the English kill Germans with it?"

"It was simply a gift." Potter put down his glass in such a fashion as to suggest he wanted to leave.

"Come, sit down. I ask too many silly questions. It makes men angry sometimes." With the glass in her hand she sat on the edge of the bed, her dressing gown falling away to expose her crossed legs. Her eyes were still on the gun.

"Just one more question. Okay?"

Potter nodded, looking down at her, cradling his glass with both hands.

"Is the gun loaded?"

"No, I don't think that would be a good idea," he replied. A red blush covered his face and neck. He felt as if he were going to die. As he stood a few feet away from Lollia, he had a full erection; the front of his trousers bulged out like a tent. He placed both of his hands in his front pockets and clenched them like a fist to hide the obvious. Rather than distracting Lollia's attention, it drew her eyes downward. He'd never had an erection in the presence of a woman before. He felt sheepish, then disgraced that he couldn't control his bodily reactions. The first response was to run out of the room, down the stairs, up the cobblestone street and catch a taxi back to his hotel. But Lollia's warm, comforting smile riveted him to the spot where he stood.

"Why don't you show me how the gun works?" asked Lollia, glancing from Potter to the Revelli M15.

"Yes, of course," replied Potter, walking over to the mounted submachine gun, both fists still in his trouser pockets.

"Take your wine."

"I'm not very thirsty at the moment," he replied.

As the night closed in, Potter knelt before the Revelli's smooth, long barrels and explained how the submachine gun operated. Lollia listened contentedly, refilling her glass of wine several times. Potter, once again back in control, held out his glass for her to fill. He told her about Uncle Foss and the trouble he'd experienced with perfecting his pistol. After another glass of wine, Potter reflected on John Moses Browning's contribution to the science of modern weaponry. Lollia listened, her head cocked to the side, as if transfixed by this young Englishman; a little knot twisting occasionally above her nose.

They were both relaxed. Potter stretched out on the floor beside the Revelli M15, and Lollia on the side of the bed facing Potter, with her arms hanging over cradling the wine glass. A small lamp illuminated the bed. Potter sat up in the half shadow. Again he reached out with his glass. Lollia silently poured the last of the bottle. A tiny rivulet of red wine spilled down the side of the glass, over Potter's hand and onto the pure white carpet. He stared at the little red pool between his knees. Lollia leaned over, touched the spilled wine with her finger and put it to his lips. He felt the erection again as her finger lingered for a second too long.

She let the empty bottle slip to the floor. Rising to her knees on the bed above him, she let her dressing gown slide over her shoulders. Potter could still taste her wine-soaked finger on his tongue. He sat there, head spinning, watching Lollia undress. He didn't know what he was required to do. Do you kiss her? Say something flattering? Pretend that it's not happening? Who's supposed to do what to whom? He wished that he was much older and had had many experiences to draw upon.

Lollia knew exactly what she wanted to do every moment. She reached over and switched off the lamp. Climbing out of bed, she went to the window and drew the curtains and opened the french doors to a small stone balcony. As she turned, the profile of her body was defined by moonlight. In silence she stood in front of the window, as if feeling the night air on her body, while looking down at the Revelli M15. Then on tiptoes she began to step slowly forward, swaying her body, her hands folded together as if in prayer. She was circling the submachine, as if dancing some ritual. Then turning and twisting she lowered herself. Potter watched as one of twin barrels touched the inside of Lollia's thighs. She seemed to hang in the moonlit air for a moment. Her eyes closed, her tongue touching her upper lip, she began to rock up and down, moaning and groaning. Her breathing accelerated, legs rising and falling, and finally a muffled scream. Potter thought he'd stopped breathing; his face scorched with the fire of this vision. Her eyes opened slowly and she smiled down at him, and reaching out with her hands pulled him forward. He rose to his feet and followed her onto the bed.

There was the smell of gun oil on her body. It filled his nostrils. The smell of the new order of things in the world. His head buried in her hair, he closed his eyes and saw himself seated behind the Revelli M15, staring through the opened doors and firing; his finger locked against the trigger shooting into the night as if he could shoot down the moon and stars and heaven and earth.

CHAPTER 11

MY law school class gathered for the last time at the Stanley Park Pavilion for a formal reception. Parents and guests were invited. Most of that afternoon mother cuddled a bottle of brandy. I assumed that she stayed in her room drinking in preparation for going outside the house with Edgar and me that evening. I was partly right. About an hour before the reception was to begin, I was in my bedroom dressing. I stood before a full-length mirror looking at myself: black tie, silver studs in my shirt and cuffs. As I took my trousers from the closet, mother came into my room unannounced. She sat on the edge of the bed while I put on my trousers. Her eyes were bloodshot from drinking and lack of sleep.

"If you're not feeling well, then you shouldn't go, mother," I said, hanging the empty hanger back in the closet. She had done her hair and made up her face, but was still dressed in a blue dressing gown belted at the waist.

"I'm almost ready," she replied. "I'll be fine." As I combed my hair, I could see her seated behind me in the mirror. She was tracing the patterns on my bedspread with her finger.

"I'm very pleased you're coming," I said, watching her reaction in the mirror. Her hand tightened around the brandy bottle.

"Do you remember a very long time ago when we talked about the two types of princes?"

"I was almost thirteen."

"And now you're twenty. A month from now you'll be in Oxford."

"Where all the princes are educated," I said, half laughing.

She paused, poured herself a brandy, and took a long drink. "Then you'll remember that all serious artists use betrayal as their constant theme. They break it down in two ways. Comedy and tragedy. This is more than just laughing and crying about life's deceptions. The biggest deception is that it's all tragedy. Except—except, a sense of humor lets you carry the tragedy in a funny, colorful bag. Every time you open it, you know what's there. And every time you examine it, you start to laugh. Macheath's infidelity was no worse or better than Rubashov's. Only their scale of activity was different. Even if we could reverse their fates. Hang Macheath and spare Rubashov the final bullet. What would it have mattered? The tragedy wasn't their ultimate fate. The tragedy was the structure of their lives. Only Macheath's was bearable. So, my son, you have no choice but to accept tragedy as the only true explanation of what will come your way. But you can keep your distance—at least for a while—with this."

Mother held up her brandy bottle and waved it like a railway man's lantern. She looked up at me from the edge of the bed with tears forming in her eyes.

"Or this." She forced a bright smile onto her lips.

"And finally, you can always close down the curtain." She pressed a finger to her head like a pistol, dropped her thumb.

"Bang," I said.

"Only when the funny bag breaks apart." She reflected over her brandy as I leaned down to tie my shoes. I faced the mirror again looking myself over and glancing back at mother sitting motionless on the bed. "On your twentieth birthday, you'll be receiving a twenty-thousand-dollar-a-year income."

"Is that from your funny bag?" I asked, not taking her seriously. That was a mistake, not to take mother seriously the very few times she ever decided to talk to me.

"The income is from a trust your father set up."

I concentrated on her face in the mirror. How drunk was she? I was trained as a lawyer and I knew only very wealthy people had trust funds. My father who'd gone missing in the Spanish Civil War couldn't have accumulated enough money for a trust. Edgar with his modest medical practice—or so the story had always gone—had considered me a permanent liability. Had Edgar known all along about my trust? Did Mother also have a trust? Was this why Edgar had married her—for her money? Suddenly, I had a thousand questions.

"Who is the trustee?"

She smiled, obviously with some sense of comedy in her mind.

"It's called the A.O.C. Trust. That's all I'm allowed to tell you."

"Allowed? Allowed by whom?"

"The trustees."

"But why the secrecy?"

"The basic point, Matthew, is that you'll be well off. Just remember one thing. Money isn't one of three options you have in this life to battle what's in the bag."

No amount of argument or pleading moved mother to divulge any more information about this unexpected windfall. She hadn't told me earlier for several reasons. The terms of the trust prohibited a prior disclosure. Also, she said even if she'd been free to do so she wouldn't have told me earlier. Knowing that a large sum of money was to fall due on my twentieth birthday might have ruined me. She'd seen how money had destroyed other young men. Men who never had any incentive to digest the difference between Brecht's and Koestler's approach to life. Having learned these things was like having a chaperone for the money; I wouldn't get raped, molested, or have taken advantage of it in a tight spot.

AT the reception, classmates I'd never seen dressed in business suits arrived in rented dinner jackets. Yates and Cook, hair greased back, roamed around the large room, looking like ushers at a working-class wedding or funeral. Dean Scime circulated through the crowd, shaking hands with parents and patting students on the shoulder. He looked the way I imagined Spencer Tracy, decked out in a dinner jacket, greeting his public on opening night. The face and body loose, relaxed, a sparkle in the eye and a satisfied grin.

I stood between Edgar and mother as Dean Scime came across the room, his hand extended. Edgar reached out with his hand.

"Doctor Burlock," said the Dean, pumping Edgar's hand. "How nice to see you again. And Missus Burlock. What a pleasure to meet Matthew's mother."

Dean Scime glanced at Edgar and then me at several times. Why hadn't young Matthew died, he must've been saying to himself. He was, in many ways, a better actor than Spencer Tracy. As he was about to depart for another set of parents, he sunk his fingers into my upper arms and squeezed; his old routine from my first term at the law school. No question about it. By some miraculous means the tumors devouring my body had evaporated. I thought he was about to say something as he turned to Edgar. But he didn't. He probably thought it wasn't the appropriate time to discuss the possible frauds used to gain my entrance into the law school. Tiny beads of perspiration formed on his brow.

"Matthew will do well at Oxford," he said to my mother. It probably crossed his mind that Edgar had told them I was dying of cancer so they would accept me.

"We are very proud of him," she replied. Those were the first words she spoke since we left the house. Her heart had only threatened to shoot out of her chest like a racehorse out of the starting gates; Edgar had run a yellow light near Stanley Park. He gave her a mild sedative before we got out of the car. She was still on edge and looking at her watch.

As Dean Scime moved on, Edgar said to mother, "The Dean looks ill."

"He was sweating," added mother, taking comfort that someone else appeared to be at the meltdown point in the large crowd.

Call it an omen, but I sensed something was about to break at the reception. Something in the air. I couldn't put my finger on it. Classmates and parents noisily drank, chatted, and laughed around us. Then Joan arrived. She was about one hour late. Her hair tied in a bun, she was with Rod, her new boyfriend, who had his arm around her thick waist. She saw me across the room and waved. I waved back. By our third year in law school Joan had started to go her own way. Our trips down to Wreck Beach to eat sandwiches in the abandoned gun tower had stopped altogether. But we occasionally studied together and sat together in her class.

"Who's that?" mother asked, nervously fingering the diamond brooch above her left breast.

"That's Joan."

"She's not—"

"She's in my class," I said, before mother could finish.

Mother had an acute sense of class; it was a tragedy that people were so divided, an important source of betrayal. But the dividing lines, once they touched family, became rigid. After all, my grandfather had been just a fireman; mother, through marriage to a doctor, had crossed to the other side.

"Oh, I see," said Mother. "You two seem quite friendly."

Edgar smiled at mother, and nudged her with his shoulder. "Darling, don't make up absurd stories."

I'm not certain Edgar realized that such a command would come very close to rendering mother completely mute. In any case, the rot had set in; from the moment they laid eyes on one another some unconscious wound that women open between themselves began to fester. It must be sort of specialized female Wongness that men don't really understand.

"Matthew, just one more question," said mother, eyeing Joan on the opposite side of the room.

My leather leg holster with a Beretta snapped tight against my calf muscle as I flexed in anticipation of mother's question.

"Exactly—" mother paused, as Joan and Rod slowly approached from our left. "Exactly what does her father do?"

"He's a butcher in Burnaby."

A very sweet smile crossed her lips. "Oh, I do see. A butcher."

"Sort of like Edgar. Except Joan's dad sells his meat." I was immediately sorry that I'd said that. But I was defensive about Joan in their presence. For someone locked away inside the house most of the time, mother hadn't lost her skill of cutting up people of a lower social class. Her attitude seemed to be in exceptionally bad taste. Again she glanced down at her watch. She'd had enough and wanted to leave.

"Think of this as a Brecht play. It turns out all right in the end. A pleasant comedy," I said to mother, as she took a drink from a passing tray. The lines on her face eased slightly.

As Joan filtered through the crowd, my heart started to pound. She was a complete mess. Her hair half-undone, lipstick smeared form ear to ear, and some large creases roughly the size of Rod's hands on her blouse. Rod followed behind in a busman's uniform, his hat cocked to one side. The rumpled blue shirttail stuck out from his gray trousers. He was drinking from a beer bottle and tipping his hat to the women in the crowd. Under his armpits were large, damp, circular perspiration stains; as quickly as he drank a bottle of beer, it leaked out of his armpits.

Joan called Rod the "Flesh Eater." According to her, Rod liked very rare steaks. But I doubted the explanation from the beginning. Also I discounted that the name had anything to do with her father being a butcher. From the way they wove across the room, I suspected Joan had something less than a cordial farewell to the class in mind.

In the three years of law school she'd learned much about power and ceremony and solemnity. This night, however, was the final act she'd written. We were about to become her opening night audience. Dean Scime turned pale as he shook the Flesh Eater's hand. Joan stared at the Dean with the disquieting smile of a gravedigger leaning on a spade.

I felt the tension building in the room. The impact was particularly profound on mother. Her hands started to shake, and she leaned against Edgar. You could see the terror in her eyes; someone was about to go missing-in-action. Edgar stared into his drink. Joan ran over and kissed me on the lips. She smelled of wet grassy lawns outside the pavilion, and of beer. Mother was growing paler, as if she had trouble breathing. Standing in front of her was the Flesh Eater with what appeared to be an enormous erection in his bus-driver trousers.

"This is my fiancé," said Joan, wrapping an arm around the Flesh Eater. He had an intoxicated, gaping grin. Joan pulled off his cap and placed it on her head.

"We're going to live in a gun tower on the beach and breed," Joan said in the general direction of Edgar and mother.

I didn't understand how the Flesh Eater could maintain an erection for so long with all that beer in him. I wished that

I'd lasted in science for a few more weeks. All that mysterious biology of capillaries, veins, and muscles would have given me some hint about the Flesh Eater's condition.

"You know how I met Joan?" Rod asked Edgar.

Edgar peered over his spectacles with the quizzical expression doctors have in the presence of a clinically dead patient. All right, nurse. Pull the plug. That was Edgar's face.

"We met on my bus in Burnaby. Joan didn't have any change. I gave her a loan. We started talkin' and hit it off. Didn't we, hon?"

"You mean I fucked your brains out," she replied. The Flesh Eater wrinkled his nose and laughed.

In the catalogue all of martyrs, saints, lovers, criminals, no one had ever maintained a rigid erection while drinking beer and talking about bus fare in a black-tie crowd. And there was little excitement in his bloodshot eyes. How did he do it? Only Edgar seemed not to question the Flesh Eater's state. There must have been something about this in Gray's *Anatomy* which explained Rod's powers. I saw Edgar glance down several times at the Flesh Eater's trousers, his fingers clamped around his glass. Maybe Ray had been a bus driver before he ended up hanging as an exhibit in Edgar's study.

There was defiance in Joan's eyes as they met mother's. If hell was a state of mind, then for that instant Joan and mother occupied that landscape together; the glowing coals, the screams of anguish, the piles of victims, and endless stack stretching to the sky. Mother had the same look as Wong when Louise dropped dead on his back. If my briefcase had been opened, I'm certain she would have thrown up inside it.

"I feel that I know you, Missus Burlock," said Joan. Mother stood motionless.

"I—I—" mother stammered and then broke off, finishing her drink in one gulp.

"You never told me that," said the Flesh Eater.

"Shut up, Rod," Joan snapped, taking off his bus driver's cap. The four Horsemen of the Apocalypse were riding in the far distance behind mother's eyes. Rubashov was being led down that final flight of stairs. "I've thought about your mother travelling across Canada many times over the past three years." A glimmer of a smile crossed Joan's lips. "Didn't Matthew tell you that Dean Scime tells jokes about your mother in class?"

"Knock if off, Joan," I said.

"It's true. He does."

"Are you articling with a city firm?" Edgar interjected, holding up mother by the arm.

"Mister Ambassador. So good to see you again. In answer to your question. No . I'm a butcher's daughter. That's an unfortunate combination for a city firm. But I'm certain things are different in Haiti."

She dropped her hand and expertly unzipped the Flesh Eater bus driver's trousers. "But working-class people have their ways of surviving in the world." By now a number of people had crowded around us. Mother's face was lifeless. I doubt that she had a pulse. Her eyes were pin-size. From Rod's trousers Joan removed a seven-inch vial. She raised her hand above her head and slowly pivoted around. No one was talking now. All eyes focused on the butcher's daughter, standing on her toes, smiling, and the vial cradled in her hand. But when she once again faced mother the smile was gone and there were tears in her eyes.

"The system forced your mother to eat these to live. Some day that's going to change. When it does, we'll make the system eat slugs."

No one spoke. Joan looked around the room, then raised her hand, and hurled the vial against the wall. It just missed Yates' head. The splattered glass, water, and slugs slowly drained down to the floor. Then Joan ran out, the Flesh Eater following quickly behind her. Mother had fainted and Edgar knelt on the floor beside her. A light hum of conversation filled the Pavilion. A waiter had started sweeping up the broken glass and rubbing down the wall. Other waiters began pouring and serving more wine. I called an ambulance and with Edgar took mother to the hospital where they revived her. But she refused to stay overnight. She only wanted to go home.

AROUND two in the morning, with my black tie in my pocket, I sat on a wooden bus bench on Alma between Tenth Avenue and West Broadway nursing a bottle of gin. I waved off three buses which had stopped. Then a Dunbar bus pulled to the curb and the pneumatic doors opened. The Flesh Eater smiled down at me from the driver's seat. He tipped his cap. I saluted back with my fifth of gin, and slowly staggered from the bench and climbed onto the bus.

"Hi, kid," said Rod, the Flesh Eater, as I turned out my pockets looking for loose change. He lurched forward, half hanging out of his seat, and glanced towards the back. "Hey, babe. Look what's come on. The world's first teenage lawyer." As I walked towards the back, Rod gunned the bus forward across Tenth Avenue. Except for Rod and Joan, the bus was empty. Joan sat near the window on the long rear bench at the back. She was drunk. Like mother, the blood had gone from her lips. The fine tapered smile that remained looked like it had been put on with an engraver's needle.

Halfway down the aisle, I turned back to Rod. "I'm not a teenager," I said, my pockets turned inside out and a bottle in one hand.

He looked at me through the mirror. "How old are you, kid?"

"Twenty."

"Fuck me. That old?"

"Fuck you and your bus asshole," I said, swinging from side to side as he climbed the hill. He was shifting gears and watching traffic pass on his left. I don't think he heard me. I was about to repeat myself but he started yelling back at Joan about some driver who'd cut him off.

"Twenty years old. Think of what's ahead. You can vote. Bet on the horses. Get fucked. Drink legally."

"A wonderful improvement," I shouted back. He laughed, and as he stopped for the lights on Sixteenth and Dunbar, I made my way back to Joan. I slid into the seat beside her.

"Who you calling asshole?" she asked.

I drank from my bottle, wiping my mouth on my coat sleeve. "You for one," I said. "I told you my mother's the nervous type. We had to take her to hospital."

"So you waited for Rod's bus just to call me an asshole?"

"Something like that."

"Sometimes you have to be an asshole to survive." She reached over and took my bottle of gin. She took a short drink and passed it back where I cradled it between my legs. Rod was pretty drunk. I could tell by the way the fifteen tons of bus lurched forward. He was starting to sing.

It was *Mack the Knife*. I'd told Joan about mother's obsession with Brecht and *The Threepenny Opera*. After she first read the play, she told me it was shit. Then she reread it several times. She said it was a good example of how men fucked women around. One day she was going to write a *Threepenny Opera* and make Macheath a woman. Her performance at the reception I suspect was a rough first draft of what she had in mind. The lyrics drifted to the back as Rod continued to sing.

> Oh the shark has pretty teeth dear
> and he shows them a-pearly white,
> Just a jackknife has Macheath dear,
> But he keeps it out of sight . . .

For a moment Uncle Foss flashed through my mind. Of course Macheath had only a jackknife. It was arming the Macheaths with submachine guns that he feared and led Potter to Revelli's factory. I looked over at Joan; her eyes closed, she was humming along with Rod. It occurred to me that the Rods of the world now had access to submachine guns. Had Uncle Foss been wrong? Rod was driving a bus and not out shooting people down in the streets. And the only weapon was the jackknife from a song. But that night and that year, the IRA, the PLO, and the others did not yet exist.

We passed deserted side streets, darkened houses, and Chinese grocery stores. Rod kept on singing *Mack the Knife*, beating out the tempo on the steering wheel. As we sailed down Dunbar Street I emptied my gin bottle and dropped it on the floor.

Rod called back. "It's all right to be young, kid." We passed the cinema. "Floyd Patterson was only twenty and he beat the livin' shit out of Archie Moore." He went back to humming *Mack the Knife*. I guess things drifted in and out of Rod's head as he drove. He didn't expect a response. It was enough to boom out what he was thinking about at that moment.

Joan opened one eye, and looked down at the empty gin bottle rolling across the floor.

"I've been looking for you," I said.

"Want a drink?"

"Sure, why not." She passed me a bottle of rye. Rye has that funny, damp, black-powder smell like an expended shotgun shell. I held the bottle to my lips and drank.

"At the Pavilion you were staring at Rod's pants," she said, laughing to herself.

"There are basic laws of gravity and nature."

"Thought it was a big fucking erection."

"Of course. What else was I supposed to think? That he had a bottle of slugs hidden inside?"

I passed the rye bottle back to Joan. She put it to her mouth, and then stopped. Lowering it, she said, "Do you feel like a lawyer?"

I leaned over, resting my head against her upright knees. "I don't know what it's supposed to feel like."

"I feel like a whore," she said. I thought she was going to cry. Lifting my head I felt her hand softly ruffle my hair. "A very tired used-up whore. Three years of mind-fucking. Think of what we've been through, Matt. Thousands of cases, laws, books, articles. It's all up here." She lightly tapped my head with the bottom of the rye bottle. "Nice virgin boy like you with a fraudulent case of cancer ends up with a psyche all covered with festering sores. Your mind's been fucking the unclean, diseased rules. Even when you sleep."

In his Louis Armstrong voice, Rod's words echoed through the silent bus, *"Just a jackknife has Macheath dear . . ."* We passed within three blocks of my old school and Alpha House. At the bottom of Forty-first Street, Rod pulled into a looping drive and drove out the other end. We were backtracking into the city. The bus moved in a lilting rhythm, my head rolling slightly against Joan's knees.

"And you're going to Oxford for advanced mind-fucking," Joan said, playing with my ear.

"I'm doing this one for Potter. I owe it to him."

She lit a cigarette and put it in my mouth. "You mean the Haitian Ambassador didn't tell the Queen you had cancer?"

"Of the balls," I replied. "You can laugh. It won't kill you."

"You piss me off."

"I piss you off? What about tonight? That was a real piss-off."

"Burlock, your problem is that you've got a fucking feudal mentality."

I rose up and pulled the black tie out of my pocket. "I'm going home."

"Hold on, Matt. Sit down for a minute." As I sat down, she leaned forward and kissed me. Then she pulled back, tears on her cheeks. "Remember when I asked you to fuck me on the beach that time?" I nodded. "I'm asking for the second and final time."

At Joan's command, Rod switched off the interior lights. We stretched out on the back bench. Joan unzipped my trousers and leaned back. It was after three in the morning. After all we'd drunk, I collapsed on her. I remember feeling her fleshy thighs close in around me, the oscillating motion of the bus and Joan crying and moaning beneath me. I buried my face in her neck, my nose halfway into the crack between the seat and the back. I could smell bubble gum some kid had stuffed into the crack. From the front of the bus, Rod, who was no longer stopping for passengers, was still nattering away.

"Elvis Aaron Presley's just a fucking kid. About twenty just like Floyd Patterson. The Champ. You know, I think it's a kid's world these days." He broke into a rough rendition of *Heartbreak Hotel*. By Hastings Street we were both sitting up and smoking a cigarette. Outside, winos slept on street benches with newspapers over their heads. So that was my first time with a woman. A twenty-year-old lawyer, his mother whisked off to hospital, a large trust-fund income, in the back of a Vancouver bus listening to an Elvis tune, my head resting against a butcher's daughter.

CHAPTER 12

WE sat in the Alpha House kitchen in silence for a long time. Potter smoking his pipe, and examining a Pisztoly 37M, a Hungarian pistol. He was pleased to add it to his collection. I sat back in the wooden chair in my new brown suit; my new shoes reflecting the morning light; and my hair neatly cut, parted, and combed. I smoked a cigarette and watched Potter handling the pistol.

Although he was looking at the Pisztoly, I knew from the way he sucked on the pipe that his mind was on my impending travel. He pulled the clip from the bottom of the pistol and squeezed out seven rounds of 7.65 mm ammo. One by one he placed the rounds on the table.

"The British Empire collapsed once we stopped believing in it," Potter said. "The same thing happened to the Romans, the Hungarians—and now the Americans."

With the tip of his pipe he pushed the first round. It struck the tabletop with a dull thud. In rapid succession the remaining six rounds fell like dominoes. Slowly he reloaded the magazine.

"I should know what happened to Wild Bill. And I think you know," I said, as Potter slammed the magazine back into the Pisztoly 37 mm. In one week I'd leave for Oxford. I wanted to clear the boards about my grandfather. The question wasn't unexpected.

"I've been waiting for the right moment, Matthew." Until that morning, after I'd become a twenty-year-old lawyer, the true nature of my connection with Potter was as inaccessible as the dark side of the moon. I'd grown up with his stories; and he had grown older listening to my dreams. It was like we'd spliced frames of film together all those years; not knowing the final picture. There I was like a firefly exposing a long film, one frame at a time. Now it was nearly finished except for the frames with Wild Bill. He was a central character who was kept in the shadows. When the camera started to focus on him, he faded down a canal, along some bend in the road, slipped over a wall. Wild Bill stayed one frame ahead of the one Potter and I witnessed.

Potter knew it was my birthright to shoot those last frames before I left for Oxford. The location of that final shoot was, to my surprise, South Africa.

February 24, 1900
Paardeberg, South Africa

CRONJE, the Boer commander, was holed up with nearly four thousand men, uncounted thousands of women, children, wagons, oxen, and horses. In the cold rain, British artillery shelled his position. Downwind at the Canadian bivouac along the Modder River, Wild Bill Anglin crawled out of his blankets. There was an overwhelming smell in the air: a sweet, sharp poisonous smell, like incense and disintegrated, rotting meat.

The smell had been suffocating in the tent. Blanket wrapped

around his shoulders, Wild Bill slipped out and walked down to the riverbank. The smell was stronger. Entering the consciousness; absorbed by the entire body. In the dark and rain, Wild Bill looked for shelter, some relief from the stench and the shellburst across the Modder. He knew soon enough the cause of the odor.

Cronje, through a messenger to Lord Roberts, requested a one-day armistice to bury his dead. The British shells tore up the earth in and around Cronje's camp, uprooted trees, wagons, and supplies scattered in pieces across the grounds, hundreds of horses, cattle, and oxen split open and dead. Volley upon volley, the shells relentlessly penetrated beasts, men, women, and children, ricocheting and flying fragments among the dead and living, creating a mountain of carrion. The smell of the slaughter drifted down the Modder and through the British position.

Lord Roberts would only accept Cronje's unconditional surrender. That message was sent back to the Boers. The shelling continued throughout the night. A steady pounding, with an eerie lyrical sound, registering against a background of heavy rain. Sitting on the riverbank, Wild Bill tried not to think about the stench and the noise. Why had he come to the banks of the Modder in South Africa? Like many others from the colonies, he'd answered the call of the mother country. Like a child, he, like the other Canadians, travelled to South Africa to fight the Boers to fulfill his sense of duty.

The Canadian contingent was ordered to storm the Boer trenches on a Sunday. Tired, hungry, and exhausted, an English colonel marched the company of Canadians against Cronje's well-entrenched machine guns. Soon after the guns opened up, the colonel abandoned the troops under fire. Wild Bill wasn't with the men of Paardeberg that Sunday afternoon. But he heard how the Boer machine guns had torn them to pieces, drenching the veldt with young Canadian blood. At the time, he'd been talking cricket matches with his friend, Captain Vincent Fosbery, an English officer. Wild Bill, an excellent cricket player, formed a close friendship with the captain. Both were gun collectors, and would discuss long into the night the design, use, and advantages of various types of weapons. That Sunday, Captain Fosbery had requested the colonel for permission to allow Wild Bill to remain behind. He was needed to assist in the inspection of a new shipment of rifles. Permission was granted. While Wild Bill and the captain inspected rifles, the Boers cut the Canadians into fine pieces of lace; lace with a pattern no mother would recognize.

Half an hour after Wild Bill sat on the riverbank, Captain Fosbery, a pipe clenched in his teeth, silently sat beside him. Wild Bill coughed, holding his side and spitting out a little blood. He shuddered against the rain. The men didn't speak for some time. Captain Fosbery tried to light his pipe but it wouldn't stay lit in the rain. The smell of pipe tobacco, any smell for that matter, would have come as a welcome relief.

"They're taking a terrible beating," said Captain Fosbery.

Wild Bill nodded, his blanket hooded over his head.

"About last Sunday," said Captain Fosbery, breaking off with a sigh. "Your chaps caught a bit of bad luck."

"Colonel Allworth of the Cornwalls took five bullets. I guess you could call that bad luck," replied Wild Bill.

"The man was a fool, Willy."

"Bad judgment. It's like this smell. It rolls right over you."

"He was quite mad, Willy. At Oxford he was an unpardonable bore. Always looking out for himself. A pity he had to take so many of your mates with him."

Against the horizon a faint slit of light marked the approaching dawn. Still the shelling pounded away at Cronje's position with mindless regularity. Captain Fosbery watched the ghostly image of his Canadian friend disappear down towards the river edge.

"You all right, Willy?"

"Why was Colonel Allworth put in command?" Lieutenant William Anglin shouted back.

"He came well-connected."

"You mean misrepresented to the War Office."

"Falsehoods. Deceptions. Allsworth's life was a dreary lie."

"Funny, isn't it?" Captain Fosbery covered his mouth and nose, and slid down the bank. "What's funny?" he asked, facing Lieutenant Anglin.

"How none of the men killed with him had been to Oxford." The sense of outrage of Paardeberg overcame the smell from the river for a brief moment.

"Don't talk rubbish. That had nothing to do with it."

Something floating down the river struck Lieutenant Anglin above his right knee. The force of the blow knocked him backward and onto the wet, cold mud. "Goddammit," he cried out. Above him, Captain Fosbery shoved the bolt of his Enfield forward, and crouched staring around in the half-light of dawn.

"Willy, you all right?" In the morning light, the rain falling, Wild Bill sat in the mud, eye-level with the river. The river had become a psychopathic nightmare. In the shallows, against the rocks midstream and along the banks on both sides, were the slaughtered carcasses of dead horses, cattle, oxen, men, and women. Lifeless, broken, smashed bodies entangled with each other. Upstream from the British camp, Cronje, denied the privilege of burying this mass of dead, sent his reply to Lord Roberts. He dumped the carnage into the river.

Lieutenant Anglin rose to his feet, the blanket around his shoulders caked with mud, the rain running down his face, and surveyed the horror. Captain Fosbery stood next to him. The sun was above the horizon, and fell upon the splintered and shredded remains of beast and man. Decomposed parts of a horse drifted into a cow; the bottom half of a Boer floated along the side of an oxen. Death reconstructed the river into a floating sewer of garbage, burnt flesh, and broken bones. Hundreds of bloated, limbless animals bobbed near the river's edge. In the face of such slaughter how did the Boers continue the fight? If the French Canadian Prime Minister, Sir Wilfrid Laurier, had known he'd sent Canadian men to the border of hell, would he, with great regret, have declined Her Majesty's request for troops?

"It's barbarous," murmured Captain Fosbery. The rotting carrion whirled past, bouncing off rocks and formless hunks of flesh. "It's inhuman. It's absolutely unthinkable. Cronje will be shot for this outrage."

"But he requested an armistice to bury—to bury this," Lieutenant Anglin said, the blanket covering his nose and mouth. There were no words to describe "this." Cronje wanted a short lull to dispose of a nightmare.

"Willy, you don't believe that. Cronje wouldn't have buried his dead. The time would have been spent fortifying his position. And then where would we be? More dead on both sides."

Captain Fosbery turned back towards the camp. As he stepped forward, he stumbled over a water-sodden Boer corpse washed up on the bank; its clothes and sex cannoned away. Before he could catch his balance, Captain Fosbery fell and in the morning light he found himself eyeball to eyeball with a Boer without a jaw and mouth. He started to vomit and shake. Lieutenant Anglin lifted his comrade over his shoulder, carried him up the bank, and laid him on the blanket. Maybe he understood Cronje a little better, kneeling down over Captain Fosbery. Cronje, drenched, soaked, and cold and up to his knees in death and grief, merely shifted the load down the river to share with his enemy. And the enemy couldn't bear this load any more than Cronje and his men.

Without shells to match the British, he used his dead to spread a plague through the British army. A very rough-and-ready, yet effective, chemical warfare that caused sickness to spread among the British side—the side that drank from Cronje's river of the dead.

Captain Fosbery had spoken in anger when he vowed to have General Cronje shot. Because in the end the British didn't shoot him. He surrendered with the survivors of his camp on Majuba Day, February 27, 1900. Wild Bill Anglin and Captain Fosbery were among the officers on the British side who rode with Lord Roberts into the Boer camp to accept the surrender. Among the dead, stacked like cords of wood along the river, they found an old man, his white hair and beard burned and black from shellbursts and dust. Dressed in tweeds, he was shoeless. Like the old beggars who roamed through Regents Park on a Sunday afternoon feeding bread to the pigeons; except this old man fed his dead to the river.

Lord Roberts climbed down from his horse, saluted the old man. There was an ironic smile on Cronje's face.

"You made a most gallant defense, sir," Lord Roberts said, dressed in his parade uniform. Lieutenant Anglin felt slightly uncomfortable that he'd come from British Columbia to help the British vanquish an old man. Cronje's wife, grandson, sister-in-law, a nephew, and his servants nervously watched the British troops ride into their camp. The mounted men began rounding up and disarming the nearly three thousand Boers who stood in clusters, their hands raised above their heads. Lieutenant Anglin and Captian Fosbery slowly rode their horses through the crowds of Boer men. The pale, dirty faces of the defeated Boers stared up at them; faces with eyes that didn't fix on any object, strained, exhausted faces full of anguish and fear.

Captain Fosbery suddenly turned his horse around. "Willy, we're going back to camp."

"May I ask why, sir?" Lieutenant Anglin rode up to the Captain's side.

"Look at these men."

"They're worn out."

"Look at the number who survived."

That was an odd observation, thought Lieutenant Anglin. The dead were everywhere. To think of large numbers of living Boers as a disappointment disconcerted him. All around the men of the Canadian Regiment, the Gordon Highlanders and the Second Shropshires were lining up and searching the prisoners. Those images remained in his mind as they rode back to their camp.

In front of the stockade, Captain Fosbery and Lieutenant Anglin dismounted their horses and tied them to the rail. The lieutenant in the entrance saluted Captain Fosbery as he entered. Lieutenant Anglin followed behind, wondering why they'd abruptly left Cronje's camp.

"Lord Roberts has given us orders to accompany Martin Scheidel to Cronje's camp," Captain Fosbery said. "He wants all prisoners together."

Lieutenant Anglin remained silent though he knew his superior officer and friend had just told a lie. A short time later two guards dressed in khaki uniforms appeared through a door with Martin Scheidel between them. Although in his early thirties, Scheidel was balding, his beard patchy along his cheeks, and his eyes were a deep blue. A German national, he'd been captured by two men of the Second Shropshire and interrogated by Captain Fosbery. Lieutenant Anglin participated in the questioning over a two-day period. Scheidel wasn't an ordinary German advisor sent to assist the Boers' war effort. His grandfather, Hugo Borchardt, a Berlin inventor, had perfected a revolutionary pistol named the *Parabellum-pistolen*. Later the name would change to Luger and become the standard pistol carried by the German army through two world wars.

Young Martin knew and admired the Webley & Scott revolver manufactured in Birmingham. Grandfather Hugo had given him an 1896 Webley-Fosbery self-cocking revolver. Both men were from weapon-manufacturing families, and talked easily between themselves. Scheidel, under Captain Fosbery's orders, had been treated as a gentleman; he had separate quarters, away from the other prisoners, and better rations.

By the end of the interrogation, Scheidel had confided that he had his own innovation ready to transport back to Germany after his release. An admission he would now regret. It was made over wine, talk of home, and the discussion of pistols and rifles developed in Europe and America. They'd forgotten about the war and that they were enemies. With all the interlocking relationships that was an easy oversight. After all, the Kaiser was the grandson of the Queen.

The day the Canadians were abandoned in the charge of Paardeberg, Lieutenant Anglin and Captain Fosbery rode with Scheidel along the Modder River, across the veldt. They stopped at a cache Scheidel had left below the base of a small hill. After an hour of digging, they dropped their shovels and unearthed weapons and food. Scheidel sorted through the weapons, removing one wrapped in a blanket, and proudly handed it to Captain Fosbery. He pulled off the blanket. All three men looked at a strange weapon. Roughly the size and shape of a rifle; but there the similarities ceased. This "rifle" had a ribbed barrel, a wooden stock and handgrip that extended below the barrel; in front of the trigger guard hung a black ammunition magazine.

Scheidel said the gun fired eight hundred rounds per minute. The bullets left the barrel automatically by a mere squeeze on the trigger. It wasn't a rifle or a Gatling, but a gun to be carried by the common soldier at a dead run firing at the enemy's position. For the past five years Scheidel had been secretly experimenting with the concept of a rapid-fire combat rifle. After his grandfather's firm sent him to coordinate gun shipments to the Boers, Scheidel kept working on the weapon with a supply of tools smuggled into the country. Not two weeks before his capture, he'd perfected the breech-loading mechanism and the gun was complete. Still in the flush of success, he found it difficult not to confide his breakthrough to Captain Fosbery and Lieutenant Anglin. They could appreciate what he had accomplished. Besides, they had captured the gun with Scheidel and ultimately would have figured out what he had invented.

As Cronje's position was being shelled, Lieutenant Anglin stripped down the Scheidel rapid-fire scores of times, studying the breech-loading mechanism, firing pin, magazine, barrel, and chamber. He could take it apart and put it back together again in his sleep. The two officers didn't report their findings to their superior officers. The original reason was quite simply that they weren't sure what they had captured along with the prisoner. Later the reason became more complex; Captain Fosbery, as intelligence officer, distrusted Lord Roberts, and perhaps, thinking about his own gun-manufacturing future after the war, he decided to keep his light under a bushel.

The day Captain Fosbery and Lieutenant Anglin rode back to the camp Scheidel had been reading in his cell. It was the first time in many days that the pounding of the shells allowed some peace of mind. When the guards brought him out of the cell, he thought how peaceful the world suddenly seemed.

"How good to see you chaps," Martin Scheidel said, stepping forward from the guards. His English was faultless, which made it difficult to think of him as being a German national.

"General Cronje's surrendered," Captain Fosbery said, as they walked outside where a private was bringing around a horse for Scheidel. There was a tense, nervous timbre in the Captain's voice. He mounted his horse. "There's a German prisoner who can't speak English. I thought you might assist us."

Scheidel's face collapsed a little; he knew that it was highly unlikely that any German sent to South Africa wouldn't be fluent in English. Scheidel was further aware that despite what had passed as friendship between them, a British intelligence officer wouldn't use one captured German to interrogate another. He looked up for a long moment into the Captain's eyes, then mounted his horse. The three men headed away from the camp.

"It's a good day for a ride," Scheidel said, looking at the horizon. "Not so much rain."

"After the war, you'll come to British Columbia," Lieutenant Anglin said. "We'll do some salmon fishing. The Fraser's a much nicer river than the Modder."

Scheidel forced a smile. "Not so many bodies." He glanced over his shoulder. "And you, Captain. Maybe I will go to England to hunt the fox."

Captain Fosbery's face was flushed; he had the same expression as when he fell over the badly mutilated Boer near the river. He said nothing as the camp disappeared and they crossed the veldt. Scheidel rode stiffly in the saddle a few yards ahead. He talked about Berlin. How his grandfather was a big, old bear of a man, ordering around his employees and firing anyone who was as much as one minute late. There was stale beer in his beard at night. You could smell it when he leaned over to kiss you goodnight as a child.

By then it was evident they were riding north and away from Cronje's camp.

"You'll write my family," Scheidel said finally, with a strong, distinct voice. "Tell them that it happened quickly. I think that's how you say it—" Then he kicked his horse hard, turned him to the left in a gallop.

Captain Fosbery raised his rifle and followed Scheidel for several seconds. There was a loud report that echoed across the veldt. Scheidel's riderless horse doubled back, heading for the camp. The Captain put his rifle back in the saddle holster, and trotted up ahead where Scheidel had fallen. Lieutenant Anglin, head in his hands, stayed behind. A moment later, Captain Fosbery, his pistol extended, placed a single round in the dead man's head.

"It's finished," he called back to Lieutenant Anglin. He rode up to the Captain, circled him and the body.

"Why kill him?" Lieutenant Anglin shouted. "Goddammit, Vince. He was our friend." He dismounted his horse and knelt down by Scheidel. A thread of blood trickled down his head.

"He was our enemy."

"No, he wasn't. His grandfather knew your father, for God sakes."

"Don't be a sentimental fool."

"It's sentimental not to want to kill someone in cold blood?"

"It had to be done, Willy."

Captain Fosbery walked back to his horse, untied a flap, and pulled out a spade. He began digging Scheidel's grave.

As he straightened up with the first spade of grass and dirt, he took a right hook to the jaw from Lieutenant Anglin. Grass, dirt, and blood went flying. The Captain fell next to Scheidel, his head on the dead man's chest. Lieutenant Anglin, fists clenched, stood over him.

"Get up," the Lieutenant yelled.

"How many did we lose taking Cronje's camp?"

"Get up!"

"You know how many, Willy? Thirty killed. Another ninety wounded."

"I don't care anymore. I just—"

"Just listen for a minute." Captain Fosbery sat upright on the ground, feeling his jaw and looking for signs of blood on his hand. "Think of the slaughter if they'd had Scheidel's gun. Hundreds. Many thousands dead. You think this is the last war we'll ever fight? No, Willy. There'll be others. Other Cronje's. Other battles. One man's life is the cost. Just one man." He rose back to his feet and put his arm around Wild Bill's shoulder. Lieutenant Anglin fought back tears and then turned away.

"He was our friend."

"And I'm sorry for that. But we're not on holiday in British Columbia. This is South Africa and we're at war."

Later that afternoon they buried Scheidel with his gun on the South African veldt. Captain Fosbery got his Canadian Lieutenant to pledge an oath of secrecy. On the way back to the camp they invented the obvious story for the high command. Scheidel had promised to lead them to a secret Boer camp. On the way, they'd been ambushed by several Boers, and in the ensuing fight, Scheidel had been killed. After the war, back in England, Captain Fosbery wrote a letter to Hugo Borchardt in Germany. He explained how his grandson had died quickly. He had lived and died a gentleman. That was the most important thing.

CHAPTER 13

IN October, 1957, shortly after the Russians launched Sputnik, I arrived in Oxford dressed in a new tailored suit. My first meeting with my Oxford don came the following day. In a hand-written note left at the porter's lodge, Buckland asked me to attend his rooms off staircase eight at 2:30 that afternoon. I crumpled the note in my hand as I entered the staircase to his rooms. When I arrived I found Buckland seated behind an ornate desk, back erect in his leather chair, his eyes framed in wire-rimmed glasses. He didn't look up as I closed the door. I was a little late, confused by the system of a porter's lodge and the staircases.

I stepped forward. A fire roared in the stone fireplace in the corner. His room was large, with a couch, chairs, a table, and ceiling-to-floor bookcases against two walls. In front of the couch, on a low glass-topped table, were two crystal glasses with long stems and a crystal decanter full with sherry. I politely cleared my throat. Buckland licked his forefinger, slowly turned the page of his book. Finally, closing the book, he looked up with a stare that seemed a million miles away. He was preoccupied with his thoughts. He stared right through me. Then he recited lines which I later read many times again:

Know the nature of human life? Don't think you do.
You couldn't. Listen to me. All mortals must die.
Isn't one who knows if he'll be alive tomorrow morn-

ing. Who knows where Fortune will lead? Nobody can teach it. Nobody learns it by rules. So, rejoice in what you hear, and learn from me. Drink! Count each day as it comes as Life—and leave the rest to Fortune. Above all, honor the Love Goddess, sweetest of all the Gods to mortal men, a kindly goddess! Put all the rest aside. Trust in what I say, if you think I speak truth—as I believe. Get rid of this gloom, rise superior to Fortune. Crown yourself with flowers and drink with me, won't you?

A small smile crossed his lips. I thought the passage sounded like something that mother could have written with a brandy bottle clutched in one hand. I responded as I would have responded to her. "Sure, I'll have a drink." I didn't know at the time that he was reciting Heracles' speech from *Alcestis*; I'd never read Greek plays in school. I don't think Dean Scime did either. It struck me that Buckland welcomed each of his new pupils with this philosophy. No one in the college had warned me about Buckland; but then I'd not formally met anyone in the college.

"Euripides," said Buckland.

"I'll try a glass," I replied.

"No, Euripides the Greek playwright. Not a brand of sherry. Of course, coming from Canada I'll have to make certain allowance. For, shall we say, certain deficiencies in your basic education."

The classic Oxford humiliation, using Euripides to establish a plateau of superior intelligence that can be admired from the distance but unfortunately could never be scaled down to the level of someone with my deficiencies. Buckland rose from his leather chair and walked over to the fireplace, picked up a poker and raked the coals. He was in his early forties. Dressed in a shabby tweed suit, fresh white shirt with a spot of blood on the collar from his morning shave, and an Eton tie. His shoes were scuffed like those of a small child in a school playground. Tall and thin, his hair was graying. He'd mastered the self-importance of the small-time concertmaster. As he turned back from the fire, he decanted the sherry and filled both glasses. I was still standing, almost suspended in gloom, near the door.

"British Columbia's a very long way away, Mister Burlock." He nodded for me to be seated on the couch. "I trust you had a pleasant trip."

"I've recovered from the boat," I said, taking the glass of sherry and sitting back on the couch. Buckland, his legs stretched and crossed near the fireplace, raised his glass, touching the tip of mine.

"Cheers and welcome," he said.

He was staring into space again and it made me uncomfortable so I started a conversation. He seemed to have the attention span of a small child as well. "The Russians have really blown the lid off things with their rocket, Sputnik." It had been in the English dailies, and I thought it was a suitable topic to break the ice. It was, after all, the Canadians and English against the Red horde and their satellites.

"People often get excited over new inventions," said Buckland, sipping his sherry. He didn't seem to concern himself with anyone or anything which hadn't placed the greatest weight and value on Euripides, Sophocles, and Aristophanes, in the original Greek, of course. Such people might well invent things but would never understand the implications of their inventions, and certainly would lack the training to be responsible for their consequences. He glanced into his glass. I thought this was another Oxford custom so I looked into mine. This was Buckland's method of concentration and not to check the level.

"There was something in your Rhodes scholarship which struck me as curious."

My heart pounded in my temples. I thought a mistake had been uncovered—or worse, some fraud. Joan might've been right about Edgar exporting the cancer story abroad. Buckland's eccentric behavior feathered my worries and sent my imagination into flight. "What might that be, sir?" I asked, my voice cracking.

"Oh, nothing much. Just the way you satisfied the athletic requirement. Quite unusual."

Potter had warned me that using guns to meet the Rhodes athletic requirement might become the subject of comment.

"Marksmanship isn't really a sport in England," said Buckland, once again thoughtfully stoking the fire with the poker.

"I won the Rhodes in Canada," I said.

"Yes, that had crossed my mind," said Buckland. "I'm not criticizing the Rhodes selection committee, or indeed your qualifications as a crack shot with a pistol. It's just . . . Shall we say, that here—we're accustomed to basketball players or rowers from America."

"Canada."

"Sorry?"

"I come from Canada. Not the States."

"Quite. More sherry, Mister Burlock?"

I held out my glass. Two members of the selection committee were Potter's personal friends. Unlike Edgar there was no nonsense about cancer and Oxford being my last earthly dream. He'd brought up two bottles of vintage port from his wine cellar. The men sat together in the Alpha House sitting room, sipping port, talking of their days at Oxford, the high table, dons, scouts, porters, and getting slightly drunk. Although I wasn't there, Potter told me how well they'd all gotten on together. That the port had been shipped specially from France before the war; that the bottle of port on the day the Allies stormed Anzio Beach had been directly above my line of fire as a seven-year-old schoolboy. He told them I was Oxford material. Apparently that was some special code. They all nodded, smacked their lips with the fine taste of the vintage port. The next week Potter's cronies on the selection committee had given me the nod.

I suffered very little guilt over Potter's involvement in the selection process. After all, my grandfather and his Uncle Foss helped Rhodes maintain the DeBeer Company as a profitable venture in South Africa. Without Wild Bill's marksmanship abilities where would Rhodes have been? Why shouldn't his grandson benefit from some of that scholarship money? It didn't come out of thin air. The Rhodes fund owed its very existence to the rifles of Wild Bill, the other Canadians, Australians, New Zealanders, the Scots, as well as the English. Gun care and marksmanship should have been a precondition to receiving a Rhodes. Of course this was so much self-justi- fication. The reality was different. Since I'd been seven, Potter had set his heart on an Oxford education for me. He was well- intended; in that way, he was like Edgar.

"You seem distracted," Buckland said. From the mouth of someone like Buckland who appeared permanently distracted that was quite a bolt.

He'd startled me and I spilled sherry on my new tailored suit. "I was thinking about my sport," I said, dabbing a hand- kerchief on my trouser leg.

"We must really consider your academic plan," he replied. "You won't be shooting pistols around the college."

"No, sir."

"Quite. Perhaps you might try your hand at rowing or rugby. Just leave it to me. I'll find a proper game for you," he said, walking over to a large oak bookcase with glass doors.

"I came to study law," I said.

He opened one of the bookcase doors. "To read law," he corrected. "Read for the Bachelor of Civil Law. Foreign stu- dents often don't do well on the BCL. That's why you should take up a sport."

"Why won't I do well?"

He cleared his throat, taking a book from a shelf and closing the glass door. "The competition is keen at Oxford. It's not quite the same as at—" he said, pausing to reflect.

"UBC."

"Yes, the University of British Columbia."

"Not all my classmates were stupid," I replied.

Buckland circled around the couch and sat in a stuffed chair across from me. "Of course they weren't. But English chaps reading for the BCL already have proved themselves with a first in Jurisprudence. They're well-versed in English law. And that gives them an advantage."

"English law. That's all we studied at UBC."

Buckland smiled wisely. "English law?"

"I guess Canadians prefer it to their own."

"How extraordinary. American law is very different. I spent one year at Harvard some time ago."

"But I'm not an American."

"So you said before."

Buckland strained forward out of the chair and handed me the book removed from the case; it was Fitzgerald's *The Great Gatsby*. The mysterious, rich, and Oxford-educated *Jude the Obscure* of American literature who'd been found dead at the bottom of his own pool. A tragic, haunted figure who'd gone through life without reading Greek playwrights. Buckland thought I was another Gatsby in the making.

"I thought you might find this book of interest."

He might have found some interest in the 1903 Browning under my jacket. But given his views on marksmanship I decided to play the unarmed Gatsby for the moment. I rose to my feet, put down the sherry glass, and left his rooms with *The Great Gatsby* tucked under my left arm, just below my gun.

MOTHER wrote a letter once a week. Anyone who goes to Europe is potentially missing-in-action was a common theme of the letters. The first paragraph would open with her grief over the loss she suffered because of my absence. Reading these missives, I had the idea she'd probably written similar ones before. Fortunately, her bridge friends had been kind and thoughtful, and encouraged her to write so that I would know

I could always come home. I read and reread these letters, double-checking the address on the envelope, wondering whether the porter had mixed my post with someone else in the college. In these letters, I saw a new side to mother; a strong, committed, loyal sense of obligation. But I sensed I was a surrogate.

Such letters didn't obey the natural laws of common sense. I barely knew this woman who was so inconsolable in my absence. And she didn't know me very well either. As far as I could recollect, we'd only had two conversations of substance in my life, and then she'd been pretty drunk. In one letter she asked for a recent photograph. A touching request from a mother. But Danielle saw through the sentimentality of mother's brandy-laced request. She wanted a photograph because she couldn't remember what I looked like. That's what had made her so sad. She didn't have a record of me in her mind. Danielle was capable of such insights, and this quality in her reminded me of Joan.

The photographer's shop was tucked away off Turl Street. A little bell over the door rang as I entered. The waiting room was empty except for a young woman seated in the corner reading a tattered copy of Vogue. She watched me look around the room, hands in my pockets.

"You spilled something on your trousers," she said. Those were Danielle's first words to me. The stain left by Buckland's sherry over my left knee looked more like a badly healed scab. I didn't want them cleaned. No one around the college looked very clean and I wanted to fit in.

"I didn't come to have my knees photographed," I replied, sitting down in the chair opposite her.

"Castell sometimes takes pictures of my knees," she said, raising the Vogue in front of her face.

"Who's Castell?"

Danielle lowered the Vogue magazine, eyebrows knitted together. "The photographer. Are you sure you're in the right place?"

She didn't have an English accent. She looked European;

a delicate, soft, girlish face; enormous brown eyes, and high cheekbones. Long, willowy legs coiled beneath her like Louise in death. Above all these erotic sights, it was Danielle's mouth; full, sensual lips that seemed to be making love with each word. I felt a stir in myself.

"An estate agent is next door," she continued. "People looking for a house often wander in by mistake."

"I don't want a house. I just want my picture taken. And I have an appointment," I said, trying not to stare at her lips for more than a second at a time.

"Americans come in by mistake all the time," she said.

"I'm a Canadian." Why was everyone from North America automatically an American? I was a little steamed with her.

"A basketball player from the prairies?"

I nodded with an evil little smile. I leaned forward from the chair, and pulled the Vogue magazine down from her face. Our eyes met a few inches apart. "I'm a good shooter. And I'm from British Columbia." Her eyes followed mine down the leg of my soiled trousers. I'd raised the cuff high enough for her to see the 1903 Browning, and with a sudden flick of the wrist my trouser leg dropped back over my shoe.

"I think I'm going to like you," she said.

A French Canadian from Montreal, Danielle was in her second year on a Clothworker's Scholarship at Somerville, reading French and Latin. Between her tutorials she modelled for Castell: swimsuits, dresses, slacks, nylons, panties and bras. She didn't model to make ends meet. She would have managed nicely even without the Clothworkers' Scholarship. Her father, a Montreal high court judge, and her mother, who was Jewish, had family money. On her mother's side, there were a number of textile mills. The roofless, toothless employees of those mills lost fingers, went blind making dresses and pants, and died young. The family established a scholarship fund for children of textile workers to assuage their guilt. Then Danielle slips in and ties up the fund for three years. It came close to Potter's intervention on my behalf.

Secretly Danielle had a desire to become famous. Some people decide they need a public. The actress who's stopped on the street by admirers from Montreal to London, New York, and Paris. Danielle aimed high and for the bull's-eye on the target. Castell was just a warm-up target practice for what would later come. With her perfect, protruding lips, it would have been possible for her to suck up the vast lump of mankind and spit them out into servile, absent-minded slaves.

I asked Danielle if she'd teach me French.

She asked if I'd teach her how to shoot.

I knew that I wouldn't learn any French. The summer at Alpha House with Potter convinced me that foreign language instruction and learning the language of guns didn't really mix.

BUCKLAND disapproved of my decision to move out of college. That was near the end of Hilary term. And I hadn't taken up a proper sport. He probably blamed Cecil Rhodes; his scholarships were the vehicle for pumping the products of inferior colonial educational systems into the backdoor of the world's greatest university. I neglected to tell him my reason for moving; that Danielle and I had taken a flat on Divinity Road. Night storage heaters and an East Indian landlord. Not even Canadians were allowed openly to behave in this fashion. Some things were better left to be read about in Greek plays like *Oedipus the King*; left to an abstract process of metaphorical exploration.

After the move, neither of us dined in the college regularly. I bought a bicycle and rode the mile from our flat across Magdalen Bridge for my tutorials. Danielle had an MG that we used for weekend outings to the Cotswolds. Danielle dragged me along to French films. I fell asleep in the middle of *Le Amiche*, which was being shown at the Oxford French Society. Late into the night, drinking cheap wine and smoking cigarettes, we debated with friends whether national sovereignty was compatible with the concept of the Commonwealth.

Danielle attended the Oxford Drama Society until an English girl from St. Hilda's said only people from deprived families could ever understand the pain and anger, all the emotions an actor had to reproduce spontaneously on stage. Later I dropped out of an organization called the *Canadian Left in Britain*. Because of Joan, I'd been attracted to that group. The club president, D. Bradley of St. Peter's Hall, had been kicked out of the Oxford Guitar Society during Michaelmas term. He'd demanded they play only left-wing songs. In the two meetings I'd attended, D. Bradley made everyone sit around while he played Woody Guthrie tunes, and during intermission he handed out copies of Clifford Odets' *Waiting for Lefty*. D. Bradley, a Rhodes from Halifax, knew considerably more about the "Left" than he did about Canada. I avoided the rifle club. Rumors spread quickly through the colleges.

Most of our first year we huddled together in the cold flat, sitting on the floor around the gas heater and feeding in shillings to enrich our East Indian landlord. We fell into a nightly routine. Drank red Italian wine, read each other's letters from home, studied, and made love in varied places and positions, our clothes and bottles and letters scattered across the worn carpet. The room took on the smell and look of a cage for two untrained, quick, and dangerous animals. We crawled around on all fours like strange children who'd learned to fuck before they could walk. We lost track of the time and the day of the week. The lace curtains were always drawn against the gray Oxford sky and the street below.

In the warm, soft candlelight, naked on the blanket, I'd cradle one of my pistols in the palm of my hand. Danielle's eyes would narrow slightly. I sat very still for a long time, saying nothing. Sometimes I'd hold the pistol behind the candle and watch the rough image of the gun against the wall. The disfigured shadow seemed tame; a pale offspring of the guns I saw in my nightmares. Like primitive man, I gave this inanimate object a mystical quality. I'd smuggled five pistols in my luggage into Britain. I had a Colt .45 (the one I dispatched Louise the Boa with), a 1903 Browning, a Webley-Fosbery self-cocking revolver, a 1915 Beretta, and a Mauser Hsc. During those first few months the sense of Wongness in the world seemed far away.

One evening, as we lay stretched out on the floor, arms wrapped around each other, Danielle opened her eyes. "We're creatures of technology, Matt. The English are creatures of social status in the cultivated, classical mode."

The observation stirred me to reconsider my relationship with Potter. His England was feudal barons; ties of blood, school, ceremony. These were the substance of his society. Blind faith and trust were expected and received. It was like living inside a comfortable silk cocoon which protected everyone from Wongness. Potter had been torn out of that safety and went to Italy and later to America. He'd learned the language of guns. On the payroll of professional adventurers, inventors, the men who controlled the politicians, he'd seen men place their faith and trust in guns. He realized, despite his background, that tools with speed and power created a new social order in the name of protecting a dying one.

That's why Buckland ignored Sputnik and kept to the Greek plays. And why Potter had insisted I go to Oxford. Oxford was my final examination after all my years at Alpha House. A trick card Potter knew I had to play. While I never did learn French from him, he was concentrating on something more important. How to play the scene and watch the landscape. A fragile game requiring the skill of a diplomat, the discipline of a soldier, and the neutral, cold detached eye of a marksman. I'd been trained all along for something we'd never openly discussed.

Halfway through the second bottle of wine, I lit two more candles. Danielle stood beside one of the candles in an Arabesque. Nose pointed towards the ceiling. She was in her actress mood that evening. I watched her turn on point. Without knowing it, I fell asleep on the floor. Danielle said that she continued to dance for some time afterwards just for the sheer pleasure. When she dropped down to my side she heard me talking in my sleep. Eavesdropping on an old dream. Wild Bill, his arms stretched out from his sides entered the room, carrying the burning cross on his back. He wasn't alone this time. He was in a hotel room and two men watched him consumed by the flames. It was like a ceremony and Wild Bill was their sacrifice.

One of the men wore leather cavalry boots and had old-fashioned sideburns. His eyes were more than solemn; he had a dead zone for pupils; and Wild Bill's flames danced in the tiny pinholes. He held an oil lamp in one hand. The other man clutched a Browning in his right hand. The man with the gun was Potter. I recognized him in dark mourning clothes. He wore a hat. I remember thinking I'd never seen Potter in a hat. It looked odd. Not the hat, but that flames didn't flicker in his eyes.

There was another image caught in his eyes; that of a boy in a flat-bottom boat. The boy was punting down a river, and rolling green pastures like clusters of salad burst out along the banks. I couldn't make sense of it. His eyes fixed on the fire and destruction; yet they projected this image like a Constable painting.

Outside our flat, still lost in my dream, a car backfired climbing the steep hill. It sounded like someone had discharged a gun. When I awoke I wasn't crying. I jumped to my feet and standing in the middle of the sitting room I crouched in a military stance, both hands wrapped around the Browning. Danielle's face looked up at me from between the gun sights. She didn't move; in that moment as she stared up at the barrel, I saw myself naked in her eyes. Only then was I aware the dream was over. I lowered the pistol and let it fall from my hand onto a pillow. She cried softly, burying her head in the blanket. She'd never been close to death before. Her body shook with fear.

I sat beside her and touched her shoulder. She had goose-flesh. She thought I was going to kill her. Already I'd told her about Potter and Wild Bill. That night I told her the rest. Two days before I left Vancouver I had the Wild Bill dream again. At two in the morning I went to Alpha House and banged on the front door. Potter appeared in his dressing gown, hair messy from sleeping. He let me in and we went down into the basement. Potter knew the Wild Bill dream wouldn't go away. We sat across from each other at the table. All my dreams had been leading up to some truth that he'd always kept back. As we sat there, Potter openly wept. He put his pipe on the table and wept without shame. Then he told me the story that had been in his dreams for all of those years. In the candlelit flat on Divinity Road in Oxford, I told Danielle how my grandfather Lieutenant Wild Bill Anglin, Boer War veteran and Vancouver firefighter, died in 1917.

CHAPTER 14

JOHN Moses Browning had been disappointed with the Revelli M15. He disliked the double-barrel design, and the retarded blow-back system was less than reliable. Potter, however, having completed his tasks, returned to Oxford. But his studies were interrupted again midway through Michaelmas term 1916, when Uncle Foss summoned him down to his Surrey estate. The letter said it was a matter of great urgency, and Potter took the train at once. Uncle Foss' star was rising in Whitehall. From his Boer War connections, and the family weapons manufacturing business, he had come to know Churchill, Kitchener, and Haig, and through these contacts his firm received a contract to supply the army with the Webley-Fosbery self-cocking revolver.

The British troops fought with the gun in the Battle of the Somme. Fought may be a poor choice of words. The revolver jammed and clogged in the mud and dust. The battlefield had been littered with hundreds of revolvers that no longer worked. Many British soldiers died with the useless revolver clutched in their hands, rushing the German position. A million died at the Somme. Uncle Foss couldn't comprehend such large numbers of dead. He remembered the dead cattle, horses, and Cronje's men floating in the Modder River. But there was no French river wide enough to carry the English dead downstream from the Somme.

In 1916 no one on either side had grasped the horror and misery, and there was little hope that the war would end. Like a plague where death no longer has meaning; tucked in long columns of numbers. Mourning the dead was the new life-style.

When Potter arrived at the Fosbery estate, a servant showed him into Uncle Foss' study. He was standing at the window, watching the rain fall on the manicured lawns. Like a condemned man who hears the footsteps of the warder and chaplain but wants one last look at life before turning away. Maybe he saw Scheidel out there with the trickle of blood on his face. Or maybe he no longer clearly saw anything that made sense.

John Moses Browning sat on a couch across from Uncle Foss.

"There's our boy," said John Moses to the stranger next to him.

"Hello, Mister Browning."

"Still working away on those dead languages?"

"I'm giving it my best."

"I bet you are. Here, I want you to meet a friend of mine. Colonel Thompson." The stranger was Colonel John Taliafero Thompson. A moment later a servant appeared through the door and told Uncle Foss that he had a phone call from Whitehall. He looked back from the window, nodded to Potter, and then sent the servant away. As Potter watched him leave the room, he noticed how his uncle had aged. The red-rimmed eyes, the eyes with that blazed, war-zone, combat-fatigued glaze. His face startled Potter. Within a year Uncle Foss had become an old man with gray hair and a deeply lined face.

Army high command withdrew Uncle Foss' Webley-Fosbery revolver from the active service. Then he was passed over for promotion. Old friends stopped calling in at the estate. Cut off, filled with guilt, and his career shattered, Uncle Foss desperately wanted to rehabilitate his reputation. When the first call came from Home Office asking if he'd lend his services in dealing with certain Americans, he readily agreed. But why Uncle Foss? Because the Americans had asked to deal through him. That had been John Moses Browning operating in the background. The Americans wished to negotiate the terms for their entry into the war.

When John Moses slapped Potter on the back his initial impulse was to pull away. He knew that this man had some hold on his uncle. The situation was very different from that eighteen months earlier when Uncle Foss remained clearly in control.

"I've heard a lot about you, son," said Colonel Thompson.

"Colonel Thompson arrived from America three days ago," explained John Moses, refilling his glass with sherry. Since Potter had last seen him he'd changed from beer to sherry.

"That's a dangerous crossing with the German U-boats," said Potter, his eyes on Colonel Thompson. The Colonel, a tall and lanky American, was about the same age as Uncle Foss. The resemblance stopped with age. Uncle Foss' eyes had gone dead with defeat; Colonel Thompson's were filled with the glitter of influence and power.

"I think we can be frank, don't you?" asked John Moses, as Uncle Foss came back into the room. "I was just telling your nephew that we need to get things on the table."

"That's quite a good idea," replied Uncle Foss, looking at Potter for a moment and walking back to the window.

"This war's like a long-tailed monkey that needs to be tamed," continued John Moses. "But you people are stalemated with the Germans. You're bogged down. Not getting the job done." As John Moses Browning spoke, Uncle Foss filled his pipe from a leather pouch. Potter waited for some response from his Uncle. But he said nothing.

"Does that mean America will enter the war?" Potter finally asked.

"We all know who the enemy is," interjected Colonel Thompson. "But the hard truth is that to win any war you've got to do two things. Take land. Kill the enemy who tries to stop you. You kill people. Move on and kill more of their people. You don't keep your troops living in trenches for years. That's just killing people without taking land."

No one denied the accuracy of Colonel Thompson's assessment. But the extraordinary bluntness chilled Potter. He saw a brittle smile on Uncle Foss' lips, as he lit his pipe and sat down at his desk. The thought of all that torn flesh, bone, and viscera covering the fields of France counting for nothing in the end chilled Potter even more.

"America's not interested in sending her boys to get gassed and machine-gunned in foreign trenches," said Colonel Thompson. "That's a view shared by President Wilson."

Potter put his empty sherry glass on a table, and walked across the room and stood beside Uncle Foss. He looked down at his uncle and then over at John Moses and Colonel Thompson.

"What do you want from me?" asked Potter.

Colonel Thompson lit a Havana cigar clenched between his teeth. The Americans were silent. Not the contemplative silence of an Oxford library but the silence in the stop-action movement of a wolf stalking a lamb.

"I like this boy," said Colonel Thompson. "It's damn time to get down to business."

"The Revelli M15 won't do the job," said John Moses.

"We need a gun with more fire power," interjected Colonel Thompson.

"The Germans are working on a submachine gun at this moment," said John Moses, leaning forward from his chair as if to confide a secret of state.

Colonel Thompson took the cigar from his mouth; his eyes

narrowed as he looked at Uncle Foss. "And if they develop one before us—you people are on your own." Uncle Foss flinched ever so slightly. The Colonel had delivered a clean hit. He'd probably delivered several more before Potter had arrived. Uncle Foss was on the ropes. Potter wished these Americans would leave Uncle Foss' house. He wished England didn't need such people.

"We have a little mission for you," said John Moses, head nodding as if to cue Uncle Foss.

"We've decided you must go to Canada. Just a short trip," said Uncle Foss, looking up from his chair.

"It'll be no different from the trip to Turin," said John Moses. "That wasn't so bad, was it?"

"Why Canada? I'm in the middle of term," replied Potter. He watched an ash from Colonel Thompson's cigar fall on the carpet. All three men exchanged glances. "Would someone tell me what's going on?"

Colonel Thompson became their spokesman. "Because you're going to find the gun that will win this war."

"I'm afraid I don't understand. This gun's in Canada? And you want someone in England to get it for you? Why don't you go yourself?" asked Potter.

"We've tried," said John Moses, again nodding to Uncle Foss.

Leaning back in his chair, Uncle Foss sucked on his pipe for a moment. "An old friend has a submachine gun. He won't help Mister Browning or Colonel Thompson. You see, he doesn't like Americans." The truth was that Wild Bill hated Americans. Where were they during the Boer War? Where were the Americans in 1914? Lieutenant Anglin had kept up a correspondence with Uncle Foss over the years. Colonel Thompson removed a file from his briefcase and handed it to Potter.

"This is what your uncle means," said the Colonel.

Potter looked at his uncle. "It's all right, have a look."

ON February 28, 1914, in the reviewing stands at the Vancouver Horse Show Building, Wild Bill Anglin and his wife were seated behind two Americans. An American-Canadian tour company performed a concert: songs from the *Two Grenadiers*, some Irish ballads, Verdi; and ended the program with *God Save the King*. Wild Bill and his wife rose to their feet and started singing with other members of the crowd. The two men in front remained in their seats. Wild Bill leaned forward and politely asked them to stand. The Americans waved him off. Wild Bill asked them again.

"God screw the King," replied one of the Americans.

"Fuck the King," said the other. There was a good chance that both were drunk and were jesting in a crude way. But Wild Bill didn't see it that way. Wild Bill's crossover left hook caught the first man in the right eye. As the other one rose from his seat, Wild Bill caught him with an uppercut to the chin. The orchestra played on and people kept singing as the police arrived, broke up the fight, and arrested Wild Bill.

The one American had a broken jaw; his friend took eight stitches below the eye. They were fairly banged up, from the newspaper photographs. A *Vancouver Sun* reporter dubbed Lieutenant William Anglin "Wild Bill." When the full story came out in the papers, Wild Bill became a local hero. He'd taken on two men who'd shown disrespect to the King. Wild Bill's picture was in the newspaper several days running: "Wild Bill, Boer War hero, teaches Yanks respect."

The two Americans, after they left hospital, were arrested for disorderly conduct. One letter to the editor suggested treason would have been a more suitable charge. The Americans, who no doubt read the mood of the locals from the papers, left town before trial. "Yankee troublemakers flee to States," reported the Vancouver Sun. Wild Bill, who'd been persuaded to dress up in his Boer War uniform for more pictures, was quoted as saying he would have done it all over again, that he was proud to be a Canadian, proud of his British heritage, and proud that the anthropoid ape in the White House wasn't a Canadian.

One of the newspaper photographs had stopped Uncle Foss'

heart for several beats. In the picture Wild Bill had a rifle cradled in his arms. The caption below described the rifle as a modified Lee-Enfield from the Boer War. Uncle Foss knew that Wild Bill had fed the reporter a misdescription. The rifle was the Scheidel submachine gun. The last time he'd seen such a weapon had been in South Africa.

In a later letter Wild Bill confirmed what Uncle Foss already suspected. Wild Bill, who'd studied the Scheidel day and night for two weeks, had memorized every detail. From memory Wild Bill had managed to recall those details and, after much trial and error, reproduced a "Scheidel" submachine gun for his private collection. But he'd made just the one. He apologized for carrying that particular gun the day of the photograph. He thought it was perfectly harmless. He hadn't ever spoken of the Scheidel to anyone. No one else knew of the existence of such a weapon other than Uncle Foss. Of course, the photograph changed that forever. The American consulate in Vancouver had sent the photograph to Washington, and the military experts had called in Colonel Thompson. Two attempts to get the Scheidel proved abortive. Colonel Thompson tracked down Wild Bill's military record through sources in Ottawa, and had asked his old friend John Moses Browning to contact a Colonel Fosbery in England.

A Catch-22 had arisen. Uncle Foss was perhaps the only man alive who could convince Wild Bill to hand over the Scheidel to the Americans. But the Home Office firmly refused Uncle Foss' permission request either to bring Wild Bill to England or for him to travel to Canada. He suspected the Americans had a role in that decision. John Moses would have vividly remembered Uncle Foss' attempted doublecross over the Revelli M15. One of his men had been intercepted in Italy where he'd been instructed to take the submachine gun from Potter and personally take it back to Fosbery's gun factory. This time the Americans were taking no chances. The compromise was to send Potter. Uncle Foss' cooperation was acquired with a guarantee from John Moses and Colonel Thompson that no harm would come to either his nephew or Wild Bill.

As Potter closed the file of letters and clippings, he looked down at Uncle Foss. His lips were tightly drawn. He couldn't meet Potter's eyes. Without a word he rose from the desk and walked over to the window. It was raining outside. Uncle Foss' thoughts were of the young Canadian officer he'd commanded in South Africa. A man whose life he probably saved by keeping him back the day of the Paardeberg massacre. He'd grown very fond of Wild Bill over the years. He thought of Potter following Wild Bill along a twisting stream, the water running cold and swift, with Douglas firs towering to the sky. Hadn't Wild Bill invited Scheidel to go fishing in British Columbia after the war? The same man who sat on the South African veldt and openly wept after Scheidel lay dead at his side.

Secretly he was glad he didn't have to face Wild Bill. He'd killed a perfectly honorable man for what? So that the Scheidel would never be used in warfare. And now he'd agreed to hand the weapon over to the gun manufacturers of America precisely for that reason. If only Wild Bill had left the gun buried in the past—now it would go on a silver platter to the people who sat while the band struck up *God Save the King*.

Uncle Foss had prepared Potter's visit to Canada with a letter to Wild Bill. In the name of the Empire, Wild Bill's services would be required one final time. His nephew would be arriving with the precise instructions. He wrote that his own ill health prevented the journey. The lies around the Scheidel had always been thicker than the bullets pumped out of the barrel. Uncle Foss stopped feeling and thinking. Potter, John Moses, and Colonel Thompson watched him trace a pattern on the window with his index finger. It was a rough image of the Scheidel.

Perhaps Wild Bill and the Colonel always knew that the Scheidel was like a glacier, moving slowly over the years, tearing up mountains, making lakes, ripping boulders from the earth, and once set in motion, there was no stepping out of its path. As Uncle Foss watched the pattern dissolve on the windowpane, he turned to Colonel Thompson. "I have your personal guarantee as a gentleman?"

Colonel Thompson took the cigar from his mouth, extended his hand to Uncle Foss and said, "You have my personal guarantee."

The Scheidel mission outlined by John Moses and Colonel Thompson suggested a North American replica of the earlier venture to Turin. The two men tried to put Potter's mind at rest by promising that this would be the last time they'd call on his services. Uncle Foss stood by the window and said nothing. Then John Moses pulled back his jacket and removed a 1903 Browning. He presented the pistol to Potter as a token of appreciation.

"This isn't any pistol," explained John Moses, turning it over in his hand. "It has a special history." He handed it to Potter.

"What sort of history?" he asked.

"A boy named Gavrilo Princip used it to kill the Archduke and his wife at Sarajevo."

"With this gun?"

"That very one."

Potter carefully examined the pistol. He glanced over at Uncle Foss, who was watching him from the window. His Uncle nodded with approval.

"Since a boy started this war," said Colonel Thompson, "We felt the boy who'll end it should have the gun."

Potter tried to comprehend the capacity of a single gun, a small gun at that, to alter the course of history. But was it the actual pistol Princip used in the assassination? Potter thought of his Oxford classmate, Gennaro, and the Shroud. Was the image on the Shroud of Turin genuine? There was no clear evidence one way or another for either object. This much was clear: each artifact had an important historical link with betrayal. And that was the look he saw in Uncle Foss' eyes as he stared down at the pistol in Potter's hands.

THE first day after his arrival in Vancouver, Wild Bill showed Potter the marks left by a crowbar on the backdoor. Two men had tried to break in while he and his wife were asleep in the house. He'd crept downstairs with a shotgun. At the bottom of the stairs the men saw him and bolted out the door. They had been going through his gun collection. Nothing, however, was taken. A week later they had returned when the house was empty and gained access through a back window. By this time Wild Bill had hidden the Scheidel, and the intruders, having ransacked the house, left without taking anything. They hadn't returned. Why had he suspected they were after the Scheidel? Uncle Foss had apparently warned him in a letter that once the photograph was circulated he should expect trouble. He didn't believe him until after the first break-in.

The next day Wild Bill took Potter along to the fire station. Lieutenant Anglin wanted an opportunity to show off his old Captain's nephew to the men at the station. Later, after the work, they planned to retrieve the Scheidel. That afternoon, the station received a call, and Potter rode next to Wild Bill on a horse-drawn steam pumper. The whip came down from over Wild Bill's head onto the three horses. They galloped west on Georgia Street. Most of the other fire halls had converted to motorized steam pumpers. But Fire Hall No. Two on Seymour Street continued to cover the downtown area with the horse-drawn fire engines.

Lieutenant Wild Bill Anglin steered his horses around the streetcars, past the heavy Georgia traffic of motor cars, horses and carriages. Again a lieutenant, this time in a fireman's uniform, and like in South Africa, again a second in command. Little had really changed for him since the Boer War. Except the shift from starting fires to putting them out. He'd not aged as much as Uncle Foss. Square-shouldered and a large bushy moustache drooping over his lower lip, the reins held in his left hand, Wild Bill charged through the heart of Vancouver to a house fire on Richards Street.

Two blocks south of Georgia Street, they saw a vertical column of smoke rising. At Richards Street, Potter climbed down from his seat, and Wild Bill asked him to make himself useful and hold the horses. They looked different from the fire hall. The two outside mares were pure white and lathered with sweat; the center mare was black, except for a white blaze between the eyes, and was wheezing and sputtering. Potter held the bridle of the mare Wild Bill called Elly while the other firemen connected the hoses to the steam pumper. While the firemen were setting up the hoses a small crowd began to gather.

Several police constables arrived and kept the crowd from pushing too closely to the fire engine. Flames covered the roof of the two-story house. The thick black smoke made the horses nervous. Ears pricked up and eyes wild with panic, the horses seemed ready to bolt at any moment. Potter stroked Elly's nose, trying to calm the mare. As Potter looked up, he saw Wild Bill emerge from the house carrying a cat in his arms. Otherwise the house had been empty. The old tom, the fur singed about the neck, clung to Wild Bill's sleeve. He stroked the cat's chin, strolling out to the pavement. A woman in front of the crowd began to clap. Part of the inherent human tendency to sentimentalize a dumb animal as a house leaped with flames.

To Potter's relief, Wild Bill ignored the woman; he dropped the cat to the ground and helped the men with the hose. He tried to imagine this man under Uncle Foss' command in South Africa. Wild Bill was shouting orders to the other firemen, walking back from the hose to the steam pumper, supervising the operation. His men scattered around the front garden with ladders, axes, and hoses.

These people were far removed from the recoil of the nightly bombs and heavy guns in and around London. Explosion and fire spread across the London night. Whole neighborhoods in London were being raked with flames. No one was applauding the saving of a cat. The London fires of war weren't caused by some careless act; the knocked-over lantern, or the dropped cigarette end. The object of the London fires was a single-minded dedication to incinerate the English. They were the ancient tribal fires of Europe falling from the skies. The one fire on Richards Street was a dim flicker to the sea of flames that washed through buildings, streets, a city, scooping the sky with ugly tongues of black, thick smoke.

These people—these Canadians—were like children who'd been spared the harsh realities, the embittering tragedy, and the numbing horror of the daily attacks. The children of the Empire lived in complete isolation from the real fires consuming their motherland. Potter's stomach knotted. He'd arrived uncertain what to expect in Canada. The excitement of the trip rapidly faded as he watched Wild Bill, his men, and the crowd. The knot soon turned to hard cramps doubling him over. Was it the food from the ship? Or perhaps it was the smoke. The cramps took away his breath. He gasped for air, and moved back from the horses. Holding his stomach he fell to his knees. He looked up at the horses, and saw them spinning together, and then it became dark.

When Potter awoke hours later in hospital, he saw Wild Bill, still in his fireman's uniform, and smelling of stale smoke, seated near the edge of the bed. As he opened his eyes, he saw Wild Bill, legs stretched out and arms crossed, peering at him. And Wild Bill, his brow furrowed with worry lines, smiled as Potter tried to sit up. Potter felt disoriented, like someone pulled out of a wreck. Neither the hospital room nor Wild Bill was in complete focus. There was a dull ache in his right shoulder. Wild Bill rose from the chair and sat on the edge of the bed. He gave the plaster cast on the shoulder a little tap.

"You took a bad fall, lad," said Wild Bill, narrowing his

eyes. "And Elly's little dance on the shoulder didn't help matters."

"Elly?"

"The mare on the right side of the steam pumper."

"—I remember now," Potter replied, feeling the cast with his left hand.

"Accidents can happen at a fire. It's my fault. I should've left you back at the fire hall."

"I'm glad you didn't."

"You're quite some lad. Got Captain Fosbery's blood in you for sure." In the palm of Wild Bill's hand was the 1903 Browning. He laid the pistol on the bed. There was a small scratch on the butt. Had Gavrilo Princip scraped the butt end of the pistol during his training, during the nightmares that haunted him on the 27th of June 1914, or during his struggle with the police in Sarajevo?

CHAPTER 15

HOSPITALS rank with the stage for best acting performances. Sick people often play aesthetic or spiritual roles. Misery makes them prone to sensationalism. I remember the image of Potter, as a boy, lying in bed with Wild Bill tapping the plaster cast on his right shoulder. It came back to me as I sat with Edgar who didn't have a broken arm; he had cancer. Edgar lay against his pillow in a paisley shirt unbuttoned to the navel, a gold medallion of Aquarius matted in his damp chest hair, and his gray hair tied in long braids. He stared up from the bed much as Potter must have looked up at Wild Bill.

Joan sponged Edgar's face and neck. I watched her run the washcloth down his cheeks and around his chin. In the 1960s when everyone started to sleep around Edgar began sleeping with Joan. Her performance on our graduation night had not been forgotten; indeed, it may have provided the ultimate attraction. Ten years after that night, divorced from mother, Edgar married Joan. The first woman I ever slept with became my stepmother; a role for which she'd prepared me for while we were in law school. Then Edgar got cancer just about the same time he decided to give up medicine and devote himself to world peace, universal brotherhood, fair distribution of property. He stopped reading Koestler, and took up Thomas Pynchon, Joseph Heller, Ken Kesey. He traded Rubashov for Yossarian.

I spent long periods at Edgar's side. Most of the time we were alone in the room. I'd read to him about McMurphy's thick red arms and scarred hands and Big Nurse. I would play the role of Chief and told him I was planning our escape from this hospital. In the evening Joan would come for two hours. She'd ask me how Chief Bromden was today. Joan and I knew that our McMurphy was doomed; but we played along, trying to show a good face.

I carried the 1903 Browning in my jacket. Many evenings after Joan left I thought about ending Edgar's misery. He was taking such a long time to die. Once his eyelids flickered, then flared open for several seconds, long enough for him to see that the Browning in my hand was pointed at his temple. He closed his eyes, smiling. "Chief Bromden help me escape," he muttered. Edgar was slightly crazy towards the end. It was mainly due to all the drugs: the ones given him by "Big Nurse" and the ones Joan smuggled in during her evening visits. Why didn't I pull the trigger?

Because I was Chief Bromden and not Gletkin.

Because I was a gun collector.

Because I was a lawyer.

Because I still believed in Brecht's *Threepenny Opera* where the play ends with a pardon from death.

And because each time I looked down the barrel of the 1903 Browning I saw Potter. A wounded youth full of idealism. A youth who'd slipped unnoticed through history and lodged himself as a fixture in my childhood dreams.

White hospital drapery around Edgar's bed fluttered each time "Big Nurse" went inside to change pans, insert tubes, needles, clean up the debris of newspapers, dead flowers, and put on fresh sheets. Meanwhile the cancer performed the frontal lobotomy inside Edgar's head. During these interludes Joan and I were left alone seated next to each other on wooden chairs. She was in her mid-thirties, and had trimmed down since law school. Once again, ahead of her time, Joan had taken up serious exercise, running, lifting weights, cycling, and a strict diet. But the crow's-feet appeared around her eyes, and streaks of gray shot through her hair. I tried to remember the way she'd been; and I tried to remember that she was now my stepmother. We said little about the past.

I was never certain whether Rod, the Flesh Eater, had dumped her or if she'd just walked off his bus one day and never went back. One night she told me that Rod had left Vancouver with a twenty-five-year-old grocery-store clerk. She'd ridden his bus each day into the city where she worked. Joan, who was liberal-minded in most matters, said this woman had the morals of a logging-camp rat; blond hair, enormous tits, and you could have swung a helicopter blade inside her head without hitting anything. Mostly Joan talked about what a wonderful, enlightened, visionary man Edgar had become; and how happy they'd been living together in the second floor of an old house in Kitsilano overlooking English Bay.

I was never certain what to expect when "Big Nurse" pulled back the white curtains, exposing Edgar in his freshly made bed. He looked like a capsized sailor who'd been attacked by eels. Someone who'd been bullied, violated, and conquered; his miserable remaining life serving only to advance scientific study of medical students who viewed Edgar as some kind of rites-of-passage ceremony. Any medical student straying from the pack immediately was seized by Joan and cross-examined about his views on Vietnam and jogging. After Edgar got out of hospital they were going to Hanoi. This plan made Edgar happy and hopeful. He'd flash Joan the peace sign. It was a harmless little bullshit delusion. Part of the script all of us had a hand in writing.

We passed many hours with Joan's lectures on stopping American aggression in Southeast Asia. My idea was to infiltrate the American command system and issue each GI new orders: abandon victory, violence, and VC, and embrace the gentle Gods of cocaine and heroin—shoot-up, space-out, and ship-off to Honolulu. One day we were all joking together, and Edgar croaked. He just stopped breathing with his eyes wide open. He was dead for nearly an hour before we noticed. As "Big Nurse" and the doctors flooded into the room, Joan, her hand on my shoulder, in an astonishingly ugly mood, said that Edgar had been the only man who'd ever satisfied her, and that most of her life had been wasted among men with unnatural deficiencies such as myself and the Flesh Eater. Grief makes people say hurtful things. The play was over and the main actor had left, and all that remained was for the rest of us to go home.

Outside the hospital Joan caught up with me. She'd been crying. I put my arm around her waist and she tucked her head between my neck and shoulder. We walked for several blocks in the night air. I confided to Joan that I wish I knew how to contact mother. In the ten years since the divorce she'd vanished. Like Grandmother Anglin, I had visions of her drinking slug juice along the road in Alberta. All attempts to locate her had failed. She just disappeared.

She said something very odd as we waited for the streetlight to change. "Your mother found someone else. She divorced Edgar. Didn't know that?"

"Who?" I said, dumbfounded.

As we crossed an intersection she said one word: "Potter."

"Where are they living?"

"Potter, you're joking?"

"No joke."

"Maybe on one of the Gulf Islands." Joan refused to say which one.

D. H. LAWRENCE, while watching a Zeppelin raid on London in 1915, wrote: "So it is the end—our world is gone, and we are like dust in the air."

CHAPTER 16

COLONEL Thompson waited about four days before he telegraphed instructions to Harry Bliss in Chihuahua City, Mexico. Bliss, not much older than Potter, was a large man, with a whey-colored face, and was in Mexico supplying guns to General Trevino, and to Villa and his men. On the scrub-bush desert floor of Mexico, Harry Bliss was dressed in pin-striped trousers held up with wide braces. His size, complexion, and dress made him appear ten years older. To the Mexicans he appeared as a heavyset bank clerk, handing out guns instead of cash. When he met Villa in his conservative European clothes, the Mexican bandit laughed and snapped the braces on Bliss' shirt. Bliss reached up and pulled Villa from his horse, dropped him to the ground and pushed a Browning against the bandit's head. Villa's men, their guns drawn, watched, waiting for the order to kill Bliss. But the order didn't come. Bliss let Villa rise to his feet. The bandit dusted off his clothes as Bliss put the Browning into his side holster strapped on his right leg.

Harry Bliss earned his respect. And Villa got his guns. Bliss had been trained as an explosives expert and skilled gunman by John Moses' special export department at Fabrique Nationale d'Armes. His first job in 1916 had been disposing of an aide to Colonel Fosbery who'd been sent to intercept the Revelli M15 from Potter. He carried out the assignment with efficiency. Later Bliss had travelled through London, Paris, Rome, Berlin, and Moscow less visible than a division of angels.

Two days after arriving in Vancouver by steamer, Harry Bliss tracked down Potter at the Vancouver arena. Potter and Wild Bill had gone to watch the Vancouver Millionaires play Portland in the Arena. During the ice hockey match Harry Bliss, who knew Potter from his 1916 mission to Turin, sat in a seat above and to the left of Potter. Bliss said nothing until the first period interval. Wild Bill had shoved off to the concession stand leaving Potter, his arm in a plaster cast and listening to the organ music below.

"Seen the paper?" asked Bliss, leaning forward over Potter's shoulder with a copy of the *Vancouver Sun*.

Potter turned, looked up at the large man, and then down at the newspaper shoved in front of his face. On the front page was the picture of a newsboy standing in Trafalgar Square.

"Read what it says on the billboard in the picture," said Bliss. "Two Zeppelins destroyed on the east coast." From the cold air inside the arena, Harry Bliss' breath seemed labored; he breathed in through his mouth, exhaled enough dead, stale air through his nose to fill a dozen circus balloons.

"Have we met?" asked Potter.

"Maybe once, briefly. More to the point, we have common friends. They're worried about you," replied Harry Bliss, twisting the newspaper into a knot and dropping it on Potter's lap.

"Tell them everything's under control." Potter swung around in his seat, and faced Harry Bliss directly.

"This isn't hide-and-seek," said Harry Bliss, tapping Potter on his cast.

"Go away."

"Our friends want to know if you have the Scheidel."

Potter felt as if he were sliding down the side of a mountain;

after a long, pleasant hike, he'd lost his footing, and the world below was a small heap of green, melancholy earth. He suspected that Colonel Thompson and John Moses might have sent someone to keep an eye on him. But they'd also given Uncle Foss certain guarantees; facing Harry Bliss he became unsure whether the promises had been communicated down the chain.

"On a train in Mexico I met an Englishman," said Harry Bliss, who was American, as he slid down into the empty seat beside Potter. "He's a writer. Named Lawrence. Maybe you've heard of him?"

"Maybe," said Potter, staring straight ahead as the players returned to the ice.

A breathy sigh escaped from Harry Bliss' nose like the sound of a whale clearing its blowholes after a long, deep dive. "You should keep up. This guy Lawrence knows a lot about the war. Like thwarted love, he said. People and nations in ruin. Humbled and wasted. Thwarted love—"

Potter couldn't imagine Bliss making love with anything but war. As the buzzer sounded for the second period, Wild Bill edged down the row carrying two cups of coffee, the steam rising like a little trail of fog in the ice-chilled air. Thumbs hooked around his braces, Harry Bliss waited until the last possible moment before standing. He greeted Wild Bill with an oily smile, his cheeks pink from the cold. From the vibrations that passed between the two men, Potter was convinced that Wild Bill could smell Americans.

Harry Bliss, in his broad New York accent, broke the silence. "I'm an old friend of Potter's family."

Well, American or not, that made it all right as far as Wild Bill was concerned. An awkward smile crossed Will Bill's face as he handed one of the cups to Potter. "You know the Captain?"

Bliss had been well briefed. "His Uncle Fosbery's been real worried about him."

"Nothing to worry about. Just a little accident," said Wild Bill. The fans seated behind started to yell for Wild Bill and

Harry Bliss to sit down so they could follow the action on the ice below. Ignoring the grumbling above him, Wild Bill sipped his coffee and continued. "Got sick from fire hall food. Then Elly did a little dance on his shoulder. But it's healing fine."

"Sorry he's been through so much," said Harry Bliss, brushing against Potter's good shoulder. "Tomorrow, we'll be headin' back to England."

Wild Bill looked down at Potter with alarm. "That soon?"

The discontent of the fans above them was growing. "Must be going," said Harry Bliss. "I have a room on Abbott Street. I'm at the Dixie. Come there tomorrow at four. No later." Before Wild Bill or Potter could reply, Harry Bliss, like some rum-sun-stricken priest, scuttled away, glaring at the fans above him and to his right. Afterwards, there was the faint smell of dust, sweat, and gun oil in the air.

Wild Bill sat down in his seat, warming his hands with the coffee cup and glancing down the row as Harry Bliss disappeared. "You didn't mention you had friends in Vancouver."

"I don't," replied Potter.

"Maybe there's something you're not telling me about."

"It's nothing. Uncle Foss is concerned. I should've been back in England by now. But with the accident," Potter broke off, staring down at the ice. "They just want—"

"I know," said Wild Bill. He nudged Potter and leaned over. "You know where your friend's staying?"

"The Dixie." Potter watched one of the Vancouver players give a hard check to the Portland left forward, knocking him to the ice. The referee blew the whistle and called a penalty for roughing. The Vancouver player skated over to the penalty box. Play resumed. He wished Uncle Foss would have skated on to the ice and blown his whistle in Harry Bliss' face; taken him out of the game.

"Yes, the Dixie. That place's a brothel. Like the Sun Rooms on Powell. And the Harbor and Manitoba Rooms on Cordova. Whorehouse. Funny place to be staying."

Only a handful of men would ever know that the fate of

Europe hung in the balance inside a Vancouver brothel. As in Turin, Potter would end his journey shooting at the stars while another man's whore lay at his feet. But it was more complicated this time. Harry Bliss didn't stay in the shadows as he'd done in Turin. The arrival of Harry Bliss like a Vatican emissary with the latest papal bull reinforced for Potter the deceit he'd been party to; that the cutting edges of reality in Vancouver and Turin hovered under a guillotine of menacing lies and self-deception.

Wild Bill, a man whom he'd grown fond of, the man who'd taken him into his house, and the man who proudly introduced him around the fire hall to the men, now had to produce the Scheidel so Potter could courier it back to Colonel Thompson and John Moses. It was time to transact the business at hand. The problem was Wild Bill was not a businessman in the same league with those Potter represented. With his wife, Wild Bill lived in a modest house and led a reasonably domesticated life. A life that now crossed at right angles with his old Captain. The Canadian who'd served Captain Fosbery in South Africa was like a salmon returning from the sea to the river. Sooner or later the strong, instinctive desire was to return home and die where it'd been spawned. Wild Bill was that species of Canadian colonial blind-faith-inspired men and women who didn't believe that upstream the mother well was filled with a monster ready to devour all in her path.

Walking back to the Anglin house from the hockey game, Potter explained Colonel Fosbery's plan—which had been approved by the Home Office—to commence mass production of the Scheidel. Wild Bill, grim-faced, listened as Potter fretfully recounted Uncle Foss' disgrace over the revolver. How the battlefield at the Somme had been covered with the dead and his mud-jammed revolver. He'd lost his friends, reputation, and his spirit was broken over the affair; he retreated to the privacy of his Surrey estate, tottering around the garden, drawing patterns on the windowpanes like an old, defeated man. The news clipping of Wild Bill in his old army uniform holding the Scheidel had rekindled a last ray of hope.

That night neither Wild Bill nor Potter slept. They sat together talking about Uncle Foss, the war, and South Africa. At two in the morning Wild Bill was ready to leave the house. With a lantern, they went around the back and hooked up the horse to the carriage, and, in the snow, rode west towards the forest in Point Grey. Three hours later in the pitch black of a winter's night they wearily rode back from the hiding place where the gun had been safely kept. Potter sat beside Wild Bill, the Scheidel across his lap. On the deserted streets, the only sound was the plodding of horse hooves on the pavement. Potter removed the glove from his hand and touched the cold steel. Uncle Foss had told him the flame of bullets from the end of that barrel would ignite the world.

WILD Bill had personal experience with the occupants of Dixie's on Abbott Street. The house was around the corner from the Seymour Street fire station. Harry Bliss, having tracked Wild Bill for almost a week, discovered that he paid biweekly visits to Dixie's. He was a regular customer of Sally Roberts, a young, dark, Peruvian woman, who sauntered about the premises in silken dresses and boas made from ostrich feathers. She wore a large opaque pearl that dangled from a gold chain around her neck. Harry Bliss had gotten to know her, but she had no idea what he meant when he asked where Wild Bill had hidden the Scheidel. There was an off chance it had been hidden at Dixie's. After a two-day search of the rooms, basement, and rafters, Harry Bliss decided the Scheidel probably wasn't in the house.

At four o'clock Wild Bill and Potter arrived; the winter night had already set in and the lanterns were lit in the windows of the house. They stomped the snow from their boots on the porch. Wild Bill pushed open the front door which led into the main hallway. The Scheidel, wrapped in a canvas bag and placed inside a case, was carried by Potter. Inside the door, Potter set the case on the floor. A young woman emerged from one of the rooms off the main hall carrying a glass of whisky.

"Hi, Bill," she said, blowing him a kiss. "Sally's upstairs. Hey this one's cute. Why don't you leave him downstairs with me?" She glided up the stairs, looking back and winking at Potter.

Self-consciously warming his hands in the hallway, Wild Bill nudged Potter. "Appreciate it if you don't mention this to the Captain."

"Not a word," smiled Potter, unbuttoning his jacket.

Wild Bill stood at the bottom of the stairs, cleared his throat and shouted up to the woman who stood facing them halfway up. "Besides, Mae, we're here to see Mister Bliss. We have an appointment."

"Ah, yes. The man who likes inspecting our basement and attic."

"Attic?" asked Wild Bill. "What was he doing there?"

"Why don't you ask him?"

Potter ran his eyes along the slit up Mae's gown which ended at her thigh. She leaned forward on the oak railing, one arm connected like a tea cup to her waist; she had, thought Potter, the personality of a slot machine.

"All right, I will. Be a good girl and say hi to Sally for me," said Wild Bill.

She carried on up the stairs, glancing back at Potter with a semiprecious-gem smile. Wild Bill paused at the bottom of the stairs for a moment. "Ah, I'll tell Sally myself," he said, half to himself and half to Potter. There was a light, comic grin on the old soldier's face as he swung around to Potter and held up one finger. "I'll be just a minute." He shot up the stairs behind Mae. Near the top he caught up with her, pinching her bottom. She squealed and slapped his hand.

Potter bent down and picked up a large white cat with his good arm; it had been purring against his legs, walking down the hallway, stopping by the door to the billiard room, and then scampering back to his side. Potter walked down the hall, and peered inside the room. Two men were in the midst of a game; one chalked up his cue while the other stretched over the table to make his shot. Inside there were more cats; purring in the laps and at the feet of women with bottled faces. Some of the women watched the progress of the games; others chatted among themselves, stroking a cat. Potter gathered with the snow falling that it was a slow night.

As he watched, the billiard balls cracked with an echo that bounced off the walls. Their sleeves rolled to the elbow, their waistcoats undone, the two men stalked around the billiard table like cats stalking prey. Money exchanged hands with each shot. Potter circled around the far side of the table and quietly sat in an overstuffed chair. He placed the cat on the floor and watched it dart across the room and affectionately slide around the ankles of two women. The cat's sense of loyalty made him think of John Moses.

He leaned to one side, reached forward, and pushed back the white lace curtains. He thought of Oxford, Uncle Foss, John Moses, Colonel Thompson, Lollia—and Harry Bliss; how his life had been slowly overtaken by people and events and places. The snow against the streetlamps was so white, the flakes falling as big as the stars hanging over the night sky in Turin. He traced an outline of the Scheidel on the windowpane and watched the snow; when it dissolved he traced another one. The billiard game had ended and another one was nearly finished when a tall, thin woman, older than the others, touched his outstretched hand on the window and whispered his name. With astonishment he glanced up. It was Mae. She looked much older close up. Over her shoulder he saw Harry Bliss framed in the door, the case with the Scheidel tucked under his right arm.

Then the alarm rang out from an adjacent room. "Fire. There's a fire!" came the frantic cry. The billiard balls cracked one last time as people started clearing from the room. The smell of smoke quaffed through the room. The cats scattered across chairs, the billiard table, and out the door. There were loud voices filtering into the hallway as men and women fled their rooms. The front door was open and people in their nightclothes streamed out into the snow.

"Let's go," said Harry Bliss, motioning to Potter. Mae pulled back, and with fear on her face, turned to leave the room. Behind her, the room smelled of perfume and smoke.

"Where's Bill?" asked Potter, climbing out of the chair. "Mae, where is he?" But she didn't stop to reply, disappearing past Harry Bliss with a cat in her arms. "Bill," shouted Potter, but his voice was lost among all the other shouting in the hallway.

Harry Bliss stood blocking the door. Walking over to Bliss, Potter held his good hand on his plaster cast. As he reached Bliss, he swung with the cast striking the American below his rib cage and doubling him up. On the way down, Potter caught him under the chin with his boot. Bliss was out cold on the floor. Potter stepped over him and into the hallway. Smoke billowed from the stairs as Potter raced up, taking two steps at a time. He tried each room down the corridor. Finally, in the second to the last room he saw thin wisps of flames around the door. He kicked open the door. Inside, the curtains, bedding, and furniture were in flames. On the bed was the body of Sally Roberts curled up as if asleep. Across from her, Wild Bill had been tied with his arms stretched on the closet railing. He must have hidden in there when he heard the knock on the door. He had a single bullet hole above his right eye; his head tilted to the side.

When Potter returned to the billiard room he found Bliss starting to regain consciousness. As he watched Bliss moaning on the floor, he took the Scheidel out of the case. Potter placed the barrel under Bliss' chin; the heavy set man looked up. "Just following the Colonel's orders," he said. For what seemed like an eternity Potter kept his finger firmly pressed against the trigger. Outside there was the sound of steam pumpers, bells clattering.

"We'll leave it for another day," said Potter, smashing the barrel against Harry Bliss' face. The blow opened a wedge of flesh and Bliss fell into the hallway. Potter watched him stumble down the hall and out the backdoor.

The official report was that Lieutenant William Anglin of

Fire Hall No. 2, Seymour Street, Vancouver, B.C., had died in the line of duty. He'd been trying to rescue a woman in a hotel fire. The inquest lasted only half a day. The hero of the Boer War, the man who punched the two Yanks for God and King and Empire, was lowered into his grave with an untarnished reputation.

On April 6, 1917 the United States of America declared war on Germany, and the Thompson submachine gun was about to be mass-produced.

After the war Potter became a member of Colonel Thompson's Auto Ordnance Corporation. He personally supplied Al Capone with the Thompsons used in the St. Valentine's Day massacre of the Bugs Moran gang. In return, Capone had promised to find Harry Bliss. Through the gang warfare of the 1920s, the mob rolled across Chicago and elsewhere in the United States but they never found Bliss.

In 1937 Potter was on assignment in Spain. The Civil War was raging and he was supplying guns to the Communists. He was captured by the Facist troops, imprisoned, and sentenced to death. He spent two years in a Spanish prison while the Auto Ordnance Corporation negotiated his release. It was a long drawn-out process. A man named Harry Bliss, who was an influential ally of Potter demanded a personal hands-off guarantee for Potter's release. After two years of being missing-in-action and presumed dead in England, Canada, the United States, Potter agreed to leave Bliss alone and was released by the Spanish authorities.

PART TWO

CHAPTER 17

AT the bottom of the page I typed THE END, pulled the final sheet from the typewriter. I tore it up. On a fresh sheet of paper I typed Fin. A touch that Danielle would have liked. I reached over and opened the Delrose Hotel file, and flipped through my Bench notes. Below Fin I typed judgment for the plaintiff, motion denied, action dismissed, and case adjourned. Taking out the final sheet, I pondered over the options. Should I award the insurance money to the hotel owners? Why not? I thought and circled "judgment for the plaintiffs." I felt my resolve slip away. I crossed it out, and then circled "action dismissed." Extra dividends for the United Federal Insurance Company's shareholders. I stared at this decision for a moment, growing more uncertain by the second. A formal adjournment was out of the question. I had run out of options and drew a line through all three. I wrote in the side margin: Personal arsenal dismantled but still a drift in the probabilities of what or whom had caused the hotel fire and without a tentative conclusion. Of course, I worried that certain material facts—essential evidence bearing on the medical question in issue—might be misinterpreted when Hershey studied my autobiography.

I stuffed the manuscript into a manila envelope, sealed it, and wrote Dr. Hershey Rosen's name on the front. I pushed the envelope to the side and poured a glass of wine. I had no idea what time it was. I opened my desk and removed the

Seiko watch Danielle had given me for my thirty-fifth birthday. It was eight o'clock in the morning. Sunday morning. I rinsed my mouth with the warm white wine, adding up the hours I'd been writing; it had been over two days. I swallowed the wine and, refilling my glass, I rotated around in my chair and opened the curtains. I leaned back in the chair. I had finished writing something. Hershey's advice had accomplished that much. I glanced down at the envelope; it was proof that I wasn't permanently blocked. It was an exciting feeling; the sort of thing you want to share. My fingers tapping lightly over the envelope, I swung back around and picked up the phone.

I phoned Joan Bildson's number. The phone rang eight or nine times before she answered in a sleepy voice.

"Jesus Christ, Matt. Do you know what fucking time it is?" she said with a voice thick with the nightly build-up of smoker's phlegm.

"I've managed to get it all down on paper."

"What are you talking about?"

"The story about you, Edgar, Potter, mother and me."

"Send a copy to the Chief Justice," she said, clearing her throat. In the background I heard her light a cigarette.

"I want you to read it."

"I don't have time."

"Then give me the address where I can reach Potter and mother. I want them to read it."

She went silent for a moment, exhaling smoke into her end of the phone. It had been over two years since I'd asked her to disclose their whereabouts. She'd given them a promise to disclose neither the reason for the years of silence nor their residence or phone number.

"Haven't you given up yet?"

"Then you send them the manuscript. What's the harm in that?"

"You can be such an asshole, Matt."

"It's important—urgent, Joan."

I heard another phone ringing in the background. "Just a

minute, I've got to take this call." I overheard her talking to a film distributor in London. I knew that in the last six years Joan's practice had moved into entertainment law. She had clients in Toronto, New York, and London. She was still jogging and lifting weights, and rubbing elbows with directors, producers, and film and television stars. It never quite fit together that she ran this type of operation out of Vancouver, and still got written up in *People* and *US* magazines.

After ten minutes she picked up the phone again. "You remind me of a New York producer I once met in London," she said, sounding awake at last. The cigarette had opened her nasal passages and her voice didn't sound so hollow. "He got a case of the running shits drinking the water in London. For three days he was between the bed and john shitting and puking. He was staying on the twelfth floor of the Grosvenor. The night of the fourth day he thought he was okay, got out of bed, dressed, and took the lift down to the lobby. He leaves his key at the front desk and walks out into the streets. Half a block later he gets a cramp in the gut. He turns back to the Grosvenor. By the time he gets to the front desk the cramps are closer together. There's a lineup for the keys. It's about ten at night. After a ten-minute wait he's in agony. Almost doubled over with pain. He makes it to the lift. It's nearly full. Each floor the lift makes an abrupt stop, the doors open, someone gets out. By now his cramps are whacking him like labor pains. He's dying each time the lift stops. When he finally gets to the twelfth floor, he puts the key into 1250. The door won't unlock. He tries it again. Nothing. He looks at the key number. The front desk's given him the key to number 1215. He's got no choice. He walks down the corridor. He's panic-stricken. He opens number 1215. He sees two people sleeping in bed. He quietly goes into the john and unleashes one of the most ghastly shits ever to hit London. He can't flush it. If he does, he'll wake them up. So he quietly leaves the room, softly shutting the door behind him. The next morning he lies in bed wondering about that couple in number

1215. Blaming each other for the shitting unflushed mess in the toilet. Neither one accepting the word of the other. Pushing open windows; opening the door to the corridor, shouting at each other for such disgusting behavior. This is what you want me to do for you. Sneak into your mother's and Potter's life and leave five pounds of runny shit on the bedstand."

"I'm just asking you to read it. Cut out anything you don't like."

"I've got work coming out of my nipples. Distributors coming into town for film deals—" The other phone rang again, cutting her off. "Okay, send me a copy. But no promises, okay?"

After she rang off I slid another sheet of paper into the typewriter. Flames were seen rising from the rooftop of the Delrose Hotel at four o'clock Sunday morning, the twenty-eighth of July. After that sentence, fingers poised above the typewriter, I waited. There was a long lull. I reread the sentence and noticed I got the date wrong. Then there was an empty void. Rather than getting better I was deteriorating. Exhausted and dispirited, I laid on the sofa near the window. For a while I listened to the dull, barren vibration of my electric typewriter which I neglected to switch off. With my eyes closed it sounded like a distant train; the hypnotic, constant metallic rhythm washed over me, and I found myself seated in a compartment, watching forest and mountains passing in the distance, the tracks curving gently and crossing a bridge heading west above the sea.

On all sides the train was surrounded by the sea, speeding farther away from land, my eyes fixed on the still blue sea below us, I looked out for some crack in the blue, a signpost, something other than the polished clear surface of water. The train appeared to pick up speed but it was hard to judge; there were no reference points. I left my seat and walked down the aisle looking for other passengers. But I was completely alone. I went from empty car to empty car until I came to the main engine and opened the door. The engineer looked over his shoulder at me, a pipe clenched between his teeth. "All the nautical instruments are working. It must be this map," he said, holding up a copy of my manuscript. "Here, you have a look. Can you tell where we are?" He lit his pipe and turned away. I looked down at the manuscript and it had been translated into French. I couldn't understand a word.

"Why didn't you teach me French," I screamed at the engineer.

The engineer pulled back the window and threw the manuscript out. I dived after it, the sheets of paper drifting all around me as I slowly descended. Above me the train was a tiny thread of steel against an ocean of blue sky and sea.

CHAPTER 18

DIGBY Finch, the Crown Counsel, took a tissue from his jacket pocket, wiped his nose, which was the size of a gladiator's bicep, glanced up at me seated behind the bench, and then over at Mr. Temple in the witness box.

"Mister Temple, wouldn't you agree that you were often bellicose with your wife and daughter?"

Mr. Temple, who looked at ease in a cheap suit, frowned, seeking some guidance from his legal aid lawyer. "Would you like me to repeat the question?" asked Digby Finch, with an edge of contempt in his voice.

"I only went to grade nine, Mister Finch. What is bellicose?"

Leaning back in my oversized red leather chair above them, a pair of plaster lions rearing on hind legs in a cage of Latin phrases behind me, I pressed a pen to my lips to erase a smile. I watched Digby Finch slowly cross the courtroom and deposit a wadded-up tissue in the wastepaper basket. I made another stroke on the side of my notepad, and then counted them.

That was the seventh tissue he'd used in less than an hour. What was the cause of the nose problem? Vancouver is the capital of cocaine. But a Crown Prosecutor? I reexamined the septum in his nose; it was still intact. Probably just a lingering cold.

"Bellicose means warlike. Aggressive, Mister Temple."

Mr. Temple nodded that he understood. "I was too young to serve in World War Two. But I had a brother who fought in Korea."

Digby Finch produced yet another tissue and dabbed the end of his nose. His short stature, small bones, and red hair and tiny green eyes gave him the appearance of a superannuated Irish terrorist. Slightly stoop-shouldered, he raised his index finger and pointed at Mr. Temple.

"I suggest, Mister Temple, that you were physically aggressive with the members of your family. Isn't that true?"

"I don't know what you mean, physically aggressive."

"Come on, Mister Temple. You threatened Laura, didn't you? You said that if she didn't take these pictures you'd beat her. You said that."

"She wanted to take the pictures."

"That isn't what I asked you. Did you ever hit her?"

"You have to put down the law sometimes."

"I'm not talking about the law, Mister Temple. Didn't you say on May 15th that if Laura refused to take these photographs that you'd beat the shit out of her? Weren't those your exact words?"

"That was earlier. She was told to sweep up. It didn't have anything to do with the pictures."

"But you used coarse language with your daughter."

"You mean bad words?"

"Obscene language. You used it often. It gives you a thrill to use it. Just like the photographs gave you a morbid thrill."

The legal aid lawyer rose. "Objection, m'lord. Mister Finch is confusing the witness."

All eyes in the courtroom rose toward me. Digby Finch silently blew his nose and waited for my ruling. I wondered what he looked like naked; a translucent, hairless body lined with tiny ruts from the heavy traffic of years of dreary routine. Had Mrs. Finch ever aimed a Polaroid OneStep at Digby's desiccated body and pushed the little red button? Not unless it was a last-ditch effort to supply Oxfam with further evidence of the incomprehensible suffering of someone from the Third World.

"Mister Finch, would you confine yourself to asking the witness one question at a time," I said, as he twitched his nose.

After a short pause, Digby Finch continued his crossexamination of Mr. Temple. "You admit to having used foul language in the presence of your daughter?"

"Sometimes. Lawyers probably do the same thing."

"But we're not talking about lawyers, Mister Temple. It's your conduct and that of your wife which is at issue. How often did you sexually abuse your daughter?"

The legal aid lawyer was again on his feet. A young newly called lawyer, a head taller than Digby Finch, he wore a close-cropped beard, and had puffy eyelids. Perhaps he was also writing his life story for Hershey Rosen. His name was Norman Perkins. "Objection, m'lord. Mister Finch is asking the when-did-you-stop-beating-your-wife question again."

There was a pause. Digby Finch looked indifferent; Mr. Temple loosened his tie and rubbed his throat. In the public gallery, Mrs. Temple silently moved her lips as if she were plugged into an internal telephone system with her husband in the witness box. Behind Mrs. Temple, in the last row of public seats, twelve-year-old Laura Temple, in a blue dress, her dark hair tied behind her head, sat with her eyes fixed on the Star-Wars-like lighting system affixed to the courtroom ceiling.

"M'lord, I'll rephrase the question," volunteered Digby Finch.

"Thank you, Mister Finch," I replied.

"Mister Temple, did you ever sexually abuse your daughter?"

"I don't understand. You mean did I hit her?"

"Did you ever have sexual intercourse with her?"

"I never did that to her."

Digby Finch looked up at me to see my expression. "You never did that to her," he repeated with ironic disbelief. He wanted to drive home that in his humble view the witness was lying.

"I never would," added Mr. Temple, looking up at me now.

"And did you have Laura taking photographs of you and your wife during sexual intercourse?"

Digby Finch stared at Temple as if he were a virus. There was something of the censor's mentality in this type of case, unwinding the most private, personal details of sexual perversion; observing every lurid event with revulsion, and then passing on to the next, without a break or pause, an uninterrupted performance. Terrorized by his own inability to match Digby Finch in the word fight, Mr. Temple started to sob. He nodded.

"Does that mean you did force Laura to take this photograph?" Digby Finch then handed Mr. Temple a Polaroid photograph. In the back of the courtroom, Mrs. Temple dropped her head, her lips still moving. Digby Finch placed seventeen Polaroid photographs into evidence.

The court clerk, a veteran of many courtroom battles, took the photographs from Finch, glanced at them, winced, and handed them up to me. I received Digby Finch's evidence of the Temples' collective debauchery. Pictures of ordinary people with bare bodies locked together. With a search warrant, the RCMP had seized the photographs from an office at the Miracle Roller-skating Rink where Mr. Temple was manager, and his wife the ticket-collector.

There were photographs of oral sex; penetration; and close-up shots of Mr. Temple aroused. All of Mr. Temple's natural endowment was captured in the photograph; a snapshot taken by his twelve-year-old daughter. One photograph stood out among the others; it had been taken at the roller-skating rink, and the Temples were naked except for their roller skates. They were kneeling on the rink floor, like praying figures from a nativity scene. Heads bowed, they faced one another; a narrow, thin smile on Mrs. Temple's face; her right hand clasped around the stem of Mr. Temple's aroused penis. He looked half-blind with pleasure.

Around and around the rink they'd skated; Laura standing with the camera along the edge, watching her mother and father's journey in an endless circle. They were destined to go nowhere. Naked legs, breasts, stomachs, whirling in an empty building, laughing and playing and touching, gathering speed but powerless to break free. They'd shattered their family trying.

Digby Finch asked me to remove Little Laura from the clutch of her monstrous, perverse father and mother and make her a ward of the Province of British Columbia. The Ministry would place her in a foster home. A short-of-cash, government-run, social-worker-operated Alpha House where she could meet other abused children from other working-class homes. The toilet always unflushed with someone else's shit.

Digby Finch had no personal use for Mr. Temple. Roller-rink sex ignited some deep fear and revulsion. It seemed to make his nose drip. Maybe decent people sent their children to private schools and then among good friends in the hot-tub they took pictures of each other with expensive cameras. But these monosyllabic lower forms of human life let their children participate.

Looking up from the photographs, my eyes fell on Little Laura. She was out of her chair, running her hand against the wall, stroking the soft, velvet fabric, the color of beach sand. She touched her cheek against the fabric as if to seek comfort. I watched her eyes dart from the ceiling light fixtures. The lights looked like an enormous gray concrete egg carton, and inside each nodule, a nucleus of lights; only a few of the lights illuminated the windowless courtroom. She'd never seen anything like this before. It was a new world for Laura. Like Dorothy in *The Wizard of Oz*, Laura found herself at the hands of strange forces and swept into a totally alien environment. If Digby Finch was the Lion, seeking courage, then the legal aid lawyer was the Tin Woodman after a heart, and Mr. Temple the Scarecrow wanting intelligence. Little Laura brought them here—to my courtroom. And the Wizard on the bench couldn't really help any of them. Like the Wizard of Oz, I had all the splendid trappings of power, a mystical reputation, impressive robes, attracting an attentive audience. Laura saw through the sham; I couldn't change anyone. Coming to me for courage, heart, and intelligence made as much sense as putting wings on a bag of hammers and expecting it to fly. Not even the real Wizard of Oz could eliminate the Wongness spinning out of control in her world.

NANCY Rosen slowly crossed the living room. Dressed in a bikini, she carried an old champagne bottle filled with seeds for her birds. Her suntanned skin glistened with oil. From the sofa, I watched her standing on her toes in front of a large metal cage suspended from the ceiling to the left of the white marble fireplace; a matching cage hung suspended on the right. A middle-class fetish for symmetry, I thought. Inside each cage dozens of exotic colored birds fluttered with expectation as she reached to open the small door. She poured the seeds from the champagne bottle into the palm of her left hand, pulled out a retractable feeder, carefully smoothed the mixture out, and then slid the feeder back into the cage and shut the door. Beating their blue and yellow and red wings, the birds, hungry sybarites, dived and darted in frantic excitement.

"Hershey's in Mexico on business," said Nancy, moving over to the second cage.

"You call your father by his Christian name," I said.

"We're Jewish."

"Sorry. I forgot."

"It's all right," she said, shrugging her shoulders. "You called your stepfather Edgar, didn't you?" It was almost an afterthought; she said it with grace, busily filling the tray, her back turned to me.

"You read what I wrote for Hershey?"

"Hope you don't mind?" she asked, glancing over her shoulder with a smile.

"It's just—just—it was meant to be private."

"Hershey gives me most of his files to read." She finished with the second feeder. The birds in both cages, singing and chirping, flittered from their perch to the feeder, soaring to the top of the six-foot cages. "Hershey flew down to Mexico yesterday. He wants to look over a piece of oceanfront outside Alvarado. Maybe a condo development in the works. Who knows, with Hershey? Anyway, he left your file with me." She paused, her finger to her lips. "Listen to them sing. Aren't they wonderful?"

Then I remembered sipping champagne with Hershey by the pool. From that afternoon when I saw her in the door, stripped to the waist, arms stretched out and covered with exotic birds, I knew she dwelled in a region which intersected my own childhood.

A soporific melody swept through the living room. I sipped a gin and tonic, listening to the chorus of florid, rich songs. A room of mellow Latin and Asian vocals. What had this twenty-year-old daughter of Dr. Hershey Rosen thought about my childhood? Like her, I'd started early in life. Perhaps she saw a little of herself in the picture I'd drawn. So far she hadn't attached the slightest degree of importance to any part of it. This reserve surprised me. I'd reckoned that the explosive force of my pre-judge life would have melted down the most mentally stable doctor of psychiatry.

"Hershey promised to replace Rudy. He was a very beautiful parrot," she said, sitting in a tub chair across from me.

"What happened to Rudy?"

"He became an addict. Rudy O.D.'d and dropped dead a week ago."

I laughed, thinking she'd made a joke. Nancy showed little emotion; but she had an animal trainer's eyes. The eyes of one practiced in judging the mood and distance of a bad-tempered, poisonous creature. She spilled a few of the seeds into the palm of her hand; tossed her head back and popped the seeds into her mouth.

"They're pure-grade Columbian," she said. "It makes the birds sing like psychotic angels. Sometimes they get too stoned. Ones like Rudy become addicts. When he hit the bottom of the cage," she said pointing to the one on the right, "he broke his neck. It turned a dark reddish-purple color. Three thousand dollars worth of dead bird. Almost as expensive as the boa in your case history."

This popular vernacular was misleading; Nancy had a direct, almost ageless look in her brown eyes, haunting and tenacious, like the eyes of the lioness in Henri Rousseau's *The Dream*. That patient, devouring stare, betraying no confidences, waiting and eternally young, silently guarding an old, profound soul. We sat listening to the birds. She ate seeds and I drank my gin and tonic—her eyes looking for some reaction in me. With one finger she stroked the string tie holding up the top of her bikini over her breasts. There was nothing sexual in this distracted movement. She was at ease, in control, and slightly stoned. At any moment I expected her to start singing like the birds. I expected her to open the cages, remove the stoned birds and start her commune. Something told me that this was not a procedure she followed in front of patients.

"When will Hershey return from Mexico?" I asked, plucking the twist of lime from the glass and sucking on it.

"Friday night. Saturday we're having some film people at the house. Also, it's Hershey's birthday."

The living room filled with the echo of rich soprano voices from the exotic birds. Subtropical chirpings, wholesome sounds evoking the passage of swollen rivers; jungle foliage thick enough to bend voices and songs among the wet leaves. I thought about Laura Temple's custody case. I'd reserved judgment. Witnessing the effects of the Columbian seed on the vocal and motor skills of Hershey's extraordinarily expensive birds postponed my depression. They screamed like aborigines locked inside a railway car winding out of the bush. There was an audible friction against the hinged-in world they occupied. Out. They wanted out.

"I really must go home," I said, rising from the sofa. "And I'd like to take my case history."

There was little emotion on her face as she rose, stretching her arms as she walked across the room. "Okay," she shrugged. "It's in Hershey's study."

"As I said before, I hadn't intended for anyone else to read the things I'd written," I said, following behind Nancy as she led me down the cedar-panelled hallway.

"And as I said before, I read most of Hershey's files."

"But that's a breach—"

She cut me off, stopping at the entrance to Hershey's study. "Of ethics? Not really. I'm a consultant. Daddy claims me as such. Sorry. I mean, Hershey writes me off on his income tax. So I have to read the files and see patients. Otherwise he might be sent to jail."

"Jail?" I repeated. The thought of handing over the most intimate details of my life left a chirping-like sound of a stoned parrot inside my head.

"Yes, jail. Making a false statement on your income tax return. You know about that sort of thing," she said, pulling back the poppy-colored curtains, and exposing a sliding door to the swimming pool and deck. She turned and faced me. A bead of sweat hung on her chin, broke free, and ran in a rivulet between her large breasts. We were inside Hershey's office.

With a display of indifference she sat back in the leather chair behind a Louis XIV-reproduction desk. Like some large, flightless bird, I flapped around the room, weighed down with the hidden dungeon which Digby Finch wanted for Laura Temple. My mind wandered in the presence of this twenty-year-old with gilded gold breasts undertaking a scientific evaluation of my childhood, and from the heat and sun. Overhead in the beamed ceiling which ran at forty-five-degree angles to the sliding glass doors were three skylights. They hung like marsupial pouches showering the room with light. Against the wall was a wet bar with six high stools. West coast paintings, mostly of barren, rocky coastal regions from the north, covered the walls which at the far end of the room rose fifteen feet. This is where sick people came for Hershey to treat them. All the cedar beams, glass, art, comforting them in a womb of light. It was like being inside a Rubyk's cube with a blinding sun at the core.

"Hershey sees all his patients here?" I asked.

She twitched her nose. "Not really. He has an office in the city."

The response had the ring of a half-truth. To one side of the ornate desk was a Victorian chaise longue covered in a deep red velvet. Carefully I positioned one knee on the edge, and leaned forward, turning towards Nancy. A perfect resting place for someone on the run from themselves; a fortress with sloping ceiling, a well-stocked bar. I knew the kind of people who were his patients. People who show up in the middle of the night, eyes swollen, faces the color of quicklime, ready to explode, fly open, split into silvery-white fragments. I saw them in my courtroom, and like a contractor with a small bulldozer I tried to clean the ground, sliding them into iron-barred cavities with a signed order. I remembered mother when she left the house. Now that she lived with Potter did she still keep shut up and cut off from the world? Or did she see someone like Hershey?

"I'm surprised that patients don't come to the house," I said.

"Hershey discourages them," she replied, taking a pair of reading glasses from the desk drawer. They had slender gold wire rims; the glasses cut in two small half-moons. She slid them to the end of her nose, and began turning the pages of my manuscript inside a large file. She read with the calculated, cold-blooded concentration of the best High Court judge. "Would you care for another drink?" she asked.

"Is that my file you're reading?"

She avoided the question. "It's no problem getting you a drink."

"No. I'm working on a judgment tonight."

"You look ready to perish from the heat."

"And I have correspondence as well," I said, thinking of an unanswered letter I'd received from Danielle. She shoved the folder across the desk. Then, leaning back in the swivel chair, she watched me pick up the file, examining the pages with the pinched look of the wronged party in a divorce action reading the other side's pleadings. I glanced up to find her watching me over the top of her glasses. She stared like a judge as well. A judge dressed in a tiny bikini with a smooth, firm golden belly, flat as a plate. In the land of Oz the judges were all nubile and barefooted young women. Maybe Laura Temple ran her hands across the textured walls, ignoring my presence in the court, because she knew that only false Wizards give case histories to a psychiatrist. I flipped through the last pages, and stood up from the chaise longue.

"It's very clever—your story," said Nancy. "I don't believe most of it. And you probably don't either."

Would this be Joan's reaction as well? "But it's all true," I said.

She nodded with the flicker of a smile. "The question is— Did you make up Potter? I haven't decided."

"That's an irresponsible thing for you to suggest," I retorted, rising to my full height.

"Don't take it personally. All of Hershey's patients fiddle with their past. Like gamblers who hide cards or load the dice."

"Why would I fabricate the evidence?" Why does the air seem to grow thin and inaccessible at such times? Physical suffering curls around the accused. As his irregular breathing increases, the words of the past wrap around the nose and mouth like mooring-rope. But it is a splendid ceremony which puts the judge before a child and the sins of mankind are trooped down an empty parade ground.

"Truth's a paradox," she said, moving the chair gently from side to side. "Because you might lose self-control. Who really knows? There are hundreds of reasons. And thousands of disorders. That's Hershey's view."

"You puzzle me," I said.

"I puzzle Hershey, too."

"Like most young people, you draw conclusions very quickly."

"After a while, you get a feel for a file. I've been helping out Hershey for three years. It's just experience."

The protective image of the father-and-daughter relationship peeled away. "How many patients do you see for Hershey?"

"The workload varies. Between nine and twelve. It depends on how much schoolwork I have. Want an apple?" She pulled an apple from a bowl of fruit on the corner of the desk. With a steel knife she cut out the stem.

"And I was about to become number thirteen?"

"Or ten," she said, cutting the apple in half and then into quarters. "I don't keep a precise count."

"So you said."

"But I have a good success rate. Considering." She stopped and popped a slice of freshly cut apple in her mouth. The effects of the Columbian seeds made her hungry.

"Considering what?"

"That most of Hershey's patients are incurable."

"Like me?"

"I haven't decided about you," she replied, then sliding the white, fleshy slice of apple between her slightly parted lips. "But if you want my professional opinion, I'd say you're probably borderline."

"Borderline?"

"You could go either way. But that's your business. You've got your file back. So I guess you're on your own. God, it's getting hot in here. Don't you think?"

Sitting on the side of the desk, I leaned forward and helped myself to a slice of the apple. "Have another one," she said, holding a slice between the knife blade and her finger. She laid it on my outstretched tongue.

"I was trying to be honest in what I wrote," I said, feeling a tiny spasm, not quite pain, more the discomfort caused by the sense of disapproval from another. Her body glistened with a thin skim layer of oil. Putting the knife in the drawer she

[172]

pulled away from the desk and crossed the long room. "If you think there's some sleight-of-hand in what I wrote, then tell me what it is." Casual indifference is the most effective hook in the world.

"You want an example?"

"I'm entitled. Since you think I've cheated."

"I didn't say that."

"Caught in a net of deceptions then."

"It'll take a minute. Pour yourself a drink while I set up."

Opposite the bar, Nancy slipped back the curtain covering a seven-foot television screen. Underneath, she opened a case, and, squatting down, began sorting through a library of videocassette tapes. I sheepishly wandered over to Hershey's glass and chrome bar. I stared at myself in the mirror over the bar. My eyes looked puffy. Sitting on the stool, I bent forward and removed a bottle of gin and another of tonic from the shelf. As I mixed a drink, Nancy worked silently, hunting for the videocassette that would impeach my work. The thought of it. A High Court judge, the bellwether of confidence and trust, waiting for a lovely, bikini-clad girl to demonstrate that he'd betrayed the past and himself.

"Remember the bit about Potter in Turin?"

"Vaguely," I replied, blushing.

"You had him fucking the mistress of an Italian colonel. And the room was all white. Ring a few bells?"

"I'd rather talk about some other aspect of what I wrote."

She ignored me like a petulant child. "The entire way you described that scene I knew. Knew you'd lifted it."

"But that's not true," I protested, spilling my gin as I came off the stool. I might have been a lot of things but I wasn't a plagiarist. That accusation hit below the belt. She saw how wounded I looked. "Well, maybe someone lifted it from you then."

The spin of the cassette machine drowned out the drugged birds in the next room. After a short whirling noise faded, the title *Vixen Rosa* appeared on the large screen. Nancy sat limply on the floor, legs crossed, in front of the screen. A young, dark-haired woman entered a white room and sat on a canopied bed, her cleavage exposed from the bodice of a milkmaid's dress. Across the room, from a balcony, a man dressed in black crept in as the woman removed her stockings. He carried an automatic pistol. I recognized a Mauser 1916 by its long barrel. His face was covered by a black mask. But slits allowed you to see his eyes. His eyes watched the young woman, her back still turned, slip out of her dress and stretch out on the bed.

Nancy glanced back at me. "Look familiar?"

Before I could respond, an unnaturally shrill voice screamed from the television as the masked gunman pushed the barrel of the automatic pistol between her legs. It was one of the most squalid, irrational violations I'd ever witnessed. The image Potter and I had shared was nothing like this. The film was grotesque, a counterfeit stump of my mental fantasy. Her screams fell away as the gunman mounted the woman. There were no stars in the sky outside the window; the rim of the universe which Potter had machine-gunned with Lollia at his side was a blank. In the background of the film there was nothing to cut the raw edge of the whiteness. The two actors groped and fed on each other like blind animals in the snow.

"Enough. Please, turn it off," I said, turning away from the screen.

Nancy rose to her knees, leaned forward and switched off the video recorder, taking the tape, toying with it, as she swung around, a slight smile fixed on her lips. She held the cassette like a ceremonial torch. Having lit the flame, the games would begin.

"You don't want to see the rest of it?" she asked, moving to the bar. She sat on the stool next to mine and balanced the cassette on top of my glass.

"That's hard-core porn. People should go to prison for making that sort of garbage," I said.

"It's close to what you wrote."

"There were no stars."

"You never get well-known actors in these films."

"I meant stars in the sky."

"That's just a detail. A woman in a white room taking pleasure from a gun. The barrel of a gun. That's the same."

"Please don't say that."

"Maybe you added the stars."

"No," I said, my eyes falling on the black cassette on top of my glass. I tapped my fingers on the plastic casing, and put it on the bar. In a strange way the cassette looked like the clip to a MAS 1938 submachine gun. A clip shooting hot celluloid bullets, tearing out a censor's eyes at one hundred yards.

"Hershey has an interest in the company that produced *Vixen Rosa*," Nancy said, pouring herself a drink.

"Hershey made this?"

"It's not really his company. Some American company's behind the scenes. They're into a lot of things. Selling guns, fitness centers, films. You know, diversified."

"This company makes guns? Do you remember the name?" I said, my hand on her wrist.

"Hershey plays his business cards close to his chest. Besides, it's no big deal. He furnishes scripts and helps with the distribution. He's into a lot of deals. I can't keep up with him."

I relaxed my grip on her wrist. "I can't believe Hershey's involved in writing this stuff."

She perked up, lowering the glass from her lips. "Oh, he doesn't. He gets most of the stuff from his patients." She paused, wrinkling her nose. "Guess they're really my patients now. Hershey doesn't have much time for patients these days."

"Who are these patients?"

"Business partners." She paused, staring at the blank television screen for inspiration. "A lot of them are real estate agents."

"Brokers write these scripts for Hershey?"

"Yes and no."

"Either they do or they don't."

"You see, they write all about their past, their dreams—"

"Like I did."

"That's it. A short autobiography. Hershey's patients are heavy on the sex."

I employed an old cross-examination technique. Let the witness go on for a few minutes and then hit an earlier question again from a new angle. "Is the American corporation called AOC?"

"That sounds right," she admitted.

I was reduced to the muted semitone of a wrestler held in a hammerlock. The admission pinned me to the mat. Colonel Thompson's old company in the pornography business? Profit from Hershey's patients, scripting their deformed, disordered hallucinations? And I, a High Court judge, had written an autobiography for Hershey Rosen to pass on to Potter's long-time employer. It was all there in the folder, a ham-fisted account of my life stretching back to my bottle-feeding days. And it was also the history of the Auto Ordnance Corporation. In a strange way it made some sort of sense; this extension of business interest by AOC. Porn was nothing but a new form of commercialized Wongness. It was a logical progression from AOC's gun business. In London, New York, and Paris, in double rooms in the Hyatt or Hilton, a businessman, middle-aged couples, lawyers, football players watched an AOC-Hershey Rosen coproduction; bouncing off satellites, carried over scores of mini-networks, festivals of sex and violence reached every isolated hamlet in the world. Undermining and betraying the basic family structure was no longer the exclusive domain of guns; the modern weapon was the porno film.

"*Vixen Rosa* sold well in Syria. And in Texas. But one of our distributors got busted by the cops. Our lawyer got her off though. I think you know her. At least she was in your case history."

"Joan Bildson? No. Not Joan."

Nancy pushed away from the bar with a little shrug. "It's too hot inside. I'm going for a swim."

Who were these people living next to me? I felt slightly

dizzy, touching the glass to my cheek. "I can't believe any of this," I said, looking at myself in the bar mirror. "I refuse to believe it. Do you understand me?"

Nancy pivoted around on her toes. No clear response registered on her face. She studied my fingers clenched around the empty glass. "Freud wrote up very detailed case histories. And he was heavy on the sexual fantasy theory as well," she finally said.

"For medical journals. For other doctors," I said, wondering what Freud would have made of her commune with jungle birds in full view of her deranged neighbor.

"We've taken it the next step."

"Porno films with a gun company?"

"Dramatized case histories. They're invaluable. Opens up therapy for people in their own homes—and on the road."

I shook my head. "I took it seriously. The autobiography. And it was all for nothing."

Smooth white teeth showed through her half-smile. "Maybe I've got you all wrong. I doubt if you're a second-generation patient."

I pushed both the glass and cassette away and, turning on the stool, started to fix my tie. One year ago Nancy was still a teenager. But she had the technique and skill of someone who'd passed through many collaborations, countries, tested and discarded many methods and theories, and who'd come out the other end with the ability to convey messages by silent gestures, and with little difficulty in explaining the mystery of conflicting demands, desires, and loves.

"A second generation?" I asked, feeling the gin circulating in my head. Why wasn't she stoned? Birds yakking, she remained calm and impassionate.

"Patients who've seen one of Hershey's films. They write their autobiography. But half of what they write is based on *Vixen Wails* or *Vixen Sizzles* or another *Vixen* series film."

"And you thought I'd seen *Vixen Rosa?*" And was Nancy one of these second-generation patients, shopping for the ultimate sexual fantasy in Hershey's porn supermart, pushing her emotional cart down the aisle, taking one off the shelf, and giving it a private screening for a neighbor or friend, as Hershey, his back turned, stared off in the distance.

"I was pretty certain. Guess I was wrong."

"Could you have been wrong about Joan Bildson?"

"No. I'm right about her."

These were important admissions. The first real hint of friendship. She pulled back the sliding door and stepped onto the pool deck. As I walked over to the door, I saw Nancy dive into the deep end. She crossed the pool with clean, firm, steady strokes. Touching the glass to my lips, I finished the last piece of ice in my glass. The shrill cries of the caged birds were mixed with the ripples of water echoing from the pool. I set the glass down and removed my jacket and tie.

Nancy moved like a subaquatic animal. I shaded my eyes against the sun. To my far right I saw a grand piano. It was white. I walked around the edge of the pool and sat on the bench and stared down at the keyboard. Many years had passed since I'd last played. I looked at my hands arched over the keyboard; they looked like weapons covered in animal skin. Then my fingers glided across the keys; half-remembered, half-improvised Chopin. Playing after so many years the hands skipped along the keyboard as if looking for a grip or a rope near the top of a cliff; some tiny ledge to cling to.

From the center of the pool, Nancy called out. "I didn't know that you could play. It's beautiful." She dog-paddled for a few moments, her words liquid. The sound of Chopin rolled in a softly blemished fashion across the pool and garden. She climbed out of the pool and sat on the deck beside the piano. She stretched back on her arms, rotating her head with the music.

"It's wonderful. You must play for Hershey's screening party."

"I thought it was a birthday party," I replied, not looking up from the keys as I continued to play.

"It's that, too. But the Americans are coming up and we're going to screen two new films we have ready for release."

The afternoon sun was luminous on the white grand piano; a finely polished radiance, the light quivering in waves. I hadn't played since the night of Edgar's funeral. It had been a kind of praying that night. A celestial translation for my distraught mother. She'd already disappeared by then. I played in her absence, quite alone, knowing she believed in the migration of the soul. The *homo totus*.

I HELD the Browning GP forward, arms extended, and squeezed off five quick rounds, striking the target in a fist-sized cluster. The silhouette of the soldier had five holes through his cardboard heart. I handed the pistol to Nancy. She pulled back the ear guards with her free hand. "Does it jump much?" she asked.

"A little flick," I reassured her, pulling the ear guards over her ears. She was the portrait of a competitor. Self-confident and contained. The first round exploded and then a second and third. She was finding her range, readjusting her grip and stance. One round clipped the elbow of the paper target. Another missed completely. One smashed through the throat. Her final shot ripped away the crotch. Slowly she lowered the pistol, controlling a smile. Lowering her ear guards, she passed me the pistol.

"I told you I was Jewish," she said.

"That was slightly more than a circumcision. You changed his personality," I replied, sliding in a new clip.

"Here. Try again." She took the Browning and drew a bead on the last unspoiled target.

The sound of the first shot recoiled in my underground shooting gallery. Like all subterranean worlds, there were ambiguous shadows running along the edges; space defined by steel and concrete and wood, forming a hard, fixed boundary from the visible world of grass and trees and sky. All the attempts at decoration couldn't disguise that this place was well below ground level. A place where many guns and cases of live ammunition were stored. A faithful reproduction of the roughly designed shooting gallery Potter had secretly installed in the basement of Alpha House when I was eleven.

Danielle had been the only other person ever to enter this room. Danielle had fingered the cross on the chain over her breast as I emptied clip after clip in an uninterrupted chain. It was taming some dark void, long after all my fellow judges were asleep in their beds, long after the cells had been locked on the people I'd sentenced to prison. It was a transition from melancholy meditation in the great ceremonies of the day to a hidden region where fault, blame, mistake, dread, and fear lay in the half-circle heart of strong-shouldered paper targets.

"You're getting better," I said, after Nancy emptied the third clip into the target. She held the pistol out in her hand. Like an inexperienced observer of some rare artifact, she contemplated it for a second. Her attitude had changed. There was the reappearance of her sound judgment. "You don't have a piano in your house?" she asked.

Placing the Browning GP back in the case, I selected a Beretta Brigadier. I checked the clip, took up a firing position, drawing a bead on the head of the third target.

"I haven't played for years. No interest really."

"You hide things."

I squeezed off two rounds.

"It's a family tradition," I replied, and squeezed off another round. I lowered the Beretta. "Edgar pushed me into lessons at five years old. From the day of my birth musical notes were stamped on my head. I was going to become the concert pianist he'd always wanted to become."

"You wrote he wanted you to become a doctor."

"Guess I forgot about the concert pianist business."

"And your mother wanted you to become a lawyer."

"I think she did."

"And you became their battleground."

"It was a military campaign. That's why I was evacuated to the far-flung corner of Alpha House. Once there was a cease-fire I could go home."

"But you never went home."

"No. Never."

I placed the next three rounds in the right temple of the target. As I looked down, Nancy lifted a pearl-handled Browning Baby from an open case. She emptied the six-round clip at the same target where I'd placed the three holes in the head.

"Please play for Hershey's screening party," she said, quickly touching the sleeve of my black silk shirt. "And don't say no too quickly," she added.

Slowly I shook my head. "I can't." Carefully I replaced the Beretta Brigadier and removed a Walther PPK.

"I see," she replied coldly.

"You forget. I'm a judge. You know what that means?"

"You won't play the piano."

"It means I'm like a standardized round. Like a 9mm shell. I fit only in one clip. I was made for one purpose. Playing the piano for a porno film screening isn't it." With the Walther PPK I punched a triangular section through the right eye of the center target. This was a remarkably effective weapon. Nancy watched me in silence as I fed in a new 9mm round clip. She stood back a few feet as I swung to the left and fired and then to the right. Fired again. Two paper heads fell like dead autumn leaves to the floor.

The shots caught her by surprise. She had her ear guards hanging around her neck. Such hard-knuckled, abrasive, rapid violence was only on the television screen of Hershey's well-insulated world. She stared at me as if she no longer recognized my face beneath the black commando grease. My hands were covered with the same grease. She'd watched me dress with the passing interest of a stagehand wandering through a dressing room. Slipping into a long-sleeved black silk shirt, trousers, and scarf tied loosely around my throat.

Her casual interest dilated into fright. This was real; it was happening where she stood. There was no safe ban of dim stage lights between us. No curtain to drop on the performance. In this grainy diesel-engine level world where the passage of conversation and the movement of the body was as a gauge to measure selective destruction. With her right hand, Nancy touched my cheek with the tips of her fingers. She rubbed the black grease beneath her right eye. Then removed more with a flick of her fingers and drew a black path below the left one.

"One question," she said.

She pulled the Browning from the case.

"What do you really think happened to Potter?" she asked, cocking the pistol.

"I don't know," I replied. "He just disappeared one day with mother."

WHILE Nancy crossed the lawn back to Hershey's house, I went into my study and phoned Joan Bildson. There was no reply at her house; so I phoned her office number.

"Working late," I said, as she picked up the phone.

"Only judges fart around watching television at night."

"Well, did you get the manuscript?"

"It's somewhere here on my desk."

"You haven't read it?"

"Look, Matt, if you want a fucking agent, go to New York."

"I was thinking about Texas," I said. It had the intended effect of throwing her off guard. I heard her lighting a cigarette. "You know some people down there."

"What are you getting at?"

"The guy you represented on a porn charge. I was a little surprised, Joan. Years and years of women's lib and you're stinking around with the porno crowd. Funny, it wasn't mentioned in your profile in *People* magazine."

"Fuck off, asshole."

"Just send them the manuscript." She slammed the phone down in my ear. I slowly lowered the receiver, glanced at my watch. Nancy was waiting for me by the pool.

As I arrived on the deck, Nancy was shedding her clothes. By moonlight she unhooked her skirt, then pulled the blouse over her head. She stood naked, touching the water in the pool with one toe dipped into the deep end. I sat down at the white piano while she went around to the diving board. She perched herself on the end of the board like one of Hershey's exotic Latin songbirds.

"Play something nice," she called down.

"What would you like?"

"Something I can swim to." Her bare feet struck the board firmly as she bounced playfully at the end. The lights under the water spread a milky haze over the pool. From the piano bench I could make out the black grease patches beneath her eyes as she danced on the board. She was in many ways still a child.

With my right hand I began to pick out the tune to *Mack the Knife*. The melody flooded back. Nancy applauded and then dived into the pool, disappearing under the surface. Joan and I had been sitting together in the back of the bus and behind the wheel, nursing a bottle of gin, the Flesh Eater had belted out the lyrics. That was before I went to Oxford. It was the first time I'd made love to my future stepmother; it was the first time I'd ever made love to anyone. It was the last time for innocence. Downtown, Joan was sitting at her desk wondering exactly how much I really knew now and how much was bluff. If I could have guessed, she was reading my manuscript at that moment for some clue to that question.

I was playing with both hands now. In the cool night, while Nancy swam naked in her father's pool, I began to sing.

"I didn't know you could sing," she shouted, climbing up the ladder and onto the deck. "You really must play for the party." Then she listened to the lyrics before joining in:

> Oh the shark has pretty teeth dear
> and he shows them a-pearly white,
> Just a jackknife has Macheath dear
> But keeps it ought of sight. . ."

[183]

CHAPTER 19

DIGBY Finch wiped his nose with a tissue as the court clerk stood and cried out, "All rise." I played my role in this heraldry, entering my courtroom with a firm, deliberate step. Seated below the judicial coat of arms, I quickly opened my file, and nodded my consent for those present to be seated. The Temple family sat in the back of the courtroom. A matron was seated between Laura and her parents. Laura leaned forward, her elbows perched on the seat in front, her head tilted slightly as she fingered a gold earring. She flicked the clasp up and down, bored and waiting for something to happen. The courtroom no longer impressed her. She didn't smile. Her mother's moist eyes were unmet. Mr. Temple held his wife's hand, and appeared to be whispering some consoling assurances to her. His face looked like a leather sack with the eyes sewn on. I joined my hands together and leaned forward from my chair and addressed the Temples.

The night before, between the carnage of paper targets and moonlit waters of Hershey's swimming pool, I gradually came to a decision about Laura Temple. I drew some strength from the tough decisions others had made. Joan's decision to defend the porn distributor in Texas; the decision of Edgar to die flashing a victory sign; and the decision of Potter and mother to cut me out of their lives. It had been a long time since I'd made any decision as a judge. To decide had become an action verb confined to a mental wheelchair. I'd played the piano for hours on Hershey's deck. Nancy swam graceful laps in the nude. As I watched her glide through the water, I remembered Laura's hands gliding down the velvet-covered walls of my courtroom; I remembered the photographs of her mother and father in the nude, the exotic birds singing, the Revelli M15 and Lollia, and *Vixen Rosa*.

Taking a deep breath, I looked down at Digby Finch and began my judgment.

"After hearing all the evidence and carefully considering the welfare of Laura Temple, I've come to a decision." There was a slight stir. Digby Finch, based on my pattern of indecision, had presumed that I would have reserved judgment until Laura was twenty-one years old and meanwhile she could grow up in a halfway house in Kitsilano. He pulled a fresh tissue from a packet and blew his nose.

"Throughout history," I continued, "parents have taught their children the socially appropriate values and attitudes they'd need later on in life. The relationship between parent and child has remained in transition from the beginning of that history. Once children were sent on religious crusades. In the name of Christ children by the thousands were sent to die from hunger, disease, and the sword. Modern-day governments still send their children to die in war. Children are sometimes used for pious or noble reasons; sometimes for stupid, dangerous, or greedy ones. The last category is called child abuse. As a judge it ultimately falls on me to decide whether the Crown has established that the welfare of Laura Temple dictates that she be taken from her parents."

As I paused, taking a sip of water from my glass, Digby Finch exchanged a look of worried astonishment with the Temples' legal aid lawyer. I controlled the temptation to pass a comment on Digby's disapproving frown directed at the bench. Instead, setting down the water glass, I continued on a roll, talking this time directly to Laura. She was conspicuously attentive for the first time since she'd arrived in my courtroom. We had accounts to settle together. We had to find each other and establish a common link. The Wizard had to come out from behind the screen and tell little Dorothy the whole disfigured, worthless truth. As soon as I began to dissemble, a sudden, crescent-shaped smile formed on her lips.

"The crusades still wage around the world. They've been submerged within the family unit: alliance formed, battles fought, treaties made and broken, new boundaries drawn and neglected. All the little Lauras of the world are the veterans; they've been wounded, sniped at, dropped in a no-man's-land with nowhere to seek shelter. The armies move their weapons over a hostile terrain, taking hostages and recruits from the children. When we look into the Temple family through the eyes of the Crown we see a landscape littered with horrible debris. What is so monstrous about the Temples' family crusade? The Crown makes no bones about its case. Mister Finch argues that by interjecting pornography, the Temples have offended the rules that govern family war games, and as their penalty, this court must order the surrender of their one-child army.

"But I reject the premise of Mister Finch's argument. He assumes, wrongly in my view, that over the great voyages of history, some fair-minded constable could play referee with a standard guidebook of conduct. To take this court into the family of the Temples is to invite guerrilla warfare. How can I win their hearts and minds if I take their child? How do I indoctrinate them? How do I prevent rebellion from within? These aren't easy questions. If these pictures had been of strangers and taken by strangers, I wouldn't be drawn in to determine the strategies, tactics, or judgment of the Temples. We wouldn't follow them to their jungle encampments, remove their children, and interrogate them. Because that would have been a short orientation tour of sex and nudity by the family generals.

"But I have been drawn in. The classified information of this family has been put into evidence. The way Missus Temple keeps her house; the employment records and drinking habits of Mister Temple. Top-secret glimpses of the most intimate details of their family have been analyzed by the experts. All of that said, how am I to come to Laura's rescue? Do I let the Crown parachute her into some foreign battlefield where she has no allies? Or should I allow her to remain with her parents? The Wongness of the world won't stop at the doorstep of a foster home. That much I know. Thus on reflection, I've decided to allow Laura Temple to stay in the custody of her natural parents. I find there is no evidence of sexual abuse and only pornographic material which bears upon this decision. I make, therefore, the following conditions. First, I order the Temples to undertake a six-month period of family counselling. Second, I order that from this date there shall be no further nude photographs taken by Laura, with her parents' knowledge or under their direction, either of themselves or any third parties."

The last part of the order sailed over the head of the Temples. Although they knew they'd won the custody battle, the last order had the abstract vagueness of rumors circulating in an occupied territory. Digby Finch was very unhappy and agitated as he rose to his feet.

"My lordship, I seek a clarification. What is Wongness?"

I smiled, half wondering if Digby would have picked up the term. "Wongness is the betrayal and treachery lurking outside this courtroom; it is the subject matter of this proceeding and almost every other proceeding which comes before this bench."

"Wong, as in the Chinese surname?"

"Precisely, Mister Finch. In simple terms, I've abolished roller-skating in the nude because it is a kind of Wongness which betrays the family structure."

Digby Finch shook his head slightly as he took his chair. Missus Temple nodded from the gallery; she understood the implications. Both Temples understood, and by the expression on their faces accepted the disarmament order. They'd been prepared for far worse. With the panic over, Laura stood up and like a schoolgirl raised her hand.

"Can I say something?"

"Yes, Laura," I replied. All eyes turned on her as she stood next to the matron.

"What you really mean is that nobody wins," she said, her head cocked to one side. Words straight from the lips of a true survivor.

"You're quite right, Laura," I said. "No one ever wins."

"That's what I thought." And she sat back down.

THE Chief Justice was watering his ferns as I stepped into his office. Stewart Grober, our Chief Justice for the past eight years, looked like a Jewish Glen Ford. Short, plump, balding, Stew's eyebrows appeared to have been airbrushed off; his head was too smooth, hairless, and without a blemish; it had the touched-up look of a *Playboy* centerfold's belly. No one else thought he looked like Glen Ford except the cleaning lady who pointed out the resemblance. After I saw Stew wearing his son's cowboy hat I saw what she'd meant. He'd worn the hat around his house and mine for two weeks after Joe, his son, was killed in a plane accident near Cranbrook.

"I'm getting lots of pressure, Matt," he said, stroking one of his ferns. "The lawyers in the *Delrose* case are upset. They say they can't get a decision from you. They're making subtle threats. Talk about filing a formal complaint. Maybe taking you to the judicial council."

"It shouldn't be much longer," I said. I sat in a chair facing his desk. He slowly lowered the Royal Albert bone china teapot after watering the last fern.

"Why don't we talk about it, Matt."

"I know all the facts."

"Then make up your mind. The plaintiff wins or the defendant wins. It's that simple. Just make a decision one way or another."

"But that's been the problem," I replied.

He raised his hand the way I'd seen him with his son Joe.

He didn't want to hear about a problem. Joe saw that hand a thousand times raised in the air over the thirty-three years before he died. After he dropped out of second-year Arts at the university, Joe would come to the courthouse with his cowboy hat, boots, and sheepskin coat; he'd sit in the back of the courtroom and watch Stew on the bench. Later in chambers the hand would go up when father and son were alone.

"Sometimes I can't make up my mind on a close case. It happens to every judge, Matt. You take it all too personally. Why, I ask myself, does Matt Burlock get himself so worked up over an insurance case?"

I'd become Joe's replacement. When Stew sat at home drinking Pims with Gloria, his wife, he'd talk about how young Matt was getting on; how efficiently young Matt ran the baseball and football pools for all the judges; and how I'd been a boy genius at Oxford. Stew thought of me as an orphan; and himself, after the accident, as childless. Gloria told these stories to Danielle, while we were still married, and she passed them on. Before Danielle left me, she said there was a striking resemblance between Joe and me that obsessed the Chief Justice. I'd retorted that Joe and I had completely different physical builds. I'd missed the point. What she meant was that each of us had inner transmitters set on the same frequency. Like pirate radio stations transmitting an emergency distress signal on a short-band frequency and as the waves crashed in we knew no rescue boat would ever arrive in time.

"What I'm about to say should never leave this office," the Chief Justice continued, as he slid behind his desk.

This was an invitation to participate in some intimate dishonesty. A trick learned (or perhaps perfected) during the days Stew was a bagman for the Liberal Party.

"You have my word," I said. Before my appointment to the bench, like Stew Grober, I'd been a bagman for the Liberals too.

"Flip a coin," he said.

"What?"

"Take a quarter from your pocket and flip it."

I emptied my pockets on his desk. "I don't have a quarter."

The Chief Justice removed one from his desk drawer. It looked quite worn from use. He tossed it in the air, caught it and slapped it down on the hairless top of his left hand. "Heads. The plaintiff wins. Tails. The defendant wins."

"No, Stew. It won't work."

He peeked under his hand. "Tails." He extended his left hand across the desk for my examination. "The defendant wins in the *Delrose* case. Now, just go off and write a judgment covering yourself, Matt."

I picked the quarter off the back of his hand. "How about going for two out of three," I said, tossing the quarter in the air.

The Chief Justice held up his hand. "I give up. What am I to do with you? Write your judgments? What is it with the *Delrose* case? You're the Oxford whiz kid. But you're sitting on this case longer than a supernumerary." His face softened; that Glen Ford smile flickered and died. His hands thrust forward, palms out; he sighed. "Matt, you're like a son. But I can't let my feelings for you get in the way of my job. And you've got a job to do, and you're not doing it. We all have to answer to someone."

"I did make a decision today."

"In *Delrose?*" His eyes peeled open with disbelief.

"In a custody case."

"That's a start."

"Maybe it's my comeback."

"This is wonderful news. Why didn't you say something before?"

"The Crown's likely to appeal." I wanted to break the news gently to him. I could see he was anxious to phone Gloria and tell her the good news.

"Let them, Matt."

"I abolished roller-skating in the nude."

Stew's laughter rolled across the office. He thought I was

making one of our little in-jokes. He'd developed some considerable reputation for sketching while on the bench. During the long, humdrum stretches of a trial, counsel assumed from the bent tilt of Stew's bald head and the implacable attention he devoted to the quick hand movements over his trial book that he was taking down every word. But Stew was drawing. He drew jurors, witnesses, counsel; he sketched with passion. Afterwards he'd go back to his office and take out his quarter and flip it into the air.

Some sketches were of recurrent images. My favorite was Stew's runner. The sketch of this prehistoric naked runner with flexed muscles, eyes nearly closed, had a haunting, primitive, and abandoned quality. He gave me a framed and signed copy of the naked runner. I hung it in my pistol-shooting range in the house. Every judge has a plumb-line for the truth, and the naked apelike runner was Stew's. He always gave one to his au pair as a welcoming gift to the Vancouver household. These young Oriental women mistakenly believed Stew's drawings had some religious significance in Canada. Only later, after a year of service, pouring Stew his Pims, rubbing his shoulders and back, and admiring his daily courtroom sketches, did the naked runner's supernatural quality dissipate. Danielle thought I'd embroidered the Chief's naked runner with a false spiritual quality. Then she thought I embroidered many things, and that's why she left.

The Chief Justice pulled a handkerchief from his pocket and wiped the tears from his eyes. He caught his breath. His face was purple as if a small chicken bone had gotten stuck in his throat. He had merely laughed about the Laura Temple case. "I knew you'd come around, Matt." He leaned over the desk and punched me on the arm.

"Do you remember *Mack the Knife?*" I asked him.

"Wasn't he the drug dealer I sentenced to ten years?"

Stew was as pure as a snow leopard sometimes.

"No, it's a song."

"Can't place it. You don't have a copyright infringement

case?" Another undecided case would have curdled the milk of his good humor.

"It's not a new case," I replied, thumbing the seam of my robe. He cracked a Glen Ford smile.

"What's the song, Matt?" He'd relaxed again in his chair.

"There's a snatch of lyrics I can't get out of my head."

"Out with it, then."

> There's a big fire down in Soho
> Seven children burnt alive
> In the crowd I saw Macheath, who
> Could not give the reason why.

The Chief Justice turned these lyrics over in his mind. He wasn't certain if I was joking. The language of Bertolt Brecht often has that effect. Absorbed in thought, his heavy jaw loosened, he stared at me intently.

"Just write a tune for the *Delrose Hotel* case. And write it fast. Find a reason—any reason—and make a decision."

CHAPTER 20

THE fine summer mist turned to a light, steady rain. My umbrella raised, I sat on the edge of the outdoor stage, an open newspaper at my side, the late edition of the *Vancouver Sun* dripping with rain. In the soggy newsprint it was difficult to recognize my picture. Like a schoolboy I sat with my ankles locked together swinging them back and forth, knocking my heels against the wooden stage, a stage hidden in the forest of Stanley Park. A peaceful sanctuary where the soft rain cleansed the green lawns, flower beds, and towering pines and firs. I looked down over the empty benches and waited under a thin, gray canopy of sky.

As I looked out, there was a young woman beneath a red umbrella sitting in the last row. She started to clap. I could hear the applause from the stage. It was Nancy. She'd been watching, hidden in the surroundings, staying close to the trees, peering through the wet branches. She'd come out of nowhere. I hadn't seen her take a seat but my mind had been preoccupied. Her eyes were bright with mercy. Halfway down the grassy aisle Nancy stopped, tilting her umbrella slightly back and uncovering her face.

"You were right not to go home," she said.

"Reporters and news crews?" I knew how these things developed.

"The CBC and BCTV. And some radio stations. A real traffic jam."

"The judge who abolished roller-skating in the nude," I said, scooping the sodden newspaper up and dropping it over the edge of the stage. "Quite a headline."

"It'll blow over in a couple of days."

I shook my head. "I don't think so. They said I'm a racist. Calling people with the name Wong devious. You know—"

"I know what you meant." She walked across the stage and sat near me along the edge. Our umbrellas touched. She squeezed my hand, staring out at the empty rows of benches. "Wongness generates Wongness," she said.

"I was remembering while I was sitting here. When I was a child, Edgar brought me to see plays here. Mother didn't like leaving the house so we went alone. *The Threepenny Opera* and *The Chocolate Soldier* were my favorites. When it rained the ushers handed out brown butcher's paper. People shaped them into cones and put them on their heads. Row after row of these brown-coned people watching the diva in a company of Prussian officers. Sometimes a raccoon would shoot across the open stage. Straight through the legs of an actor. Or a flock of low-flying geese would bring the play to a temporary halt. All those brown-cone-headed people would cast their eyes upwards and follow the geese out of sight. Then the actors picked up where they'd left off. Once when I was very young, no more than six, Edgar arranged for me to sit in the orchestra. Right below us." I pointed directly ahead of where we sat. The wet newspaper covered the spot.

"That night I sat on a little chair next to the piano player. It was *The Threepenny Opera*. One of the constables was very drunk. He fell down once or twice. His hat tumbled over the edge of the stage and landed in the orchestra pit. The piano player reached over, picked the hat off the grass and placed it on my head. It was too large, of course, and it fell down over my eyes, the lip of the hat rested on my nose. The brown-cone people in the first two rows let out a great roar of laughter. The piano player lifted the constable's hat from my head, and handed it to a stage attendant, who quickly disappeared behind the set. Today I felt that hat slide over my head again. But there's no one who can take it off this time. And no one's laughing."

I felt closed in by the forest, the emptiness around us, the ceiling of clouds resting on the pointed tips of our umbrellas. Like the constable's helmet which almost cut off my breath as it passed over my nose, enclosed in a wet darkness, just for a split moment an overpowering, dense fear seized me.

"Sorry I was late. But—" she hesitated, touching my hand. "The new films arrived for the screening today. I watched them. One of them's called *Fireman's Wake*. It's a snuff film, Matt."

"You really shouldn't watch that junk."

"These weren't actors. A man was actually killed in this film. Two women set him on fire. He had a long scar on one side of his face and was very old. They'd tied him to a cross, doused him with gas and struck a match."

"And?"

"I went through the Delrose file again. The photographs of the room and the bodies. It was the same room as in the film."

"It was Harry Bliss." Nancy didn't say anything; she just

stroked my hand. I swallowed hard. "And the people in the film?"

"They wore masks. Lioness masks."

I looked at Nancy with a friendly surface smile. She was only twenty and had discovered what I'd suspected from the very beginning. The man in the photograph was Harry Bliss. Somehow Potter had managed to settle the score after so many years of patient waiting.

I collapsed my umbrella. It had stopped raining. Swinging my legs onto the stage, I scooted forward, my chin nudged between my upright knees. Nancy folded her umbrella and faced me. Neither of us said anything for a long time.

Nancy's hand was cold as stone as she plucked a tear from my face. The late afternoon mist closed in around us. From the stage we could no longer see the back rows of benches at the forest edge. She rested her head on my knees, and I brushed the hair away from her face. Tiny pools of rainwater had collected on the stage. It was a hallowed place for me; the last place where home and family had existed as one. It was the only place where I could stare deeply into the dark mirror of my childhood and not turn away. Here was a frontier where all the memories remained alive, like flowers in full bloom.

"What do you want to happen, Matt?" For the second time, she called me by my Christian name.

I stroked her hair. "I want you to invite Joan Bildson to the screening party."

"For what?"

"The royal messenger riding comes. Riding comes, riding comes, hark who comes, hark who comes. The royal messenger riding, the royal messenger riding." Lines I'd heard many times from this stage. But I don't believe Nancy knew her Brecht.

MY head was buried beneath two pillows. Nancy, having switched on the night-stand light, sat erect, sheets pulled to her waist. She shook my arm.

"Wake up, Matt," she murmured softly. She pushed one of the pillows covering my head onto the floor.

I turned over on my side and faced her. She leaned over and kissed me on the mouth. "You were tossing and turning. Moaning things."

"Sorry." She slid down into the bed, wrapping one leg over mine. Her voice sounded hoarse and raspy with sleep. I think she caught a slight cold in Stanley Park as well. In the dark and mist, stage left, we had made love while the CBC crews sat outside my house smoking cigarettes and playing cards, waiting for my return.

"You were having a nightmare."

"I know."

"I heard you call out Potter's name."

"He was in my dream," I said, pulling her tightly against me.

After leaving the outdoor theater we drove back in Hershey's Mercedes. Two blocks before we reached Hershey's house, Nancy stopped the car, and I climbed into the back and lay down out of sight. From Nancy's bedroom window we saw the reporters keeping a vigil outside my house. Sooner or later the racist judge who abolished roller-skating in the nude would have to come home—or so they thought. I'd simply gone missing-in-action.

"There's some wine left," said Nancy, drawing a finger down my chest. "But it's probably a little warm."

"I can hear the birds from the sitting room."

"Yeah. It's nice."

"Don't they ever sleep?"

"In shifts." She giggled like a schoolgirl.

"Like all dope addicts they have insomnia."

Her eyelashes flickered against my chest like the wings of some tiny drug-charged bird. "I wonder if they're still outside waiting."

She kicked back the sheets and rolled out of bed. She crossed over to the window. Standing naked, with her back to me, I watched her lift one of the sloping slats of the wooden window blind and peer out into the night. Ivory-colored rings rimmed her bottom and back. She stood with her weight on one foot, the other languidly crossed behind with the foot arched upwards. Her head and shoulders were in the shadows. "They're putting a rope ladder against the house."

"What?" I shouted, sitting bolt upright in bed.

She removed her finger, letting the slat fall back into place. She stepped forward and the light caught her face. She was smiling. "I was just joking. I think some of them might have left. The others are still there."

"It's a big story, I guess."

My bare back touched the brass rails on the headboard. It was like falling into a dark arctic canyon; eyes closed, the sudden chill fused my mind and spirit. When I opened my eyes, Nancy was in bed, sitting on her knees. She passed me a glass. I drank a little of the luke-warm wine. "You haven't told me about your dream," she said, as I passed the glass back. Her smile was of the clinician coaxing a patient to confess.

"I was inside an enormous building," I began. "The ceilings rose almost out of sight. Steam hissed from hidden vents, and clouds of mist billowed in the distant corners. I walked from room to room for some time. They were all empty. Then I came to a door that had a red neon exit sign above it. The room was flooded with light and there wasn't any steam or mist inside. On the floor was a large hose. Nearly eight feet high with an exterior that was a yellow, slime color. It wasn't fabric; it stretched over a series of corrugated rims that supported the skin-like covering. It looked abandoned. Like a snake made for a festival and stored away for safekeeping. At the bottom of the structure were a series of cables and cords, shooting off in every direction and disappearing underneath the wall. I wasn't frightened; merely curious, and weaving my way among the electrical connections underfoot, I began looking for an entrance into this thing. My fingers touched the silky exterior wall, and after searching for a long time, I was about to leave the room. At that point a flap between two of the ribs ruffled slightly. I ran to it, nearly tripping over the wires, cords, and cables, and grabbed the flap with both hands. I caught my breath and stepped inside.

"As I turned, the flap disappeared and somehow I knew that I would never leave this grayish-blue place. There was no sign of life; only a tranquil sea of water stretching to the horizon. My feet treaded along a very narrow path near this sea. Although the water was translucent, it was lifeless and empty. I continued to follow the passage for some time. Suddenly I felt released and at peace. Inside this grayish-blue world of crystal-clear water uncluttered with temples and clumps of ships and hoisted sails I travelled without fear, desire or thought.

"The pathway abruptly came to an end. Potter was standing there, smoking his pipe; the Scheidel submachine gun strapped across his chest. There was some kind of semiconducting layer between us. We didn't need to speak to communicate to one another. I followed him into a channel where the sea narrowed to a small tip of water. With my trouser legs rolled up, I stood shoulder to shoulder with Potter. He bent down, pulled back the sleeve on his shirt, and plunged his hand into the water. As his hand emerged, I saw he'd found something. He opened his hand, and I looked down at a building. Not just a building. It was a skyscraper. But it was compressed, flattened, and the walls black as night. All the lights were turned on, illuminating all the thousands of tiny windows. For hours, Potter and I fished these buildings out of the sea, storing them at the foot of the pathway. We stacked them like fish one upon another, window to window, but they were so small it took many to form a layer which reached up to my ankle. It was like fishing for salmon. These buildings had been running upstream to spawn.

"I caught movement off my left side. I dropped several buildings in my excitement and they sank into the sea. Stew's naked runner charged down the pathway towards us. He was wearing one of the Lioness masks over his face. Potter pushed me to one side, and pulled the Scheidel over his head, knelt and opened fire. The bullets were noiseless. They tore holes in the naked runner's chest and through his mask. He fell backwards into the sea. Potter calmly relit his pipe, the Scheidel resting by the leather strap from his shoulder. The sea turned a crimson red and began to rise, spilling over the pathway. The black skyscrapers we'd recovered were washed away. I remember crying and shouting at Potter. Nothing came out of my mouth, and the louder I shouted the deeper the red sea rose around us. Then I heard you calling my name. And I woke up."

Nancy leaned over and switched off the table lamp. We lay side by side in silence, her hand on top of mine. It was as if some creature had stung her throat and she was waiting for it to heal. She started to say something several times, but nothing came out. I felt her breathing on my neck. She cleared her throat. Then once again. Her fingernails pressed lightly against the fleshy part of my hand.

"Joan's coming to the party," she finally said.

CHAPTER 21

THE style of a man's dressing gown is the style of the man. Hershey's dressing gown was black silk and over the right breast was a fiery red Chinese dragon, tail coiled, talons of crimson flame shot out of its mouth. The night before, Nancy had taken it from a closet in Hershey's bedroom. The perfect gown for an accused racist to wear around the house. It was better than roaming around naked in Hershey's house. The birds stopped singing as I padded past. The sight of a naked judge is a rarer sight than a stoned songbird. Nancy's eyes walked up and down the gown. She bowed from the waist. She whispered playfully, *Shogun*. The man who'd seen the face of Wongness in his dreams.

Robed in the red dragon dressing gown, I sat in Hershey's kitchen, buttering a piece of toast and reading the morning newspaper. There was a picture of Digby Finch. It was an old photo. Without his name printed below I wouldn't have recognized him. He was interviewed about the Laura Temple case, and he was taking the opportunity to get his shots in. Above my picture was the headline: *The Judge who abolished roller-skating in the nude*. I had a lurid smile on my face. Of all the photos in the press file, they went with the one taken several years earlier after the annual Oxford-Cambridge Boat Race Dinner. I'd given the speech on behalf of Oxford. A speech uttered after too much port. Someone had seen fit to capture that moment, and share it with a reporter. All over Vancouver people were being put off their breakfast; a mousy molester's smile on a judge's face wouldn't go down well with ham and eggs.

"Where was Judge Burlock?" asked the reporter in the article.

I was a fugitive. On the run. Hunted by the people sitting in the television vans outside my house. They'd set up their cameras in my hedge.

Where was Judge Burlock? Holed up in his neighbor's house, wrapped in a Chinese dressing gown. I was on the lam. Digby said my decision had been lamentable for the entire community. It takes only one long-tailed monkey to scream an alarm until the chorus is picked up and repeated throughout the forest. Lawyers in the *Delrose Hotel* case detonated a few screams of their own. The legal trees were hopping with angry monkeys. Monkeys with the instincts of sharks. I pushed my toast to the side. On the inside page, there were a number of stormy letters from members of the Chinese community demanding an investigation of my courtroom slurs. Closing the paper, I thought of the red sea in my dream. I heard a door close nearby. I'd thought Nancy had returned. She'd gone to my house—through the back garden—to bring me a few items of clothing.

A strong hand with a firm grip fell on my shoulder.

"Matt, what are you doing here?" Hershey said.

"I'm giving Nancy a hand with the party."

"She told you about that?"

"It was to be a surprise. For your birthday."

"Oh, yes. My birthday," he laughed nervously. Then in a very loud voice he continued, "Matt's helping with the party. That's great, Matt." All the while he was opening and closing the fridge door. Finally, he had the presence of mind to remove a bottle of orange juice. "You're right, Matt. I wasn't scheduled to get back until tonight."

"Why do you keep shouting my name?"

"Shouting. I didn't know that I was." Hershey drank straight from the bottle, leaning forward on a hand propped on the kitchen sink. Several rivulets of orange juice channelled down his unshaven chin. In his blue-and-white dressing gown (no dragon on this one) he stood staring out the window, opening and closing his eyes. My courtroom instinct told me that Dr. Hershey Rosen was about to confess to some crime. He had the overwhelmed, guilt-ridden posture. Confession for the guilty was like morphine for an addict.

"You were shouting, Hershey," I insisted.

"Hello, Matt," came a familiar voice from behind me. Her hair uncombed, arms folded with a cigarette in one hand, Danielle walked into the kitchen, bent forward, kissing me on the forehead, before sitting down at the table.

"Honest, Matt," moaned Hershey, staring down at the sink. "I can explain everything."

"I'm certain you can," I replied, watching Danielle's face for a reaction.

She merely arched her back, stretching her arms over her head; her dressing gown—which matched Hershey's—fell open over her crossed legs; the well-tanned, tapering legs of a much younger woman. "Hershey said you were sick," she said, searching the table for an ashtray.

"Funny how we met," said Hershey, trying to change the subject. "Right out of the blue."

"In a cocktail lounge at Finisterra," added Danielle, vines of gray smoke curling from her nose.

"I bumped into her one night in the bar." Hershey looked at Danielle for confirmation and then at me, his eyes plugged with the coarse friction of lavatory lies. I said nothing, playing the wounded ex-husband in Hershey's dressing gown; a gown that I had worn to bed with his daughter; a gown which he, at that moment of domestic Wongness, rather fortunately, had not recognized.

Danielle measured the lost, plaintive look on my face; like a porter peering into a sleeping-car and wondering if it was appropriate to inform a passenger he'd missed his station several stops back. She flicked the long gray ash from an American cigarette on the plate containing my discarded toast. "I was very worried," she said warmly. Her voice had a distinct, rich ring; even simple information glowed with the sloping hues of caring. As she gestured with her hands, trails of smoke zigzagged through the kitchen air.

"What's gone wrong, Matt?" she asked.

"She had a right to know," interjected Hershey, standing in front of the open fridge.

"You've written some kind of bizarre life story," she said, with oppressive sadness in her mellow voice.

"Hershey makes them into dirty movies," I said.

A bottle of pickles fell out of the fridge door and broke on the floor. A diversion intended to look like an accident. Glass, pickles, and juice splattered over Hershey's bare legs and feet and the counter and fridge. A conspicuous splash-down, leaving Danielle slightly bad-tempered and on edge.

"Don't talk nonsense," she said. "Judges don't talk nonsense. They write judgments. So what are you doing? You write a sordid life story, and talk about porno films. Matt, have you gone nuts? I mean, really crazy?"

"I didn't say you were crazy, Matt," said Hershey, looking up from his hands and knees on the edge of the pickle-juice puddle.

"You didn't have to, Hershey," said Danielle, glancing over her shoulder. She touched the corners of her eyes. "I have these. I can see. You're sitting half-naked in Hershey's kitchen in that seedy gown reading a newspaper." She had got up a head of steam. I thought of her in our flat in Oxford. Drinking wine and eating food with me on the floor. I wanted to kiss her on the lips. She was boiling now. "What are you doing here?"

"I'm playing the piano for Hershey's surprise party."

"Another lie. You've not played since Edgar died," she said, pushing back her chair.

"I promised Nancy I'd do it. As a special favor to Hershey." I watched her circle around the debris and help Hershey clean up the mess.

Nancy didn't see Hershey and Danielle bent down on the floor as she entered the kitchen. She'd returned from my house, wearing some of the things I'd asked her to bring. To be precise, Nancy entered the kitchen on bare tiptoes wearing my black silk shirt unbuttoned to the navel, and around her waist my leather holster with the 1903 Browning packed inside. The gun Gavrilo Princip had started World War I with. My black silk scarf was tied around her forehead. She'd planned a perfectly clean, secret attack. All her concentration was on her prey; I sat at the table alone, my back to her. She pulled the Browning from the holster.

"Matt, I'm ordering you back to bed," she said with an alert, wide-eyed smile. "Hands up. This is a rape." As I turned my chair, I ducked in time to avoid the two large dills which Danielle had unleashed at my head.

"Oh, my God," said Nancy, stepping around the corner. Hershey and Danielle sat on the floor next to the fridge.

"Nice to keep things all in the family," said Hershey, stabbing a pickle with a jagged piece of glass from the broken bottle.

DANIELLE and I found shelter in Nancy's bedroom off the main upstairs corridor. Danielle's prolonged Gallic silence continued as she stood near the window overlooking Hershey's sprawling garden and pool. Below, caterers suspended a pig above an open pit; others prepared tables, setting out bowls of fruit and flowers; a portable dance floor was being assembled upwind from the pig on the spit. I watched the activity below from the edge of the king-size bed. A workman removed outdoor lights from boxes and carefully set them on the grass.

"I don't understand why you can't go home," she said with a slight strain in her voice.

"Read the newspapers."

"Have you phoned Stew?"

"Stew? What can he do?"

"Hiding only makes it worse." She lit a cigarette and threw her head back like a high-strung thoroughbred, her nostrils flared with tension. The muscles across her small, slender shoulders were knotted. "What's the cause of all this distress? This great emergency, Matt?"

"Don't be afraid for me," I said.

"Since when did Matthew Burlock take up sleeping with a twenty-year-old girl, and leave a twelve-year-old child in the hands of people with filthy sexual habits? Yes, I'm afraid for you, Matt."

Danielle had been in Mexico on business; her father's textile business—which she had taken over—and was inspecting Mexico as a branch office location; abundant resources, cheap labor, and indigenous corruption. Mexico contained all the essential elements of Quebec in the 1950s. It was like going back home for her. As she paced the room, I could see Danielle pursued by hordes of children streaming behind, kicking up dust with their tiny shoeless feet, dirty and with big, brown, hopeful eyes.

"All your life," she continued, blowing out smoke as she paced. "Some slow grind's been wearing you down. Over the years I've seen it. That's why I left. I didn't want to slide under with you. I look at you and what is really left?"

"Why did you come back? To hop in bed with Hershey?"

"Hershey thought I might help pull you out of this thing. But I guess it's too late for that now." At such times Danielle normally opened the sluice gate on her repressed religious beliefs. She'd come to "save" me. Any distasteful or painful experience was translated into a lopsided litany of strange motives and conduct.

Across from the bed, I flicked on the television set and the video recorder underneath. I pressed the fast-forward button and found the last part of the film. Reaching up I adjusted the volume. Danielle turned from the window, her head cocked trying to interpret the grunting and heavy breathing from the television.

"What are you watching?" she asked, slowly crossing to the bed.

"One of my cases," I said, pulling the clip from the Browning, my eyes fixed on the tube.

"Holy Mother," shouted Danielle, her hands raised to her face. "That's disgusting—dirty." One of the women with a lioness mask was on the bed with a young naked man. There was a close-up of the penetration. She was moaning beneath the mask; the man's face was masked with a remote sneer. Across the room another woman, also wearing a lioness mask, though clothed, stood beside an elderly man tied to a wooden cross. They were watching the couple on the bed. There'd been a close-up of the penetration followed by reaction shots from the participants and observers.

"One of Hershey's little films. Thought you might like to see it." I pointed the unloaded Browning at the television screen and pulled the trigger. I'd drawn a bead on the man tied to the wooden cross. The invisible bullet would have caught him at the far tip of the scar on his right cheek.

"How can you watch such trash?" she said, sinking onto the bed.

"The performances aren't Oscar class." The hammer hit the firing pin with a hard click again. This time I'd aimed at the penis of the man on the bed as it withdrew from the naked lioness.

"In God's name, Matthew. Turn it off." She covered her eyes and turned away.

"There's something I want you to watch first." As the camera zoomed in on the naked lioness, she was seen to remove a syringe from under the pillow and drive it into the naked man's leg. A moment later he was in convulsions, his eyes rolling up till only the whites showed. The lioness with the syringe watched him bite through his tongue. In the next shot, the two lionesses squirted liquid on the old man tied to the cross. The clothed one took a match, struck it, and tossed it at him. There was a loud *whoof* and he was engulfed in flames. The camera held on him for nearly a minute as the fire devoured his clothes and hair. His body seemed to melt and explode. I reached over and turned off the television set and put the clip back into the Browning.

"It was so real," Danielle said, pale and trembling.

"It was real."

"What do you mean?"

"A feminist snuff film shot on location in Vancouver. Shot at the Delrose Hotel. A run-down dump. Occupied by people who could only afford the services of a lawyer with a working-class consciousness."

Danielle's teeth clattered, as I put my arm around her waist. "Those men. Did they—did they really die?"

"The police report said they were two homosexuals involved in a weird sexual ritual. They were on drugs. Got a little carried away. An argument developed and one set the other on fire. The other died of a drug overdose. Nice and neat."

"Hershey did this?" She was very afraid. Had she gone to bed with a sexual killer? I poured her the last of the bottle of wine Nancy and I had left on the table. She drank the glass straight down. "Well, did he?" she asked me, as I walked over to the window and looked down at the activity around the pool.

"No. Someone else."

"Who? Why don't you go to the police?"

"Because I have no direct proof. Besides, it's better to keep some things in the family, as Hershey said." I watched Nancy directing men who carried the speaker system for the band. She walked near the pool, drawing the stares of the other workmen whose eyes fixed on her tight jeans and bikini top. One of the workmen said something to her and she dropped a tray of flowers on the pool deck and ran out of sight around the side of the house.

"I think you're deranged, Matt. I really do." She closed her eyes, her hands at her side touching the bed. I knew that look of sorrow and hurt. There was a ghastly feeling of déjà vu. She had seen me retreat to the window, taking my Browning, standing with my back to the wall, like an armed killer, eyes rotating around the room. It was a repeat of our last night together. I'd found what I thought was another lead on where Potter and mother were living on Mayne Island. We paid a private investigator to search the title records of all the land on the Gulf Island. He thought he'd come up with a possible site. We'd taken the ferry over to Mayne Island. An old couple lived in a cottage. He'd worked for the Canadian Pacific Railway company before retiring. He wasn't Potter. Danielle had snapped inside that night back at home. I'd shown her a set of new detailed plans to find them. She knew that, like the others, they would lead to empty buildings, vacant lots, or the wrong people. She tore the papers into shreds. She threw the tiny fragments of paper into the air as I stood against the wall holding a pistol. She slammed the door and the next morning was gone.

"Where are you going?" I asked. Danielle pulled her dressing gown together and walked to the door.

"You're crazy, Matt." She feebly snubbed out a cigarette into an ashtray and turned around facing me. "It was stupid to come back." As she opened the door, Nancy faced her, out of breath.

"I wouldn't go in there. He's dangerous," Danielle said to her.

"Matt, I have to talk to you," Nancy said, over Danielle's shoulder.

"All right, have it your way." Danielle shrugged, glanced back at me and left, lighting another cigarette.

Nancy closed the door and rushed over to the window. She took my hand and pulled me across the window and opened one of the wooden slats. There were two RCMP cars and a van in front of my house. Uniformed officers were carrying out my guns. The television cameras were rolling as they were being interviewed by the press. I dropped the slat and leaned against the wall. None of the guns had been registered. I'd committed a very serious criminal offense. In another hour, if he didn't already know, Stew would hear the news that his adopted son was not only a racist pro-porn judge but also heavily armed.

"I'm sorry, Matt. Someone must've followed inside this morning. I went downstairs to get the gun—and—." She began crying, as I pulled her next to me, hanging my arms around her neck, the Browning dangling from my right hand.

"What the hell," I murmured in her ear. "You go back to the pool," I said, kissing her lightly on the ear. "I have some work to do."

After Nancy left, I sat down on the edge of the bed and opened the nightstand drawer. I pulled out a note pad and pen. I thought of the *Delrose Hotel* case, and how each time I'd started the judgment, I'd written the same sentence. Flames were seen rising from the rooftop of the Delrose Hotel at four o'clock Sunday morning, the nineteenth of November. This time I kept right on writing. An hour later on the nightstand, in a neat pile, lay my handwritten judgment in the *Delrose Hotel* case. I'd found in favor of the Delrose shareholders. They hadn't torched the hotel for the insurance money. Funny, I thought. Not about the innocence of the hotel owners but the timing of my decision. My paralysis had ended at the same time as my career as a judge. The decision was made by someone under criminal investigation; it was probably void. Was it this knowledge which had allowed me to finish the decision? I wondered.

I'd been blocked looking for the one unquestioned source of Wongness—a futile task leading me to the edge of madness—and when I pulled back, although too late, I knew my job was to consider the limited consequences of this case. The problem was there were too many possible sources catalogued by Darwin, Marx, Freud, and Einstein. Many sophisticated explanations: it resides as part of our evolutionary heritage, the historical struggle of the working classes, our individual and collective neurosis, or free-floating particles in the cosmos. Just a lot of twilight zone theories about the sources of Wongness, but as mother had said from the beginning, life wasn't a choice between theories but a personal decision about survival or destruction. Either you found a safe passage through all this Wongness or you perished. Either you believed in the Prince of Safety or you went missing-in-action.

CHAPTER 22

I WAS astonished at the beauty of the night. Guests had been arriving for hours and gathering outside the pool. Under the circumstances, I decided it was best to stay confined to Nancy's bedroom. I lay in bed, fingering the Browning and watching

The Fireman's Wake on the video recorder for the nineteenth time. I knew every scene and camera angle by heart. I felt rested, almost serene, through the scenes that had caused my heart to pound in my neck the day before. I looked down at the Browning. Was this really the original pistol that some scruffy youth had used to start a war? There were many more questions, but they drifted away without any real attempt at achieving an answer. I kicked back the sheets, pushing them on the floor.

Outside I heard a splash as someone dived into the pool. There was the sound of laughter in the distance. The band was playing *Days of Wine and Roses* in the background. I thought of television and radio crews on the other side drinking coffee in the back of a van, talking politics, baseball scores, and my gun collection. The diving board thumped noisily. Another splash, followed by a shrill of laughter.

I checked the clip of the Browning once again. Closing my eyes, I saw Stew's Naked Runner floating past in the red, rising sea, and the lioness mask over his face. The sounds of love-making from the television mingled with *Days of Wine and Roses* drifting in from the open window. As the water rose higher and higher, I could taste the blood filling my mouth. There was no panic feeling. Just sliding away from the solid earth and marvelling at the extravagant sepia tones of the light below the surface of the blood-red sea.

The door swung open and the light was switched on.

"What the fuck are you doing?" asked Joan, as she slipped in wearing a low-cut party dress. She was carrying a small suitcase in her right hand. Walking over to the bed, she dropped the case beside me.

"Watching a little television," I replied, lowering the Browning from my temple.

"You shouldn't play with guns, asshole."

"You shouldn't play with fire."

She opened the case and took out a white silk suit, shirt, tie, and shoes. "You're getting out of here—now."

I leaned over and pushed the fast-forward on the video recorder. It stopped precisely at frame 982. I pressed the stop action and froze the frame of the naked lioness on the bed. It was a close-up and you could see a small dot below the right nipple.

"You know, you should have had that wart removed a long time ago. It's like a fingerprint."

"There's no time for that now. Just get dressed. Parked out front is a 1956 T-bird. The keys are in the ignition. Drive to the False Creek Marina. There's a twenty-six-foot boat waiting. It's called *Between the Sheets*. You'll find it on pier 6, third boat in."

I looked up from buttoning the shirt she'd laid out. "How appropriate."

"Take the boat across the Bay and you'll be picked up just north of the old gun tower on Wreck Beach. Put on the flashing yellow signal light. It's in the hold." Joan inhaled hard on her cigarette, her eyes running up and down the suit I'd put on.

"Your acting skills also leave a lot to be desired," I said, removing my jacket and strapping on my shoulder holster. I placed the Browning snugly inside with Joan holding out the jacket as I put it back on.

"You look like shit," she said, the cigarette spilling ashes on the carpet. She held out a white hat. "Don't forget this."

"Thanks."

We crept down the hallway, Joan leading the way. At the top of the stairs she motioned for me to wait. Outside, the party broke into *Happy Birthday to Hershey*. Then Joan signalled me to join her and we went down the stairs.

"You've got ten minutes. Then I'm tipping the reporters that you were seen in a white 1956 T-bird."

The main part of the house was empty as I walked out the front entrance. The T-bird was double-parked in the long circular drive, and the engine was running. Outside the drive, I turned onto the street, shifted gears, and headed for the Marina. As I passed my house, I saw two RCMP uniforms standing with a reporter. One was holding one of my Thompson submachine guns. Watching them disappear in my rearview mirror, I drove down Marine Drive to Granville. My arm brushed against the Browning inside my jacket. What was I doing with the Browning pressed against my head? Would I have really pulled the trigger?

I parked the car in the parking lot behind a luxury condo complex overlooking Granville Island and the Marina. This was False Creek, rolling lawns and winding paths nestled against a small inlet. On pier 6 I found the *Between the Sheets*. On the next boat I saw a couple sitting in the cabin watching television from a banquette. They were watching the ten o'clock news. I saw my face flash onto the screen. It was followed by a cut to police officers displaying my guns. As I untied the boat and climbed aboard, I glanced into the cabin one last time. A reporter was interviewing a Chinese man; there was an insert of my picture in the left bottom corner.

As my boat approached Burrard Street Bridge, I watched the cars and buses racing overhead. To my left was an outdoor restaurant with people sitting outside at round tables with folded canopies in the center. People who believed in the system; who believed in courts to protect them; who believed that Wongness happened to someone else. From the water it looked like any other party. People laughing, drinking, and swapping stories. On the surface, it was like Hershey's party with music drifting and women serving drinks from silver trays. These everyday people were the Auto Ordnance Corporation's and Hershey's market. Hershey's party-goers were in the business of furnishing a new generation of destructive weapons to these people. *The Fireman's Wake*, like the Scheidel, was a prototype weapon for revenge.

English Bay was calm that evening. A half-dozen ships lay anchored off Point Grey, the decks illuminated with lights. A few small boats passed as I navigated around the peninsula. After forty-five minutes I was in the vicinity of Wreck Beach. I had some trouble locating the old gun tower where Joan and

I had eaten sandwiches and read cases. I missed it the first two times past because I didn't expect to see a light from the top gun turret. Just like in her film, Joan was efficient, timely, and had an exacting eye for detail. No doubt inherited from her butcher father's eye for cutting up steaks on the chopping block.

About half a mile off the beach I dropped anchor. Below deck I found the lantern, flicked it on. It flashed off and on, throwing light around the interior of the hold. I found a brandy bottle. Apricot brandy. Mother's favorite brand which I'd not seen in years. I broke the seal and took a long drink before climbing back up to the deck. I set the lantern next to the wheel and relaxed back in the padded captain's chair, putting my feet up next to the instrument panel. The waves lapped against the boat, rocking it slightly. Edgar had joked about mother's brandy while he was in hospital. He said if they ever opened her up they'd find apricot seeds growing inside. But then, mother had left him, and men who are rejected, even when they're dying, can remain bitter.

Joan had done a wonderful job of organization. I sat on the deck looking towards the coastline shrouded in darkness; only the light from the gun tower pierced the blackness. She'd thought of everything; not missing a single detail. The 1956 T-bird, the year before our graduation, was now a vintage car—a collector's item provided the first leg of my escape. Then a boat, *Between the Sheets*, substituting for the Flesh Eater's bus. Engines off, waiting quietly off Wreck Beach where she'd shot her first handgun. Back to the university. I'd failed biology. My old instructor Nelson's probably still applying to medical school. Meanwhile, I've managed to fail the law. From the very beginning it was obvious that I wasn't cut out for the professions. I only knew one thing: guns. They were the only part of my life not marred by failure.

I automatically reached for the Browning as a large cabin cruiser approached rapidly on my port side. I knelt beside the chair. Within five minutes the mooring cable secured my boat to the side of the cruiser and Joan climbed down a ladder. She'd changed out of her evening clothes and into a khaki jumpsuit. I stood on the deck, the Browning dropped to my side.

"Go on, climb up," she said, as she jumped on deck. She reached around and removed a pack from her back.

"Sandwiches?" I asked, as she opened the pack.

"A little treat," she replied, switching the setting on the lantern to a constant beam. She was in much better humor than at the house. I watched her contact a wire to one side of a terminal, then contact the second wire and set the clock. "Give me your jacket." As I handed it to her she put my wallet inside the pocket and dropped it down the hold. "Let's go."

WE were nearly even pegging with Bowen Island when I saw a small ball of flame spread out over in the distance. I looked to Joan and she patted me on the back. "Boom, you're dead."

"You look better in a mask," I said.

I followed her to the stateroom below deck. As we walked in, I heard the television reporter say they'd found a car with my prints on it at False Creek. In front of the set, his pipe lit and legs stretched, was Potter. At his side, mother was adjusting the volume of the television set. Potter glanced up, removing the pipe from his mouth.

"Welcome aboard—son."

"It's a real pity they took all your guns," said mother, as if we'd just spoken together the day before. For a woman who was afraid to leave the house, she looked remarkably happy and content on the cruiser.

I stood there, the Browning hanging just inside my left armpit, glancing at Joan, then Potter, and, finally, mother.

Potter had been the man who'd gone missing-in-action and had never come back to mother. "Before I went to Spain," he said, touching mother's hand. "I'd read about 'Wild Bill' Anglin's widow. From an investigation, I learned Wild Bill

[214]

and she had a daughter. I decided to send for your mother, and she joined me in New York City."

"A week later, we got married in Manhattan," said mother. She looked at me directly as she spoke. "We stayed at the Plaza on Fifth Avenue, across from Central Park. That's where you were conceived.'

"After New York, I went on to Spain where I ran into a little trouble," Potter said. "Your mother checked out of the Plaza a week later and returned to Vancouver to wait for me—"

"But I got a letter from Spain saying your father was dead. That he'd died in prison."

Potter turned to mother, nodding. "Bliss' handy work," he said.

"When you married Edgar," I said, glancing over at Joan, who was lighting a cigarette. Presumably, Joan had known all about this for years.

"You were only a baby, Matthew. You needed a father and I needed a place to wait." Mother broke off and looked away.

This confused me. "You didn't believe he was dead?"

"I told her that in my line of work I sometimes went missing for days or weeks, but I always turned up sooner or later," explained Potter.

"I didn't know what to believe, Matthew," mother said. "I just knew, even after I married Edgar, that I still had to wait. I relived that brief time we spent in New York. It was all so clear in my mind. How in New York we'd walked around the Village, sat around the Jazz Clubs, dined in the Midtown restaurants," said Mother, rising from her chair. The memories she'd lived with for all those years with Edgar had finally found words. All those frozen images now thawed, and the swollen emotional river flooded the banks of our connected past.

"I'd leave your mother at the Plaza and in the early afternoon I'd disappear, then reappear without any real explanation. I was dealing with the Communists. They were staying downtown in the East twenties. Two of Stalin's emissaries wanted a gun deal with the Auto Ordnance Corporation. They wanted guns for the Spanish Communists and for themselves. I didn't tell your mother any of this at the time. It would've been too dangerous. Meanwhile, my client had a problem. They lacked hard currency, and their credit rating was zero. But I knew that supplying weapons to the Soviets and their allies meant great profits for the company."

Mother walked over and put her hand on my shoulder. "Your father's idea was to raise money for the Soviets in the States." I thought, Jesus, they even talk like married people. One started a story, another picking it up for a while, then dropping out and letting the other add a few key elements. Back and forth, like they'd been married forever. "So he set about organizing left-wing sympathizers in New York. From his Oxford days, he had a contact with the New York Theatre Union. They were committed to doing left-wing plays."

Mother paused, and Potter continued: "My big money raiser was Clifford Odets' *Waiting for Lefty*. With that money, I started the gun shipments to the Spanish Communists. I'd met Bertolt Brecht several years before. He was in New York at that time, and I asked him to write another smash hit like *Waiting for Lefty*. Of course, that never got off the ground once the Spanish put me in prison."

"Brecht was in rehearsals for *The Threepenny Opera* before you left for Spain, said mother, looking down at me. "We went to opening night. Five days later, alone I crossed the North American continent by train. I didn't know I was pregnant with you."

"And I was off to Spain, and planned to meet your mother in Vancouver. After I got out of prison in Spain, the export department at the Auto Ordnance Corporation had a batch of letters waiting for me from your mother. So I knew that I had a son in Vancouver. And I found out that your mother had remarried. It was a bitter, black time for me. Without my wife and son, Bliss still on the lose, Hitler sending tanks and armies out with missions of destruction."

"What was an English gentleman to do?" I said.

"I'd only been responsible for your grandfather's death. I had no right to reappear and kill your mother's marriage as well. So I received a leave of absence from the Auto Ordnance Corporation and was hired by your school in Vancouver. It wasn't the sort of company you ever really quit. I needed time to figure things out more clearly. The time slipped past. I got the headmaster, a friend of Edgar's, to enroll you in school at seven. Now, at least, I had my son."

"He didn't know that I never left the house and continued to wait."

They both paused and exchanged glances. Joan raised her glass to me from the bar, a cigarette in the corner of her mouth. Mother turned back to me, a slight smile spreading around the corners of her lips. "Then in 1962, by chance, I met your father. I was waiting for the elevator up to your law office. The doors opened, and your real father stepped out—"

"And you both disappeared," I said, not letting mother finish. The entire canvas of my past and family life had been repainted, the figures uprooted, the landscapes shifted, the sounds of Fifth Avenue, the colours and hues of Central Park, the voices of Communists, Brecht, Odets broke down the harmony, order and composition of painting I carried around inside my head of my life, Potter, mother, Edgar. Moments after I'd become officially dead, I been given a glimpse of my past: conceived in New York City, Housed in Vancouver, and schooled in the traditions of an English gentleman. The balance between foreground and background collapsed under the weight of these new alliances, misfortunes, entrances and exits. My newly formed perspective, without the false tensions and inferior frauds, came together, and for the first time, I was at peace, with the original which had been hidden for years behind the fake.

"Looks like you're carrying a Browning," Potter said, the pipe clenched between his teeth. Mother reached over and switched off the television set.

"The Browning," I said, pulling it from the holster. "Father," I added. I handed it to him butt end first, and watched him examine the barrel.

"You're right. The Browning."

"I don't think you'd be surprised if I have a few questions about what has happened since 1962," I said. Joan had crossed the room and was mixing a drink at the bar.

"I guess we can leave the details of the funeral arrangements for later. Don't you, Joan?" Potter asked, winking at Joan.

"I'll fill Matt in later, Lord Fosbery." She shoved a drink for me across the bar.

"Don't be absurd, Joan. You always call him John," mother shot back. If she ever had a genuine panic disorder, she'd been cured. Mother opened a large envelope she had stuck in the side of her chair, and handed father a copy of my manuscript. He tapped it with the end of his pipe.

"There are other matters to clear up here first," father said.

The details were largely ignored that evening and my father concentrated on the main events over the past two decades. Potter was never really Potter, Alpha House master and teacher. Uncle Foss wasn't really his uncle. He was his father. The seventh Earl had died while father was still holed up in a Spanish prison. After becoming the eighth Earl of Fosbery, father rejoined the Auto Ordnance Corporation and kept up his search for Harry Bliss. At least that much I had got right.

Why had he disappeared with mother without a word? That was 1962 and President Kennedy had begun to station troops in Vietnam. The Auto Ordnance Corporation had been contacted by the Vietcong to supply weapons. Mother and Lord Fosbery spent eight years in Hanoi coordinating the gun shipments and transferring funds to the Swiss bank account of Auto Ordance. A decision had to be made whether to disclose their location and risk a possible breach of security. Auto Ordnance, after all, was an American corporation doing business with the other side. This sort of international Wongness has certain dangers and risks. So they made a decision to keep their whereabouts secret. By the end of that war I'd been appointed to the bench and it was even more dangerous to my career to suddenly reappear without some explanation short of outright fraud. With my career in ruins, and about to suffer public disgrace and possibly prison, those reasons no longer held.

There was another reason as well. That's where Joan came into the picture. Not long after the Vietnam War, Auto Ordnance decided to go into the film business. Films had always been a weapon of sorts. Violent and aggressive pornography, like a loaded gun, would lead to violent and aggressive behavior. If you can use guns to defeat another country, then the porno film could be employed to deprave and corrupt and undermine the population without firing a single shot. Soon a number of foreign governments were paying for Auto Ordnance to produce and distribute porno films into the cities of their enemies. The idea was to make pornography as commonplace in their society, sold in the local corner store, seen on in-home television or videocassette players. It was commercialized Wongness before the eyes of every child over the age of six.

After Edgar's death, Joan had gone through Edgar's personal effects. Among his papers, she found a copy of the trust deed set up by the Auto Ordnance Corporation for my welfare. She had no idea where mother had disappeared; so she took a chance. She sent a package containing some of Edgar's jewelry to the Auto Ordnance in care of mother. They, in turn, forwarded the package on to her in Hanoi. Over the next decade they kept in touch, and through the Auto Ordnance Corporation, Joan began to receive corporate work out of Los Angeles. By the 1970s they'd started to feed her film work, grooming her for their business. Joan, as usual, had her own axe to grind in the porn business. She wanted the Auto Ordnance Corporation to make feminist porn films. If these films were going to be warfare, then women should be able to aim their own guns.

She got her chance about two years ago. Through an old CIA contact, father had discovered that Harry Bliss was living in Bolivia with an old friend from the war, Klaus Barbie. The Butcher of Lyon had given Bliss protection in La Paz. They'd sit around at night and talk about the victims they sent off to Auschwitz. All the while there were guards around the complex, carrying submachine guns. Barbie was a local celebrity, and enjoyed another man's company who could appreciate the satisfaction of catching members of the resistance and executing them on the spot. The CIA operative, who owed father a favor, had been in the encampment one night and overheard Bliss brag to Barbie how he'd been responsible for getting the first submachine gun. And how he had executed the owner of the Scheidel, the original gun made by a German.

Within a week, father had Joan fly into La Paz and negotiate a film contract for Bliss' life story. He personally transferred the twenty-five-thousand dollar bait which Joan used to persuade Bliss to fly into Vancouver to shoot the documentary. Barbie encouraged Bliss to take the opportunity. He'd basically been sponging off Barbie for many years, and this was a chance for Bliss to get some financial independence in the last years of his life. Barbie's reason was also one of national pride. He wanted Bliss to tell the world that a German, Scheidel, had changed the course of world history.

Bliss and his bodyguard had been in Vancouver for several days when Joan showed them a script. It was part fantasy and part reenactment of the actual events. That's how she got Bliss tied to the cross. Bliss' bodyguard had no objections to the sex acts in the script; until, I presume, he got the final syringe. The other lioness in the film was mother. The lady taken to hospital after Joan had thrown a bottle of slugs against the wall? Being the wife of an Earl had brought about a number of changes. The years in Hanoi, with the fighting, bombing, and destruction, made her a veteran. She wasn't going to stay in any house ever again, just in case father might go missing-in-action once more. She insisted on being at his side day and night. She even followed him along the jungle trails, the rain forests, and the Vietcong camps. She ate their food and stood at father's side while he negotiated the price of guns. She saw how the Vietnamese women fought alongside the men, and ate things in the jungle that had made Joan's bottle of slugs look tame. This wasn't a woman that Edgar would've recognized. Then Edgar hadn't been an Earl, or exported guns, or ever gone missing-in-action.

Mother flew in from the Fosbery estate via London for the film. The lady with the brandy addiction and panic disorder, who'd been reborn in Hanoi, asked father for the privilege of striking the match. Wild Bill was no longer the man who burned up because he didn't go to a proper school. His grandson would become an Earl in his own right. And royalty have a way of avenging their own. She was merely carrying out the job I or father should have done. But mother had become a feminist. It had been her father Harry Bliss had torched. No one was going to take away her right to even the score with Bliss. Joan had gone to London with her plan, and she supported mother's right as a woman to participate in the execution of Harry Bliss. Father, who'd patiently waited years for the pleasure, finally let himself be persuaded by Joan and mother. The simple route would have been to send someone to La Paz to quietly put a bullet in old Harry's head. And miss the opportunity to make a feminist statement? Mother was now teaching a butcher's daughter, who'd only seen blood on the floor of her father's shop, the need for women to assert their sisterhood, and to record that assertion for others.

Father turned the Browning over and over again in his hands, as if he had never expected to see the weapon reappear in his life. There was something on his mind; I remembered that twinkle in his eyes, the way he parted his lips as he sucked the pipe as a prelude to saying something important. I could also see that he was getting tired.

"Son, next week we'll be going to Tokyo. There's a little project we've been thinking of looking into," he said, all the while looking at the Browning.

Canada didn't seem a likely location given the circumstances, but I wondered out loud about Japan. "Why Tokyo?"

"We have a couple of people interested in artificial intelligence at the Corporation. Great possibilities for weapon invention. The Japanese are getting close. So we're told. Since you've come on board, it might be a good project for you to sink your teeth in."

"But I failed first year biology."

"And a legal career doesn't look all that promising."

I knew then he was thinking not about the Browning but the Revelli M15; his first "project," as he now called it.

"How much time do we have?"

"About six months. Maybe a year. Enough for things to blow over here. For you to pick up the language."

That's what mother had said about French. You can learn the language over a summer. I hadn't learned it after twenty years of marriage to Danielle.

"The other details we'll work out later."

As the night ended, father had fallen asleep in his chair. Mother removed the pipe from his hand and went to bed. Joan and I stayed up until dawn talking about La Paz, Barbie, and Bliss. She sketched in the arrangements that would be made for my funeral in Vancouver. It would take place in three days.

"If I hadn't been assigned the *Delrose* case, and got blocked, would I have ever found Potter—I mean, father." I was getting a little punchy by four in the morning.

"Don't be thick. You still don't understand."

"And of course you do?" I said, putting the Browning back in my holster.

"Gentlemen's agreement. Protections and guarantees. With Bliss and his people on the loose you'd never have your own life. He never let your mother out of his sight. Matt living in Hanoi for years? You were better off in a safe, cushy job as a lawyer and then a judge. The heirs of the Earldom have a history of fucking up."

"When did you switch over to the upper class?"

"Not the upper classes. Your father. Because he's spent a lifetime selling weapons to the right side. And with *Fireman's*

Wake I got to blow away Cinderella's slipper forever. By the way, don't expect me to call you Lord Fosbery, asshole."

As we went above deck, our crew had anchored off Vancouver Island. In the distance, I could make out the skyline of Victoria. The Empress Hotel, the Parliament building, and the marina loomed against the horizon. Successor to the Earldom of Fosbery, I scanned the coastline of the most English part of Canada. Soon I would be working alongside the Colonel Thompson's, John Moses', and Harry Bliss' of father's world. Is that what he'd prepared me for all those years at Alpha house?

CHAPTER 23

IN absentia burials bring out the very best in undertakers. At the church, as Joan later recounted, the mourners filed past the empty coffin; some even doubted that Judge Burlock was dead. They hadn't found a body. But it was fairly clear that no one could have survived the explosion that had destroyed the stolen boat. The police believed that Judge Burlock had been involved with a major gun ring and had been killed in a lurid double cross. This was whispered around the church. Even Digby Finch, who was among the mourners, wondered if Judge Burlock's decision abolishing roller-skating in the nude had been an accident, a counterfeit, a grotesque aberration. He sent a bed of red roses; they arrived in a bell-shape with a silver paper sword protruding from the top. There'd been a mix-up at the florist's. Digby's bed of roses ended up at a Masonic temple, the bell-shaped flowers and sword at the foot of Judge Burlock's bronze coffin.

After the main service, most of the mourners followed the black hearse to the cemetery. Joan placed two small Haitian flags on the front of the hearse; she told the driver that they were the Burlock family crest, and the Burlocks for over a thousand years had gone to their graves under such heraldic devices. She also slipped in fifty dollars, as his hand reached to take down the flags. So my empty coffin made the final trip with flags flying.

It took the undertakers nearly forty minutes to unload all the flowers they'd brought from the church. They placed them outside the cordon perimeter around the burial plot. The plot was covered with a green tarpaulin; with Digby's bell-shaped roses, it looked more like an Hawaiian picnic than a funeral. As the mourners gathered around the pallbearers set the coffin on a portable catafalque, Bishop Davies, a small Welshman, someone whom Joan got at the last moment, opened his bible; he passed the sign of the cross over my coffin. On the opposite side of the proceedings I sat in the front of a limousine dressed in a chauffeur's uniform and cap, a false moustache on my lip. Mother and father sat in the back. Father had a pair of binoculars, and handed them back and forth with mother.

I saw a very old man, standing at the edge of the main group, and looking like a dissipated Spencer Tracy, wipe a tear from his eye, using the back of his hand. Joan stood beside him, probably wondering whether this old man's cane would continue to sink into the soft lawn.

"I knew that he wasn't long for this world," said the old man. "His father told me all about it. A fine man, Matthew's father."

"Sorry, I didn't catch your name," Joan had said to him.

"Scime. I taught young Matthew. We all knew he wasn't well. Cancer, you know. Terrible stuff. I knew he didn't have much time. But I didn't let on. I promised his father. Just a matter of time. He had it bad. There was nothing left when he died. Just gone." He wiped away another tear. Joan bent down and pulled Dean Scime's cane from its hole. The Dean straightened himself. Plucking a rose from a wreath, Joan slipped it through the Dean's lapel.

"There. A present."

"Why thank you."

"Actually, I was looking for a slug."

Bishop Davies raised his voice. "Judge Matthew Burlock was a great professional man; a man who has left his mark in the jurisprudence of Canadian law. A man whose brilliant career has been cut short by a tragic series of events." He didn't elaborate. Welsh ministers, like Welsh trade union officials, have that bloodhound instinct to sink their teeth into the shank of any issue and not let go, charging down every untrodden path, hanging on until you chop off their head. But this one, out of character, stayed with the positive aspects of my life. "A first-class Oxford degree. Yes, Matthew Burlock achieved many, many honors."

"Are you part of Matthew's family?" asked Scime.

"His ex-stepmother who once screwed him."

"Really," said Dean Scime, beaming and not hearing a single whispered word.

The sermon seemed to drone on too long. The only other sounds from where we sat were distant traffic. Twisting around, I saw Joan push and shove her way through the assembled lawyers, judges, school friends, public officers, and RCMP officers circulating amongst the crowd. As Joan reached the car, she climbed in the front seat. She reached over and pulled my cap down.

"How's it feel to be dead?"

"I think it's something that grows on you," I replied, readjusting my cap. But there were, seriously, some hard parts to observe.

Danielle, flanked by Hershey and Nancy, stared at the coffin during the graveside service. After I'd disappeared, Danielle moved back into the house. She'd become news as my "widow," a bit of family fraud right to the end. The public, much taken by her beauty and charm, had begun to recognize her in shops and stores. Strangers stopped her in the street. She always wanted to be a celebrity. I thought of the foreign guests staying on for my wake, expressing their sorrow and regret; the men kissing her French-style on both cheeks, embracing her bare shoulders on Hershey's pool deck.

It was Nancy who troubled me. At the graveside, she smiled; but I could tell that she was stoned, and probably had been stoned from the moment she heard about my accident. Joan told me that Nancy had smoked dope. It was the same stuff she fed to the exotic birds. The birds that sang and sang throughout the night. When one guest had threatened before the party to machine-gun all those fucking screaming birds, Nancy, with the help of the bass player, carried them up to a guest bedroom. Before the services, Joan had been around to Hershey's house. She found Nancy in the bedroom, smoking dope. Opposite her bed was Stew's framed sketch of the Naked Runner. Danielle had given it to her.

As I turned on the ignition, I saw Laura Temple drag her bicycle from the gravel path and cross the rolling lawn, carefully avoiding the graves. Bishop Davies had finished the graveside service, and the mourners dispersed and filtered back to their cars. Laura looked lost. The gravediggers emerged and she watched them pull back the tarpaulin. She laid her bicycle on the grass. They were smoking cigarettes and talking about ferry delays at Horseshoe Bay; one of the men was planning a weekend on Vancouver Island camping. Laura crept closer, her snivelly nose sucking in the air. She carried a handful of wilted forget-me-nots; she looked at the mountains of flowers surrounding my open grave. Then she stared down at her own flowers, hesitating slightly. Father had gotten out of the car and walked across the lawn to where she stood. He later told me what had been said.

"Did you bring those for Judge Burlock?" asked father, pointing down at Laura's flowers.

She half turned, looked at the old man with his white hair, striking his pipe bowl against the palm of one hand. She nodded. "I planted them myself," replied Laura. "I got lost and everything."

"Why don't you put them on the top of the coffin?"

"I won't get in trouble?"

"No. I promise."

Laura walked past the gravediggers and pushed a wreath of roses from the head of the coffin and placed the crumpled forget-me-nots on top. She stood back, and watched the gravediggers diggers slowly lower the empty box into the ground. Father moved up beside her, resting his arm around her shoulder.

"I'm glad that I wasn't the only one who's late," she said.

"I've been a little late myself. You liked the Judge?"

"Yeah, but my mom says our case got him into lots of trouble. I thought he did a good job."

"I think he'd be pleased that you remembered him."

"And who are you?"

"An old schoolmaster."

"That's a kind of teacher?"

"That's it. A teacher." The pipe clenched between his teeth, I noticed that father's face had grown thin and narrow; the rings under his eyes looked like coiled rope.

"What did you teach him?"

"All sorts of things. Science. Maths. A little French. And most importantly, I taught him that the royal messenger always comes to the rescue."

Father squeezed her shoulder, while we waited in the car for him to walk away from Laura. She walked back to her bicycle. Joan leaned over the front seat and opened the back door of the limousine. As Laura lifted her bicycle from the grass, she watched the friendly old man climb into the back of the car, and kiss mother on the cheek.

As father closed the door I asked him what he'd finally said to Laura. "That you'd merely gone missing-in-action," he said, bringing a warm smile from mother's lips.

A moment later, as Laura Temple pedalled down the path, she saw our big black limousine speed away from the curb and disappear through the cemetery gates and turn into the street. From her vantage point it must have seemed that we were in a hurry.   •